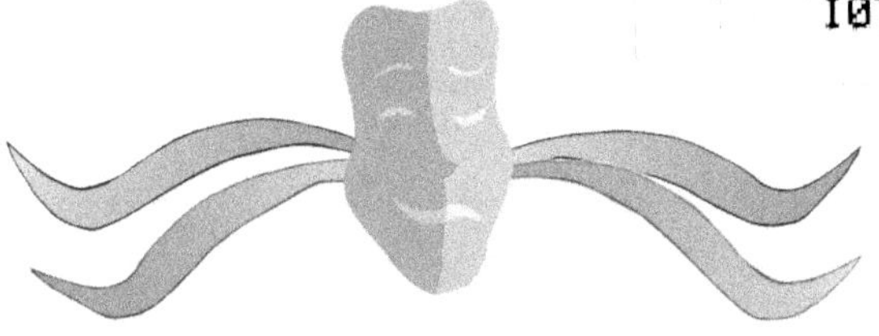

"EEEEeeeek!"

Amanita hid quickly to avoid being seen by someone running by – then peeked out as a sergeant and captain in Raven-soldier colors came out of a door down the hall.

"You realize you've roused the entire garrison, Captain Fayorn," the sergeant growled. "I can't imagine His Sorcerousness is going to be particularly forgiving that you disturbed their rest because of a *mouse.*"

"A *rat,*" Captain Fayorn corrected with a shudder as they stopped in front of another door. "Or so I thought at first. It wasn't real. Someone was trying to rattle me."

The sergeant grunted. "I don't suppose you were able to apprehend the culprit?"

Fayorn flushed. "I most certainly did."

The sergeant entered the room and emerged moments later with a 'rat' in each of his massive paws. Thony and Dae, held in place by the scruffs of their collars. Thony looked chagrined; Dae, indignant.

"*Children?*" Sergeant Sterevor said in amusement. "Go back to bed, sir. I'll take care of this little rodent problem."

Captain Fayorn glared back at him, then stalked past and went back in his room, slamming the door behind him.

The sergeant chuckled, letting go of his captives, but turning them so they both had to face him.

"So, you're the scoundrels who disturbed Captain Fayorn's beauty sleep."

"Yup!" Dae said proudly. Thony groaned.

"Hunh." Sergeant Sterevor shooed the pair of them back down the corridor.

They passed within inches of the darkened doorway where Amanita stood frozen.

How THONY Stopped a War (and Fixed a Friendship)

Book Four of the

Prankster Prince

Mangala McNamara

RISING DRAGON BOOKS

Mangala McNamara

Also available in eBook and hardcover editions.
McNamara, Kerridwen Mangala
How Thony Stopped a War (and Fixed a Friendship) by Mangala McNamara Indiana: Rising Dragon Books, 2024
 p. 1 map
(McNamara, Mangala. The Prankster Prince; bk. 4)
Summary: Runaway Prince Thony and his friends face an army of zombies created and controlled by an Evil Wizard and a vengeful Dark-elf who threaten the sanctity of the Fairy Wood. They must use pranks to save not only their world, but all the worlds in the universe.

ISBN 978-1-960160-42-3 (pbk)
1. Princes and princesses - Fiction. 2. Adolescent Rebellion - Fiction
ISBN 978-1-960160-43-0 (hc) ISBN978-1-960160-41-6 (eBook)

ISBN: 978-1-960160-42-3
First Print Edition: July 2024
10 9 8 7 6 5 4 3 2 1

For my son Griffin, who said I had to write this book
before he left for college.

CONTENTS

Prologue 1
(Because this story has gone on for long enough that now we need a re-cap)

Chapter ONE 5
Not-So-Scary Little Girls

Chapter TWO 9
A Really Nice Evil Wizard

Chapter THREE 19
Coming Clean

Chapter FOUR 25
Mischief and Mayhem, Round Two

Chapter FIVE 31
Mousie, Mousie

Chapter SIX 39
Saving the Dae – er – Day

Chapter SEVEN 45
Go Down in a Blaze of Glory

Chapter EIGHT 53
Long-term Problems

Chapter NINE 59
Fillies Before Bros

Chapter TEN 63
Existential Crisis, Part 1 (Why Are We All Here?)

Chapter ELEVEN 75
Existential Crisis Part 2 (Love is Dumb)

Chapter TWELVE 85
Existential Crisis, Part 3 (So, Why Are We *Really* Here?)

Chapter **THIRTEEN** 89
Bros Before Fillies?

Chapter **FOURTEEN** 95
Clearing Things Up?

Chapter **FIFTEEN** 101
Au Pears and Potatoes

Chapter **SIXTEEN** 113
An Explosive Situation

Chapter **SEVENTEEN** 125
When the Zombies Come Marching In

Chapter **EIGHTEEN** 145
When Push Comes to Shove

EPILOGUE 161
(Where we tie up every last little loose end – KNOT!)

Map from Captain Shalladra's Bedroom 176

Index of Characters 177

Index of Places 181

And now an excerpt from...

Thony and the Much-Anticipated Adventure
Chapter ONE: A Princely Punch 183

Author's Note 194

About the Author 197

Also by Mangala McNamara *198*

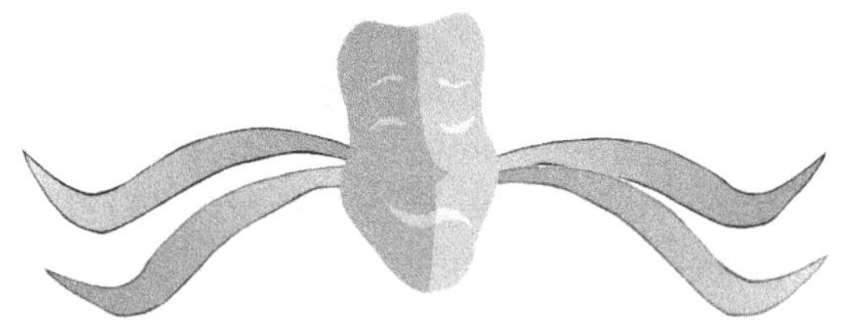

Prologue

(Because this story has gone on for long enough that now we need a re-cap)

CROWN PRINCE ANTHONY DEVINTHAL OF Aldyrwald *(known officially as 'the Affable and the Affirmative' due to an unfortunately adorable episode in his infancy, and continuing to be used despite his penchant for playing pranks... and his distaste for the title)* was faced with an impossible home-situation: his parents were planning to make him get married shortly after his fifteenth birthday.

That was, of course, a horrible idea, but the whole thing only got worse.

Papa and Mama *(aka King Bill and Queen Annabel of Aldyrwald)* weren't choosing him a proper Princess-Bride – the youngest or oldest daughter of a set of three or seven or twelve – and then setting up a proper Quest full of adventures and derring-do to win her. Nor were they going to arrange for a Worthy Miller's Daughter to go through adventures and derring-do to win Thony *(which is the nickname the prince strongly prefers to go by... well, until he's crowned. Because 'King Thony' just sounds stupid)*.

No, Papa was trying to pacify the neighbors – who want to invade on the pretext of the Devinthals having lost the Divine Right of Kings, because Thony's sister, Priscilla, was born with a bushy black tail. *(And nevermind that Priscilla – and their other sister, Joanna,*

1

and Joanna's husband, Prince Roger – have all become honest-to-goodness GODS, after some crazy thing called a Ragnarök where all of their world's Gods somehow kicked it at once.)

And 'pacifying the neighbors' meant making Thony marry a *middleborn* princess. One of the ones who wouldn't likely be able to find a husband otherwise because of her unlucky place in the birth-order. And if that weren't bad enough, it's likely to be an *old* middleborn princess – a maiden-aunt or even a maiden *great*-aunt of a reigning king. With a provision in the betrothal agreement that if Thony should die without issue, Aldyrwald and its three prosperous valleys would belong to his wife's family.

Which *probably* meant that said-wife would almost certainly be under instructions to off Thony and Papa both at her earliest convenience.

And since Aldyrwald was already one of the larger countries in the Mountain Region, that would mean that the newly-combined country would *definitely* be the largest... most powerful... and therefore *most dangerous* country. Which meant that the *other* neighbors weren't likely to let such a marriage go through in the *first* place...

...Thony might, in other words, be single-handedly responsible *(or something)* for the end of the five-hundred-year peace in the Mountain Region. Not to mention the end of the Devinthal dynasty and the existence of Aldyrwald as an independent nation.

So, what choices did he have?

None, really.

He ran away from home– erm, that is, set out on a Grand and Noble Quest to find a solution for this problem.

To find his own Princess-Bride. *(Hopefully one with a royal father who possesses a large and active military that he's willing to lend Thony – and Aldyrwald – for his daughter's protection and continued prosperity.)*

To have his *own* adventures, full of derring-do.

Or, at minimum, to grow up a little bit before getting married.

And on this brave endeavor, he took with him as boon companions, the prankster-stable-girl-*cum*-assistant-pastry-chef Amanita, and the unicorn, Twinklestar. *(More like they horned in on his adventure, but once he heard about the carnivorous plant-people he might run into, Thony was inclined to be generous about it all.)*

The three of them – and his horse, Silverfoot – bravely entered the Fairy Wood, known to be a Gateway to Worlds Unknown. Therein they met with foul monsters *(and fled for their lives)*, beautiful maidens from another world *(well, a decent-looking student-wizard and novice-priestess anyways)*, visited Fairyland and met with the Fairy Queen *(okay, that part was just plain cool)*, and were awarded a second Quest of Great Mystery. And another boon companion, the fairy-prince *(and Prankster-in-Chief)*, Puck.

And... Twinklestar decided to pick Thony as his unicorn-maiden.

And they exited the Fairy Wood onto Amanita and Puck's home-world *(because, oh, yeah, she **wasn't from around** Aldyrwald)* and got dropped into the middle of a war.

A war that's been instigated by an evil sorcerer named Valderon Raven'sWing, who seemed to be turning people into zombies to fight for him if he couldn't buy their loyalty. And who either wanted to invade Amanita's homeland *(of which she just happens to more or less be the Crown Princess, and never mentioned it, so... **awkward**)* or he plans to invade all the worlds in the universe through the Fairy Wood... possibly also including Aldyrwald.

But, y'know, stuff happens.

Of course, all that's standing between Valderon Raven'sWing and his plans to *Conquer the Known Universe* are Thony, Amanita and Twinklestar *(because Puck had to report in to the Fairy Queen about the war)*.

Oh, and also an accident-prone mercenette *(a mercenary, but she's only fourteen and way too small)* named Dae Goldeneyes. *(Who's being hunted down by a well-meaning mercenary friend who realizes that Dae does **not** belong in warzones.)*

And a trio of spies, including the famous Bard, Julanna Silversea, and the somewhat infamous mercenary-spy, Istevan Slyblade. And another guy named Davril, who seems to be in charge of taking care of Julanna's baby, Daphne.

And a gang of street-kids in the plainsland city of Flowerdust where all of the crazy seems to be converging...

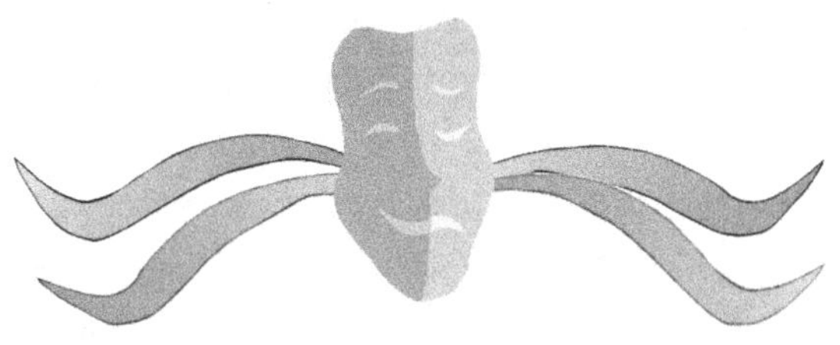

Chapter ONE

Not-So-Scary Little Girls

"**S**ERIOUSLY?" DAE WAS LOOKING OVER Thony's shoulder. "You decide to write some sort of chronicle of things and you don't even mention that I'm the most amazing warrior in the *world?* And we call them Evil Wizards here, not evil sorcerers."

Amanita peered over his other shoulder. *"That's* your biggest concern? Not that he might be *giving away our secrets?"*

Dae shrugged as Thony winced. "It's not like it's up-to-date. I mean he didn't even mention how he *rode into town on the back of Valderon Raven's Wing's horse."*

"I thought we decided we weren't going to talk about that," Thony muttered, looking down at what now seemed like a really bad idea.

"We said later," Amanita pointed out. "This is later."

She leaned onto the table he was using as a desk, resting her head on her left hand which she was propping up on her bent elbow. On his other side, Dae mirrored her, prompting the young prince *(and unicorn-maiden)* to note again how similar they were.

Those girls that he and Amanita had run into in the Fairy Wood had said something about Amanita being the *mirror-twin* of one of them, Girona Starshine. Which basically meant they were identical

5

twins born on different worlds to different parents. But Amanita and Dae had been born on the same world, and Girona had said that although there were hypotheses *(she might have said 'theories,' but Thony couldn't remember for sure. And anyways he was a Prince and knew the proper difference)* that there could be mirror-twins born on the same world, there was no evidence for it that anyone had been able to find. And anyways, the wizards Girona was studying with were apparently looking for a *theoretical* proof, not an *empirical* one, so whether they would even appreciate actual evidence wasn't clear to Thony.

All of which was basically a way to avoid thinking too hard about what the two of them were trying to intimidate him into talking about.

Luckily, two tiny girls – even if they looked a lot alike and were bracketing him like a pair of bookends – were not really all that intimidating. Not by comparison to the various embarrassments of the day, anyways.

"Come on, dude," Dae wheedled as Amanita narrowed her eyes at him.

All right, maybe *Amanita* was intimidating.

A little anyways.

He knew all about her penchant for malicious pranks and they were sharing a room right now, so she not only *knew* where he *slept,* but would have *unlimited access* to his sleeping self.

Hmmn. And considering his speculations that Dae might actually be her mirror-twin, perhaps he actually *should* be wary of... Nah. They couldn't be. Dae was way too accident-prone, and her dark-brown hair didn't seem to bleach reddish in the sun the way Amanita's did.

They were still too much alike. There must be a word for it, somewhere.

But the important thing right now was... to put the kibosh on Amanita's overly healthy sense of vengeance. As regarded himself anyways.

"Hey, I just realized," Thony said. "We should probably rearrange who's sleeping where."

"What?" Amanita looked a bit thrown by the completely random-seeming comment.

He leaned back in his chair casually... and not so incidentally out from between the two of them. "You two are both girls, so you guys should share this room. I can use the other one."

Amanita straightened up, frowning.

"Puck warded this room to keep the two of us safe," she began.

"And I like my privacy," Dae added. "Besides, it would look strange. You're supposed to be a girl, too. Unicorn-maiden, remember?"

Thony gave her a dark look. "Look strange to *whom*, exactly? Who do you think is watching *us*? According to anyone and his uncle we're just a bunch of *normal kids.*"

Yeah. 'Normal kids.' Not runaway royalty and underage warriors.

"Well, they might be watching *you*," Amanita said a bit uncharitably. "After all *you* rode into *town* on the back of *Valderon Raven's Wing's* saddle."

Abruptly she dragged the other chair around and plopped herself down next to Thony.

"What happened to you today?" she asked, her tone serious and quiet. "You told us you rode in with the sorcerer, but... did he *hurt* you or something?"

"No..." Thony sighed. He was going to have to give them the whole story. They wouldn't understand otherwise...

Chapter TWO

A Really Nice Evil Wizard

THONY HAD GUIDED THE SORCERER and his troop through the confusing, twisty streets of Flowerdust. Raven'sWing had followed the directions the incognito prince had pointed out from behind him without question, and the disapproving fellow, Fayorn, had finally stopped looking so disapproving as they made it onto streets that were less disreputable. Not that it was Thony's fault they'd come in on one of the back ways instead of the main gates. Though to be honest, Flowerdust just seemed to have sprawled out farther and farther in all directions and the 'main gates' had long been overgrown by buildings.

Thank goodness the Inn of the Starred Hoof was just off one of the *other* dusty roads that entered the town.

The sorcerer was... a very good rider.

Thoughtful of a lad riding in the precarious pillion position behind him without anything more than some saddlebags to stabilize his seat.

Full of friendly questions about things like which was the best bakery in town and when the next local festival was to be celebrated. Things that Thony had to find a way to not-quite-answer, since he hadn't the slightest clue. Though he was able to recommend a couple of food-stalls in the central market with absolute honesty.

And full of gentle questions about Thony's home and family, which he'd also had to deflect.

Based on how the line of questioning had become both more gentle and more probing, he rather suspected that Raven'sWing had come to the conclusion that Thony was either an orphan or suffering some sort of abuse at home.

Or a runaway. Which was, at least, accurate.

The sorcerer had seemed pleased that the people of the town took note of their passage and made way, but didn't cringe in fear. He remarked on it approvingly to Fayorn and the rest. Thony thought he caught sight of Jost's green cap in one of the crowds, but they were by too quickly to tell for sure.

And then they'd reached the large market square in front of the mayor's mansion and things had started to get... really weird.

The Raven-troops were clearly not expecting their Lord and Master to show up and some poor fool at the mansion gate decided to challenge the new arrivals. Fayorn snorted and made sarcastic comments about Captain Shalladra's command and training of her troops. The rest of the men with him had even ruder things to say, and one of them seemed to have unfurled a flag from somewhere and rode to the fore of the group, waving what must be Raven'sWing's personal standard in what even Thony could tell was an insulting fashion.

Raven'sWing settled his people – the ones who had come in with him, technically they were *all* his people after all – with one splay-fingered hand held level and gently lowered a few inches. His men quieted to mere mutters, and the standard-bearer backed up his horse to Raven'sWing's flank at a sharp glance from the equally-rebuked Captain Fayorn.

It wasn't even a *spell*. It was *respect*.

Thony couldn't help being impressed.

He also couldn't escape. An attempt to wriggle a little to slide off the horse *(to one side, thank you very much, he'd been riding since he was four, no matter what the Sorcerer Supreme here seemed to think, and he knew better than to slide off a horse's back end)* had been met with a hand removed from the reins and gently placed on his leg. And a quiet reminder that he'd been promised payment for his troubles and should stay until they'd sorted this out.

"Yessir," Thony had said. It was what he thought Jost – or one of his crew – would do. Poor boy offered coins, after all...

There was a hurried consultation going on at the gate, messengers running up and being sent back off in a different direction. After another couple of moments, the way was cleared and the new arrivals rode inside the mansion's wall.

The front courtyard of the Raven-HQ-*cum*-mayoral-mansion wasn't really all that large, though it seemed bigger than when Thony had viewed it from the roof-top in the night. It was seriously *cramped* now that it was lined with Raven-troops standing at attention three-deep along every wall.

Some of those troops had clearly been rousted out of bed and their salutes kept dipping down to cover yawns – at one point they seemed to be doing it in sequence, almost like a wave. Some of the rest were filtering in from the sides, huffing and redfaced and dusty and had clearly been called off of street patrol duty to make a good showing.

And then there was the fellow whose pants kept trying to fall down – Thony guessed he needed to tell Dae at least one of her pranks had borne fruit.

("Serves them right for making drawstring pants part of a uniform," Amanita said disapprovingly.

"Oh, it wouldn't have mattered," Dae said blithefully. "I messed with his belt, too.")

Thony hadn't had a full view of the panoply, peeking around Raven'sWing's back, but he hadn't seen Istevan.

And then Captain Shalladra came out and... somehow managed to *sweep* down the three broad steps from the main entrance despite wearing neither a gown nor a cape. She knelt on one knee once she reached the cobbled courtyard and bowed over her knee from the waist, spreading her arms to the sides.

Which was dramatic, but it had made Thony wince to think of balancing on his knee on those rounded stones.

"Captain Shalladra," acknowledged the man Thony was sitting behind.

"Welcome, my liege. All that you see is yours. And all that lies beyond it. I present to you the Township of Flowerdust, latest to come to your banner. What is your pleasure?"

She didn't stumble over the words, but Thony had practically heard her substituting for thees and thous.

Valderon Raven'sWing had looked around the courtyard with that same gentle smile. Thony was sure he caught a sparkle of amusement when the sorcerer's eye fell upon the fellow with the pants – so he had a sense of humor.

"You have done well, Captain Shalladra Stillheart. Rise and dismiss your troops. It grows late. We shall do a full review... tomorrow."

The woman had risen, doing so without hesitation or any visible indication that kneeling like that had hurt. A wave of her hand sent everyone scurrying off. The guy with his pants falling off moved somewhat faster than everyone else. The men who had arrived with Raven'sWing began to dismount.

She turned back and stepped close to Raven'sWing's horse, taking a firm grip on its bridle though the equine tried to sidle away. Thony had been reminded of the ease with which she had pulled the taller and bulkier Istevan up from the floor. The horse had as little chance as the man, the former controlled by the bit attached to the bridle, and the latter controlled by Shalladra's control of his... girlfriend?

The relationship between the adult spies hadn't been clear... not that Thony had gotten properly introduced to any of them.

"My lord," the pale, black-haired captain had greeted Raven'sWing more personally. There was a warm and vibrant note in her voice. Like she was, um, *personally* pleased that he had arrived, early or not.

("Seriously, Thony? You're going to keep speculating on the love-lives of all these people?"

"There's reasons, Amanita. You'll see. Just listen, okay?"

*"***Fine.*** But it was bad enough that I had to hide in that wardrobe while Captain Shalladra, um, **blackmailed** Istevan. If I have listen to any **other** gross stuff..."*

"It's relevant. You'll see."

"It better be...")

"Help the lad down, will you, Shalladra," Raven'sWing said. "He doesn't seem all that comfortable on a horse and we don't want such a helpful young man hurting himself on our behalf the first time he goes for a ride."

Which was just plain insulting. Thony had been riding since–

(*"Since you were four. Yes, we got it. Keep this moving along, dude."*)

"Certainly, my lord."

Shalladra did just that, pretty much bodily lifting Thony down, her face not revealing surprise, disgust, or anything else at his unexpected presence. She nudged him to stand back as the sorcerer swung down easily and a groom appeared to take charge of the horse. Raven'sWing lightly admonished the man to be gentle with his steed.

Thony had just time to notice that the equine's eyes were ringed with white and rolling with fear. Rather the way Silverfoot had looked when they'd fled the *glypherthryp* in the Fairy Wood. It seemed less skittish as the groom led it farther away.

Raven'sWing didn't seem to notice. "I hope our early arrival didn't inconvenience you in any way, Captain, but I thought Captain Fayorn Greensleeves ought to have a day or two to accustom himself to the place before relieving you. Fayorn," he beckoned the blonde fellow with the long, drooping mustaches forwards, "I don't believe you've met Captain Stillheart."

Fayorn's youth was somehow vastly more distinct when he stood next to his pale colleague. "I have not had the pleasure," he said, though he didn't sound like it was a *pleasure* at all. "The captain's exploits precede her, however. I know her by reputation."

Shalladra appeared to have a similar reaction and gave the younger captain a brief, curt nod before focusing those intense, ice-blue eyes of hers on Raven'sWing again.

Raven'sWing seemed... amused at the interplay. "Fayorn, why don't you have a look around. See what the place is like, eh. Take the sergeant with you."

Thony was beginning to be amused at the way Raven'sWing issued orders phrased like questions but without a hint of questioning in his tone. It seemed a useful skill to practice for the future.

(*"Enough with the editorializing, dude. We just wanna know what* **happened.***"*)

"Shalladra," Raven'sWing continued as Fayorn bowed and left them, along with a burly older man who had been one of the riders. "I'm sure you're just dying to show me all you've accomplished here. Where shall we begin?"

The smile he gave the woman was not the same kind one he'd given to Thony – or anyone else, for that matter.

Shalladra... *simpered* back at him.

(*"No* way!*" Dae was shocked. "She's a mercenary captain with a terrifying rep! She wouldn't* **simper!**"

"*Yes, way," Thony winced. "I've been simpered at by too many of Mama's ladies-in-waiting. Trust me. That's what she was doing."*

"*Ugh," Amanita said casually. "That's disappointing. Go on."*)

"I told you how docile the population is in my... communiqués," Shalladra's little dramatic pause suggested she was switching out a different word again. "So, it's been fairly routine. Even this mansion – it belonged to the local mayor. A pretentious fellow, so it's nicer than you might expect." She paused again. "The master suite is quite... adequate."

Raven'sWing's smile broadened in that just-for-Shalladra way. "Perhaps we'll have to start there, then. Dinner can be sent up, I would assume."

(*"Eeeeeewwww...."*

"*Hey, what about Istevan?"*

"*Girls, can I* **please** *just get through this?"*)

Shalladra reacted about the way one might expect at this point, but apparently wasn't so lost to military proprieties that she didn't feel obliged to answer, "Of course, sire. You should know, however, about the spy I caught a few days ago."

"Spy?" Valderon Raven'sWing's eyebrow crept up, but his tone sounded like... he was almost purring.

And Captain Shalladra practically stretched like a cat being petted. She tucked some of that straight, chin-length black hair behind her ear coquettishly – and her ear was *pointed*.

(*"So?"*

"*He's a bit of a rube, Dae. There's nobody with pointy ears on his world."*

"*A-***hem!***"*

"*Well, that I saw anyways..."*

"***ANY****ways..."*)

Shalladra did her little twisty 'oh, you're looking at *me?*' thing and elaborated.

"Well. More of a seditionist, really, I suppose. I have her locked away where she can't do any further harm. I was planning to make a public display of her in a trial in the next day or two." She made a little *moue*. "This place doesn't even have a decent dungeon, so she's in the pickle cellar."

("She 'moo'ed'? Like a cow?" Dae asked.

"It means pursed her lips and looked pouty," Amanita interpreted. She gave Thony a wry look. "I don't think it's a word people use outside of the nobility."

*"Well, then **say** that, man," Dae ordered him. "Talk like People, not Nobles."*

Thony decided to ignore that...)

"She?" Raven'sWing queried. His attention had seemed to sharpen even further, but he spared a glance for Thony. "Give the lad a few coins, Shalladra. He's done me a service."

"Yes," Shalladra told him as she opened her purse and counted out a few copper coins. "Some minstrel woman. Name of... Silversea, I think."

"Silversea? *Julanna* Silversea?" Raven'sWing demanded as Thony accepted the coins. "You *arrested* and *confined Julanna Silversea?*"

His entire demeanor had changed *again,* and now – although he still seemed incredibly *focused,* it was no longer directed all at Captain Shalladra. And she seemed to wilt a bit as he took away his regard.

"Yes... do you... know of her, milord?" Even her voice had been wilty instead of that supreme confidence and control they'd heard from her before.

"Do *I* know of her? *Everyone* knows of her, Shalladra. She's practically an icon on half the North Coast!" He controlled himself with a clear effort.

Shalladra had frowned. "Surely not. She's hardly more than an infant herself."

"We don't age the way your people do. She's an adult and an important one." The sorcerer passed a hand over his eyes and ended with pinching the bridge of his nose. Papa had done that a fair amount when Thony was brought to him on some charge or other, so he was fairly familiar with that particular expression of exasperation.

"Leaving all that aside... it is *terrible* politics to arrest a Bard, Shalladra. We talked about this."

The woman seemed to have recovered from looking a little lost. Her voice had also recovered some of its self-absorbed indifference and smug confidence.

(*"Oooh. Aren't **we** being fancy?"*)

"Sire," Shalladra said almost condescendingly. "I know that *you* are new to the idea of ruling, but the purpose of conquering a place is to control it. And that includes most especially the people who carry the news from place to place, such as Bards and Singers. Once you have eliminated all opposition and rebellion – and the remaining Singers belong to *you* – then you can exert these tender sensibilities of yours and free them to do their work."

Raven'sWing had frowned. "That's not the way *we* do it, Shalladra–"

"Milord. You said you planned to build an empire to rival any other known. One that will *last,* you said." She raised an eyebrow. "Lord Nightcreeper did just that. You took me as your advisor because I knew his techniques."

And then... she looked at Thony and... he wasn't sure what, but he found himself shivering. Rather like the sorcerer's horse.

Raven'sWing seemed to come out of some fugue right then, and suddenly he was beaming that *special* smile at Shalladra again. And her eyes were back on him instead of Thony.

"So I did, Captain. So I did. And you've been absolutely invaluable to me. Of course."

The sorcerer had reached out and put an arm around Thony's shoulders and he'd felt... safe. Safe from *Captain Shalladra,* anyways.

That beaming smile had been turned on *him,* and Thony had felt that *he* would do anything for Valderon Raven'sWing. Then the man had toned it down a little and ruffled Thony's hair.

"Go on with you, lad. But come back tomorrow and perhaps I'll have another little task for you. Ah, to have a lad like you for my own..." He had shaken his head and given Thony a shove towards the gate.

Thony had backed carefully away as Raven'sWing recaptured his captain's eye. He'd felt... rather like a baby rabbit when she looked at him. A baby rabbit that had been sighted by a cat.

"Let's get our fair Bard out of gaol, dear Captain," Raven'sWing said, putting an arm about Shalladra's shoulders, and she looked up at him all googly-eyed but *his* attention seemed to be wandering again. "I haven't seen Julanna in... a long while..."

Shalladra straightened up again, her voice gone smug and hard again. "Surely you would prefer to refresh yourself first, my lord. You've been on the road all day and riding hard for the last several to have made it here so soon."

"Hmmmn." Raven'sWing hesitated, and then he beamed at her again. "And dinner with you? Of course, dear Captain. A few hours more or less won't make a difference at this point. Erroth," he waved over one of the men who had ridden in with him, "See that the Bard is released from her – a pickle cellar did you say, dear Captain? From her pickle cellar. And provided with an appropriate suite. Under guard," he added, laying fingers across her lips when Shalladra looked ready to object.

They went into the mansion and Thony was finally able to make his escape.

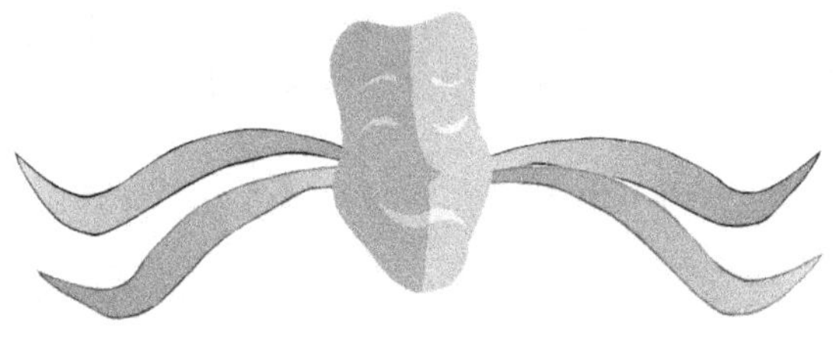

Chapter THREE

Coming Clean

"SO... WHY DID WE NEED to hear all the gross parts?" Amanita demanded.

Thony gave her an incredulous look. "There's obviously a *Thing* going on between Raven'sWing and Shalladra."

"We knew *that* already," Dae pointed out. "From those letters."

She pointed at the neatly tied bundle on the table next to where he'd been writing. All of them stared at the stack for a moment.

"Dear Goddess," Amanita muttered. "We've got to get those put back. Like, *now.*"

Dae nodded. "Tonight. We'll go in tonight."

"I agree. And we need to continue our campaign of pranking them." Amanita gave a short, firm nod.

Thony looked at them both, gnawing a little on his lip. He'd managed to avoid telling them about his... awkward conversation with Jost right before Raven'sWing had arrived. So far anyways. He should probably mention that Jost had agreed to get his crew of street-kids to help them out. If *Thony* told the girls, after all, he might be able to control how they heard it...

Thony switched to chewing anxiously on a thumb. "Are you sure about that? I mean now the sorcerer-dude is *here...*"

He couldn't give up, not with Aldyrwald in danger, but...

19

Amanita gave him an incredulous look. "*Now* you want to back off? He's just a *guy,* Your Royal Highness. He still puts his pants on one leg at a time."

"That's not necessarily true," Dae said thoughtfully, and Amanita flashed an irritated look at her.

"What do you mean?"

Dae grinned. "It *is* possible to put your pants on both legs simultaneously if you're sitting down. I do it all the time."

"You would," Thony muttered as Amanita asked "How?" in the tone of someone fascinated in spite of herself. Dae mimed it while Thony rolled his eyes heavenward.

"I'll have to try that some time," Amanita commented when Dae had finished.

"It's a real timesaver." The mercenette giggled. "I wonder which way Raven'sWing does it."

"Who *cares* if he puts his pants on by one leg or two?" Thony demanded, exasperated beyond his limits. "I know *I* don't. Him being a master sorcerer who is trying to build some kind of absolute despotic dictatorship empire across all the Worlds has absolutely nothing to do with how he gets dressed!"

He paused to glower heartily at them. "And you two aren't taking this anywhere seriously enough! Didn't you hear what I said? He clearly has some kind of *spell* on Captain Shalladra. A *love spell,* maybe. And he put some of it on *me,* at least the edges of it or something and I still... I still..."

The young prince shook his head hard and tried to blink away the frustrated tears that were coming up. "I *still* can't help thinking he's a great guy."

He looked away. "Oh, yeah. And I ran into Jost and his crew. They know I'm not a girl now. And Jost is going to have them help us with pranking the city to stop the enchanted army. Except... Except I don't even *want* to now!"

Thony folded his arms on the table and buried his face in them. Hopefully he'd done it fast enough that the girls wouldn't see those tears.

An... awkward pat on his shoulder from Amanita's side. "That's called a *compulsion* spell more generally. They aren't hard to notice... from the outside. And, for better or for worse, they're one of the easier spells to set. Almost anyone..."

Her voice trailed off and Thony guessed Dae was giving the runaway princess a significant look.

"Not *anyone*, Your Royal Highness," Dae said with as much dry sarcasm as Amanita had addressed Thony with a few minutes earlier. "Sorcerers and wizards and witches. And magickal beings. And... royalty."

"Actually, most *noble* houses have some Gifts along those lines," Amanita said in a small voice. "And... some other families with long histories who – for one reason or another – were never ennobled."

Hunh. Interesting.

That was... true to some extent in the Mountain Region around Aldyrwald as well, though it was understood that one was supposed to *suppress* one's magickal tendencies unless one intended to abdicate one's titles and go live out in a tower – or a cottage, or even a haunted castle – out in the wilds. Kings and Queens with magickal power tended to have stories that... went rather badly. For everyone, but especially for them.

For example, there was the Queen who became obsessed with proving she was lovelier than her stepdaughter – the child of her husband's first wife that he doted on. The Princess had gotten stuck in an enchanted sleep until her Prince kissed her – but the beautiful Queen had been forced to wear burning hot iron shoes and dance until she died. Exactly *whose* idea that was – the Prince and Princess or her own husband – Thony had never heard.

It had made him very, very glad that his own great-great-grandmother, Arabella, had given up practicing magick once his great-great-grandfather, Crown Prince Anthony had found her and *well* before they ever ruled Aldyrwald. There weren't any tragedies like that in the Devinthal family.

On the other hand, *knowing* what it was... he should be able to shake it off. Thony hadn't thought about the lessons he'd gotten in Magickal Defenses in ages, but it wasn't all that hard...

He sat up a bit to see Dae perched on the table and looking... disgruntled, but not particularly dismayed.

"I'm a little more concerned about just *whose* techniques for world-domination she's sharing with Raven'sWing," Amanita added in a more normal tone of voice. "'Lord Nightcreeper' sounds like it's a name I should *know*... but I can't think who it could be."

"It sounds *creepy*," Dae put in, then snickered at her own joke. "Okay, so let's see, what do we need to do?"

The mercenette began ticking things off on her fingers.

"We need to put those letters back and continue our campaign of mischief against the troops; see if we can rescue Julanna Silversea; and stop the enchanted armies." She looked up at them brightly. "Did I forget anything? Oh, yeah, I need to check in with Evrien Quickfoot at the Guildhall and make sure Kamauri and Daennor and Rainsparkle don't know where I am and what I'm working on."

"We also need to take some more supplies out to Davril and the baby," Thony pointed out. "Or did you manage to get out to see him, Dae?"

She rolled her eyes. "Yeah, he's good. *They're* good. *I* got another lecture about not being old enough to do stuff." She sighed. "I think he has younger sisters that are about our age."

"And we need to dye Thony's hair," Amanita said. She got up and pulled a paper packet out of a basket on her bed. "This stuff is supposed to make it turn black."

Thony winced. "Jost wants to be able to tell it's me as I move around the city. He says he's told everyone to recognize me by the red hair."

"That hair *is* like a battle-flag," Dae agreed.

Amanita frowned. "That includes the Sorcerer Supreme now, too, though. Is that still a good idea?" She narrowed her eyes at him. "And you say *he* knows you're a boy?"

Thony shrugged, hoping to avoid explaining in any detail.

The girls exchanged a *look*.

"I thought he was helping us because he was sweet on the 'unicorn-maiden'," Dae commented. She gave Thony a curious look. "How'd you get him to agree to help anyways?"

Thony reminded himself that his *Secret Plan* was to get Dae and Puck – if he ever showed up again – to whisk Amanita away to a safer locale, will-she-nil-she. He needed to stay on Dae's good side. And he needed to *talk* to her about this the instant he could find a chance to do it without Amanita in attendance. And within hearing.

But he couldn't seem to be *pandering* or these clever girls would figure it out. And Dae, with her big mouth, would blurt it out as soon she figured it out and then there'd be no way to catch Amanita when she wasn't paying attention.

But having Amanita – the next-in-line to the throne of Pathremir after her mother – here in the battle-zone was just too risky. Raven'sWing might or might not be able to get to Aldyrwald, where Thony could prove a useful hostage. He could *definitely* reach Pathremir according to the map that was tucked under that stack of letters on the table.

Jost had – more or less – agreed to help with this, too.

Thony had to give the girls *enough* without making them realize there was more to say.

Well... it was going to be embarrassing, but it would definitely distract them.

He avoided Dae's bright, interested gaze, and muttered something at the table's surface.

As he'd guessed, her eyes lit up further and she asked for clarification.

He mumbled again, and this time Amanita caught it.

All too sweetly, she looked at Dae. "He *says* that Jost said 'maybe it doesn't matter' that he's a boy."

Dae's eyes widened. "Oh. Oh, *wow.*"

Thony knew his face was burning red. It was fine. He hadn't sorted out that Jost was saying he might *still* be 'sweet on' Thony, even though he was a boy, until after he'd gotten back here. In that space of time when he'd had the room to himself before the girls came boiling in with having heard about him riding into Flowerdust with the sorcerer.

What was *embarrassing* wasn't that there was someone thinking about him like that – Mama's ladies-in-waiting had pretty much inured him to *that* idea after all. He hadn't particularly enjoyed their attentions, but they'd been flirting with him since he was ten or eleven years old.

It wasn't even that Jost was a boy – as he'd told the young chieftain of the street-kids, that wasn't a big deal in Aldyrwald, except for royalty who needed Heirs. Queen Arabella had been raised by her fathers – a pair of powerful wizards – and supposedly the only problem was that King Anthony had complained he couldn't make mother-in-law jokes.

No, the *embarrassing* part was that he had been so *utterly clueless* when Jost said that.

Thony had gone over the conversation in his head a dozen times now and felt more like an idiot every time.

Well, at least Jost had come to the conclusion that Thony was clueless because he 'wasn't as grown up as he looked.' Peasants at home sometimes married as early as fourteen, Thony knew, though they weren't *supposed* to until they were at least fifteen. But it was considered better to have an underage pair wedded before a baby was actually born... which suggested that they were, um, *fooling around* rather earlier than that.

Princes rarely married until they were eighteen or twenty-one, though princesses were expected to be properly rescued by sixteen or so. *(And none of that was counting all the middleborns, who didn't really count, of course.)*

At least he could probably shut Amanita up over this. And presumably Dae would wind down if she didn't have anyone to keep bouncing not-so-witty repartee off of.

"Yeah, yeah," he broke into their banter. "I need to marry a princess, not Jost. What about you, *Princess Amanita?* Don't they have princes and noblemen lined up waiting for *you?*"

Amanita stopped mid-snicker and gave him such a flash of misery that he almost *(almost)* regretted saying it – and then she went *fierce* and *nonchalant* and *utterly obnoxious* and he no longer felt guilty at all.

Chapter FOUR

Mischief and Mayhem, Round Two

SOMEHOW, THEY MANAGED TO PULL themselves back to the business at hand and plan the evening's campaign. Nothing further was said about Jost and the street-kids. Thony had no opportunity to catch Dae alone.

They went back over the rooftops to Raven'sWing's HQ, taking a great deal more care on the last outdoor bits. Security around the former mayoral mansion was much tighter than it had been the last time.

Again, they split up, each to create their own set of mayhem, with plans to meet up in the cellars when they were done to look for Julanna Silversea – or possibly Istevan Highblade.

Dae snuck about the barracks again, shortening everyone's laces a bit more, soaking the towels, and rearranging clothing. One fellow's rather lacey underthings were put out in the hallway and hidden behind large sculptures and vases. A woman fighter's outer garments were distributed among the rooms of several men.

Thony used Amanita as inspiration and switched the salt and sugar as she had done back in Aldyrwald. For good measure, he mixed up several other spice pots whose contents were of similar colors and odors.

He then drained all the oil he could find – including from the lamps – and stored it in bottles that used to hold pickles. Used to? The pickle jars had been emptied into the stew that was simmering overnight on the hearth... pickles and pickling brine together. Feeling rather pleased with himself, he went looking for a stair into the bowels of the building.

Amanita had the stack of letters and the map to replace... but discovered that it was harder to rediscover a place found by accident than finding it had been in the first place. She finally hit upon the idea that the place would be more heavily guarded and then had to divine a pattern to the movements of the various Raven-troops moving about the building in what was now the hour before midnight.

It took some time, and she had to go around the back way for the servants' passages to get into Captain Shalladra's master suite. The servants' door was locked, which Amanita found ridiculously paranoid, but definitely explained all those dust-bunnies under the bed. She carefully oiled the hinges and the lock and then picked it to let herself into the bedchamber directly.

As before, a small lamp was burning – turned down until it was just a bead of light, but her eyes had adjusted to the utter blackness of the servants' byways and that tiny bead seemed to light up the whole room. A cautious glance showed her rumpled sheets, but no occupants.

Amanita stole carefully out from her servants' door and over to the desk where she had found the map and letters. Nothing seemed disturbed on the desk, although the room had a much more 'lived-in' look overall.

She carefully put everything back and was about to leave, when a sound of voices startled her and a beam of light shot across the room from the large keyhole in the door that led to the sitting room.

Amanita's *first* thought was to dash for her own door and get on the other side as quickly as possible. She had *zero* intention of having to hide out in the wardrobe again, covering her ears.

Her *second* thought was to peer through that keyhole and see what she could.

After all, people who came into a sitting room and turned up a light that brightly were often planning to sit there for awhile. There was a very good chance they wouldn't notice that there was someone creeping around inside the attached bedroom.

And, I mean, the temptation was irresistible, wasn't it?

To her not-entire surprise, the first thing she saw was an older guy sitting on one of the comfy chairs in there. Black hair with wings of white at his temples. Or at least from the one temple she could see; she was assuming he was symmetric. This must be the sorcerer, though 'Raven'sWing' seemed like an odd usename since ravens were *black*.

Well, maybe he'd been younger when he chose it. Or maybe it had been assigned to him, like with knights in Dawil and Bards in Selavan. Amanita had no real idea how Evil Wizards acquired their *nommes de magique*.

Frustratingly, she could either *listen* at the keyhole or *look* through it. While peering through, she could get the tone, but not the sense of what was being said.

Raven'sWing had a deep, warm voice rather than the high, cold one she'd always felt an Evil Wizard *should* have. Clearly, he was breaking the rules somewhere.

And the person who answered him was a woman with a melodious voice – Captain Shalladra? No, *she* really *did* have an icy tone, except when she was being smug and superior.

This had to be...

Raven'sWing's conversation-partner leaned forwards to spoon some sweetening into her cup of tea.

It was Julanna Silversea.

And... she seemed to be having a perfectly pleasant tea with Raven'sWing.

Middle of the night or not.

Middle of a *war-zone* that he was *responsible* for or not.

Though Amanita supposed the woman might be relieved at having been extracted from – Thony had said a pickle cellar, hadn't he?

No longer able to resist *listening,* Amanita turned her head to press her ear to the keyhole.

"–ll haven't told me why you're so far from Selavan," Raven'sWing was saying.

"I'm a *Bard,* Val. Traveling around to sing songs is literally what we do."

VAL?!?

"Besides, I rather think I stirred things up enough in Selavan for awhile." There was a smirky sound to Julanna's voice. "Istevan suggested it might be a good idea for me to make myself scarce until things settle. And the rest of my family in Selavan agreed."

She didn't sound particularly broken up about that. Amanita wouldn't have taken her own family wanting her to leave nearly so well. Which was at least slightly ironic, all things considered.

"Ah, yes, *Istevan*." Raven'sWing's voice was... unhappy. "I noticed his name on the rosters Shalladra sent me of her new recruits. I... was hoping it meant that you and he weren't still *together*. But I suppose, since you're both *here*..."

Julanna actually chuckled. "We were never *together* the way you're thinking."

"Really?" If skepticism could drip... Amanita really wanted to see as well as hear, but oh, well. "He seemed fairly *proprietary* when he came up to the university to fetch you back to Selavan."

A pause where a nonchalant shrug might fit...

"He's my cousin's husband. I think he sees me as another little sister to look after."

"Your cousin – isn't Jessina quite a bit younger than you?"

"A different cousin." Julanna sighed a bit dramatically. "Those Selavani men. They just don't understand that a woman *can* handle her own life. We argued about it all the way back to Dynsfyor."

"He hurried you off so quickly... we didn't even get to say 'goodbye'."

Was the Evil Wizard going to *cry*? His voice sounded... *sad* or... *wistful* or... *something*.

Of course, Amanita hadn't exactly gotten to say proper 'goodbyes' herself when she left home... nor when she left Aldyrwald either, for that matter. So maybe she was just imputing her own feelings to Raven'sWing. Who surely couldn't feel such human things as *regret* or he wouldn't be an *Evil* Wizard... right?

"Oh, Val..." Another small sigh. "I *wanted* to... Or rather I *didn't* want to say 'goodbye' at all."

During the rather pregnant pause following that, Amanita pretend-barfed on the floor.

And when it became clear that there wasn't a lot more to *hear*... and she *really* didn't want to *look*... she started to sneak away.

Exactly why Amanita decided to try peering through the keyhole into the office, she couldn't have said. There hadn't been any changes in lighting from that side. Or any noises.

Or... anything.

What she saw, however, made her steal very, very quietly away, back through the servants' door and down stairs. She had to find Thony and Dae before they got caught looking for the no-longer-imprisoned Bard.

It was *incredibly imperative*.

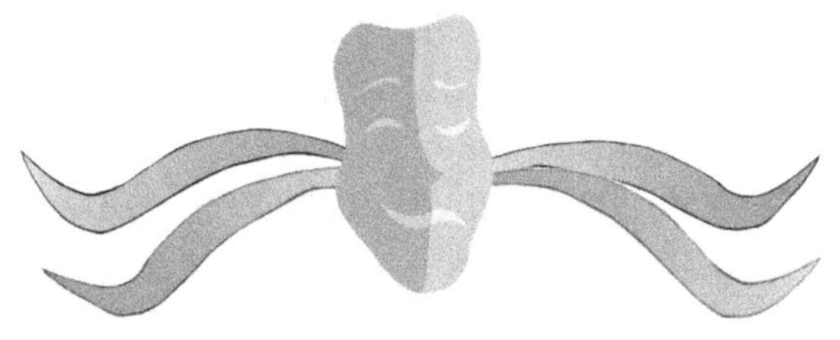

Chapter FIVE

Mousie, Mousie

Trying to save time, Amanita emerged from the dark and dusty servants' passages and into the better-lit and somewhat-less-Byzantine main corridors. It took a little while, given that she didn't want to come out near the master suite – there were Raven-troops coming and going from the office and standing guard right outside. Which she should have remembered when she was hiding out in the bedroom.

She grimaced at how she was, herself, now covered in grime. Hopefully she'd be mistaken for a serving-girl rather than an interloper. At least there didn't seem to be anyone moving around in this area of the building.

A level down *(and why did this stairwell only lead down* ***one*** *level?)* a blue-tunicked Raven-soldier passed her without seeming to notice her existence – which would have been spectacular, except that she suddenly realized it was Istevan.

Hesitating only an instant, Amanita turned and ran after him.

"Sir!" She managed to catch at his sleeve, though his long stride, tired as it was, made her trot just to keep up.

But he slowed at her importuning.

"Yes?" His tone was abrupt, his eyes haunted... though less so than the last time she'd seen him. He still looked like he needed a week of good sleep – though she had to admit *(to herself, not Thony and **certainly** not Dae)* that he would have been pretty good-looking without those dark-circles under his eyes. Even if he *was* stupidly tall.

The gentle look in his warm, brown eyes as he realized how he was out-pacing her and how quickly he came to a considerate halt rather did him a better turn in her opinion than his looks.

"Yes?" Istevan said again, but with a friendly tone. "Aren't you a little young to be on night-duty?"

Amanita caught her breath – and ignored the comment on her size. "Lieutenant Istevan Highblade?"

The man nodded, though his eyes were suddenly wary. "I am he."

"I carry word from Daphne," Amanita said, making it up on the spot. Why hadn't they planned out what they would do if they actually *did* make contact with him or the Bard?

Istevan's stared at her for a moment, and suddenly the phrase 'heart in his eyes' made sense to Amanita for the first time. He cast quick glances up and down the deserted hallway, then bundled her into a – thankfully *empty* – side room. A music room, it seemed to be, since there were several instruments including a piano. Relics of the previous owner of the house.

"*What* word?" he demanded in a quiet, fierce tone.

"'Mama,'" Amanita quoted. "'Hoas.'" She paused. The baby hadn't been awake very long while the runaway princess had been around. Had she said...? "'Steee-wan.'"

Istevan did not look terribly amused.

"Well, what do you expect?" the girl asked. "She's only a baby. Davril wants you to know they're both out of the city and safe," she added. "We're friends."

Istevan frowned, but it was easy to see it was a worried-frown, not an angry-frown. She'd seen enough of both to be able to distinguish them easily.

"I suppose I can believe you've seen them. That is how Daphne talks." His expression lightened briefly in a sort of vague fondness. Then he focused on Amanita again. "But I can't imagine Davril sending a *child* into danger just to tell me that. You can't even be as old as Kyri!"

That must be the younger sister Dae had guessed about.

Amanita squirmed a little under that concerned gaze... which was something she didn't generally do. Tad – the stablemaster in Aldyrwald could have given her that look and gotten the same response, and maybe her dad, but not a great many others.

"Well, he didn't," she admitted. "He doesn't actually know we're here. He tried to discourage us from, well, this. But we're helping him and Daphne," she added earnestly.

Istevan smiled faintly. "I've done that a time or two myself." He snorted, eyes going faraway with some memory for an instant. "And he's done the same to me. But you said 'we,' so there's more than one of you... *kids?*"

When Amanita hesitated, he added, "You look – and sound – like you're from Pathremir. You're an awfully long way from home, child. Are your friends Pathremiri, too? Why are you involved in any of this?"

She lifted her chin a little defiantly. "We may be kids, but we're involved because we don't want to go home to places that have been conquered and crushed. It's our world, too. We have a right to defend it. And we saw you and the Bard – Julanna – get arrested. So, we helped Davril and the baby. Because we were *there* and we *could*. And if everyone did that, the world would be a better place, wouldn't it?"

The man closed his eyes for a moment, then nodded. "Well said. And you've convinced me you know Davril – and Daphne. Why *are* you here?" Then he shook his head. "Silly me. You're here because *he* is."

Amanita frowned. "'He' who? Oh, you mean Valder–"

The tall, blue-clad man had his hand over her mouth before she could speak another syllable.

"Don't," he whispered. "*He* is a very cautious person and I shouldn't be surprised if he's set spells to alert him to those who use his name too casually. Or too frequently." Istevan removed his hand. "Words are powerful things. Guard yours, girl."

The ex-stablegirl/runaway princess swallowed hard. How many times had they spoken the sorcerer's name? She was *such* an idiot! She could probably set a spell like that herself – it wasn't even *hard*. Some people believed you didn't even need a spell for that – that their left ear would itch or something if people were talking about them.

Would *he* have set the spell to report back to him *who* was speaking? Or maybe even *what* they said? Though that was a lot harder...

Istevan gave her an approving look. "Good girl. Now, I don't have any reason to believe Val actually *has* done that. But caution is the course of wisdom."

Amanita nodded a little shakily, then did a double-take. "Hey, waitaminute. You sound like you *know* him. *Personally.*"

The tall man straightened up, his expression rueful. "I did. I... do, I suppose. I'll find out shortly. He sent for me. I was on my way to his rooms when I ran into you."

"Almost ran *over* me," Amanita groused habitually, then shook her head. "What do you mean you'll 'find out'? Either you know the dude or you don't."

Istevan sighed. "We... didn't part on the best of terms."

"Because he thought you were dating Julanna," Amanita stated. "Were you?"

"Hmmmn." Istevan folded his arms and looked down at her from his ridiculous height. "Who did you say you are again? And *why* did you make contact with me?"

"I didn't," the girl informed him. "And I just wanted to let you know you aren't alone. And to offer our help if you nee– if you can use it."

Guys tended to be touchy about *needing* help she remembered a little belatedly. Even Thony – look at how he'd tried to set off from Aldyrwald without her.

"We're doing what we can to hinder the, um, *sorcerer-guy's* plans for the, um, *home of the Fair Folk,*" she added, trying not to name names, now that she realized the problem. "But we can run messages, help you rescue the Bard, create a diversion so you can escape – that kind of thing – without mucking up our own operations."

Istevan eyed her with what was at least an attempt to hide his dubiousness. It wasn't *belief,* but she'd take it. Most other adults would have given her straight up sarcasm and doubt.

"Well, it's... nice... to know we aren't alone, I suppose... If you could let Davril know we're all right..." It was clearly an attempt to get her – *them* – out of danger. "You can tell him that we – Julanna and I – are still sticking to The Plan. We'll be – how did you put it – running our own 'operations to hinder the sorcerer-guy.'" He chuckled slightly, and it was a warm, friendly, if rather tired, sound. "From the inside of things. You're working from outside his bureaucracy, I take it."

Oh. Maybe he *wasn't* trying to get rid of her and her team. That was... gratifying.

"Sort of," Amanita admitted. "It's... small stuff so far. We thought we'd have more time to scale up."

Suddenly Istevan's face lit up with a sudden grin. "You and your, ah, *colleagues* wouldn't happen to be why the food was so topsy-turvy the last day or so?"

She shrugged a little, not wanting to give away too much – and she didn't really remember the details of what Thony had said he'd done in the kitchens anyways.

"Clever to use what's to hand," Istevan said approvingly, and *that* felt weirdly good, coming from him. "Now, I don't have much time – Val and Julanna will be wondering what happened to me–"

"Oh, I doubt it," Amanita couldn't help herself from muttering, and he raised his eyebrows.

"I won't ask," he said. "A good spy – or saboteur – doesn't give away most of what she knows. Or how. Or *who.* What I don't know I can't reveal. But Shalladra knows I was sent for as well and she's... someone to be wary of as well." He winced. "Particularly for me."

"Um, yeah..." Amanita said uncomfortably, remembering things she'd seen and heard... and tried *not* to see and hear. "Well, good... luck? We'll try to get in touch with you whenever we're near enough, to see if you need anything."

He nodded, but his attention was clearly elsewhere. "Try to make it just you. I don't want to even *know* who your compatriots are. And if you think of any way I can help with *your* 'operations'... just keep in mind that I have precious few resources, and if what you're doing conflicts with my work, I'm sticking to my own plans."

"Fair enough," Amanita agreed. "For right now, I just need to know the fastest way down to the pickle cellar."

"Where they were keeping Julanna?" Istevan frowned, then shrugged. "Nevermind."

He gave her directions, and they parted ways, taking turns sneaking out of the deserted room so no one would notice they'd been talking.

Amanita followed the directions, though the stupid mansion's corridors seemed to go on forever. It didn't seem nearly as large from the outside.

"EEEEeeeek!"

Amanita's blood curdled at the high-pitched screech and chills crawled up and down her back.

Someone must have seen a mouse.

That had to be it, though it was surprising that there was anyone in this blasted place who would react like that to a mouse.

Well... Amanita had a sinking feeling.

It *had* to be a mouse.

A mouse or... Dae.

Anyone wanna lay bets?

The runaway princess cursed under her breath and dashed back up the corridor she'd just dashed down on her way to a stairwell that Istevan said would lead to the pickle cellar. She was heading in the direction of that scream.

A door burst open just ahead of her. Amanita ducked into a darkened doorway as it slammed shut again and there was the sound of a frantic scrambling for keys. She was just in time to avoid being seen, then cautiously peeked out when the bobbing light – a handheld lantern – and hobnailed boots had clattered by.

There was sudden pounding on another door down the corridor in the direction she'd been heading. The door opened, then shut rather solidly.

When Amanita dared to peer out into the corridor again, a white-faced young man with weirdly long, drooping mustaches was just emerging from the second door. A chunky-looking sergeant-at-arms was following him out, regarding him disapprovingly.

"You realize you've roused the entire garrison, Captain Fayorn," the sergeant growled.

Amanita was shocked. First, by the sergeant's tone when addressing a superior officer, and second, by the fact that the apparent originator of the rather *girly* shriek was, in fact, an adult male.

"Hardly that, Sergeant," the young man's voice was shaky, but they were walking back down the hall. "They're all a couple floors up. I'm the only one who got a room on the office level. Even Shalladra and milord likely couldn't hear."

"I wouldn't bet on that," the sergeant grumbled. "The Captain has ears like a fox. And eyes like an eagle. I can't imagine she – or His Sorcerousness – are going to be particularly forgiving that you disturbed their rest because of a *mouse.*"

"A *rat,*" Captain Fayorn corrected with a shudder. "And we don't need to be delicate here, Sergeant. They weren't *resting.* And you know it as well as I know it."

"Not my place to speculate on my superiors," the sergeant said somewhat primly. They were passing Amanita's hiding place now and she pulled back farther into the doorway of... was this some kind of gaming room? "But over a *mouse,* lad..."

"*I'm* your superior now, too, Sterevor," the younger man said dryly. "And a *rat.* Or so I thought at first. It wasn't real. Someone was trying to rattle me."

"I'd say they succeeded," Amanita muttered to herself.

"They must know I'm from the eastern edge of the Mountains of Koitan," Fayorn was going on. "It was calculated and planned to affect *me.*"

The sergeant grunted, so apparently that made sense to *him*. "I don't suppose you were able to apprehend the culprit?"

Fayorn flushed, to judge by the back of his neck in the lamplight. "Cul*prits*, Sergeant Sterevor. And I most certainly did. Locked them in, too."

The sergeant grunted again. "Handy that you ended up in a room that can be locked from the outside then. Still seems damned disorganized of them not to have been ready for us. Milord is known for running a bit early on his plans – and those damned zombies already delayed us so long–"

Fayorn snorted. "As if Her Iciness would bother. And she'll get away with it, too. Milord has to work to keep *her* under control. He won't care about minor inconveniences like this."

Sergeant Sterevor held a hand out for the keys. "She's critical to making all of this work, lad. You know that."

"Aye." Fayorn sounded very sour.

The sergeant opened the door and went in.

A moment later, he emerged with a 'rat' in each of his massive paws. Thony and Dae, held in place by the scruffs of their collars. Thony looked chagrined; Dae, indignant.

Amanita pulled a hand across her face in disgust.

"*Children?*" Sergeant Sterevor said in amusement. "Go back to bed, sir. I'll take care of this little rodent problem."

Captain Fayorn glared back at him, then stalked past and went back in his room, slamming the door behind him. The sergeant chuckled.

He let go of his captives, turning them so they both had to face him.

"So, you're the scoundrels who disturbed Captain Fayorn's beauty sleep."

"Yup!" Dae said proudly. Thony groaned.

"Hunh." Sergeant Sterevor shooed the pair of them back down the corridor towards the room he'd originally come out of.

They passed within inches of the darkened doorway where Amanita stood frozen.

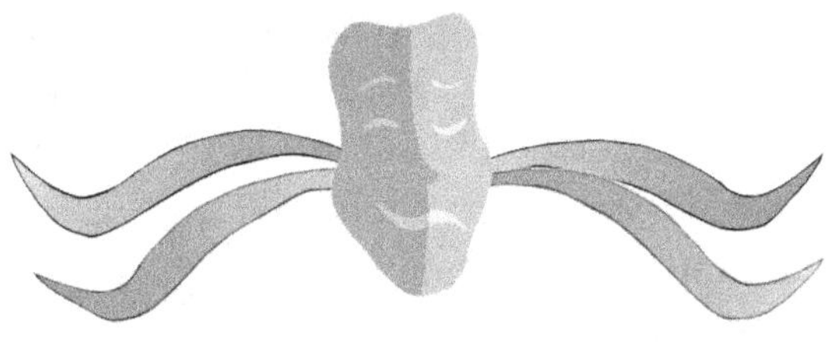

Chapter SIX

Saving the Dae – er – Day

THONY PLODDED MISERABLY ALONG THE corridor beside Dae.

This was it.

The end.

The finish.

Bye-bye, baby.

His homeland was about to be Heirless.

He was about to *die*.

The ogre-sized sergeant behind him had said he'd 'take care' of them.

Thony glared at Dae as she skipped nonchalantly along beside him. *How could she be so cheerful?*

It was all her fault anyways. Why'd she have to play that *one last stupid prank* on the new commander of the Flowerdust garrison? Why couldn't she keep the Big Picture in that flighty little head of hers?

And he'd finally gotten a chance to tell her his idea about getting Amanita out of the war-zone...

Hey! It *was* all Dae's fault.

Maybe if he could just get everyone to *see* that... Which felt kind of grim and grotty, but it was his duty to return to Aldyrwald...

It was just a miracle Captain Fayorn hadn't recognized him as the kid who had guided them in this afternoon. And he and the sergeant had seemed chummy – Thony hadn't gotten a good look, but had the sergeant been there, too?

Maybe there was another way...

Dae skipped closer.

"Remember," she stage-whispered. "It's not over till the fat lady sings."

"So, keep your mouth shut," Thony muttered back out of the side of his mouth.

"Hey!" Dae exclaimed loudly.

But whatever else she might have said was cut off by a shove from behind and she glared over her shoulder. Sergeant Sterevor's snort of amusement didn't really help.

"Into my office, mousies," he told them.

The room they entered was well-lit for day-time, let alone the middle of the night. There were tables to each side piled high with stacks of papers, a desk with more papers and writing implements... and one chair behind the desk.

Sergeant Sterevor took the chair.

"Now," he said, leaning his elbows on the surface of the desk, "tell me what you're doing here. You don't look like staff."

"We weren't really *doing* anything," Thony said – quickly, before Dae could speak. "You see, my little sister here–"

He gestured at Dae and the sergeant interrupted him with a raised eyebrow.

"Your *sister?* You don't look enough alike to be *relations,* let alone *siblings.*"

Thony shrugged. "It's the way my family is, sir. A curse or a blessing going way back when, Mama says. My older sister has hair as bright as a dandelion and eyes as green as grass."

And he could say *that* with absolute veracity.

Sterevor could apparently read that in his face. He let it pass, though he still looked skeptically at Dae. "Odd. But go on."

"Well, you see, my sister, here, didn't believe me when I said I actually knew His Sorcerousness *personally.*" They'd overheard the sergeant referring to Valderon Raven'sWing that way as they snuck around. "And – do you have little brothers and sisters, sergeant? Then you know how *annoying* and *impossible* they can be," Thony went on after the sergeant gave him an amused nod. "A guy can only take so much, y'know?"

Priscilla had complained like that... rather a lot, now that Thony thought about it.

The sergeant was regarding Thony more closely. "You do appear to be the boy who guided us through this benighted town earlier."

"*See,*" Thony turned to Dae triumphantly... and begging her with his eyes not to screw this up. "I *told* you so."

Dae put her hands on her hips with a very good look of fake skepticism. "Yeah. You tell me *lots* of things. But *he's* not the sorcerer-dude."

Thony let his expression grow thunderous and opened his mouth...

"So how did you end up in Captain Fayorn's bedroom pretending to be rats?" Sergeant Sterevor intervened in the incipient 'sibling-battle.' He'd picked up quickly on the signs Thony was taking such care to telegraph; he really *must* have his own annoying little siblings. Or maybe – he was old enough – his own kids.

"There's two doors to that room, did you know?" Dae volunteered in a sprightly manner. "But one of them locks from the inside once you go through."

Thony gave her his best 'aggrieved-elder-brother' look (*copied from... well, okay it was more copied from Master Eswith than his sisters*).

"We knew we weren't supposed to be in here, sir. So, we dodged out of sight when a guy in uniform went by... and then we heard someone coming in from the other door, so we hid, and... I couldn't *stop* her, sir." His 'explanation had a nodding acquaintance with the truth. "She has this *thing* about playing pranks on people. She just *can't* let a good opportunity slip by. Just last month she put *slugs* in my sandwich. Live ones."

Thony shuddered reminiscently. It had actually been Amanita who had done that – and he hadn't eaten food in her presence again until they embarked on this mad Quest-thing – but it got the point across.

And Dae didn't look all that disturbed at having that misdeed attributed to her. Thony suffered the unpleasant realization that he'd *probably* given her an *idea.*

Or... hunh... so far, the mansion's kitchens had been where *he* went to work...

Sergeant Sterevor was looking at them with a certain tolerant amusement. "So, this was all about a boyish boast and a little girl's prank. Very well. Promise not to try anything like this again and I'll send the two of you home with a warning." He eyed the mounds of papers around him with a certain resignation, and Thony guessed that they'd actually provided an entertaining break for the older man.

Still, no need to push this.

"I promise," Thony agreed fervently – though he held his fingers crossed behind his back to nix it.

"And you?" The sergeant turned to Dae.

Who put on her most truculent face. "But I *still* don't know for sure if *he–*" and she jerked a thumb at Thony, "–really *does* know His Sorcerousness."

The sergeant stood up. "You have my word he does."

"And how do *I* know *you* know *he* knows?" she demanded.

"*Da–phne...*" Thony switched the name halfway through to the only other one he could think of beginning with the same sound, earning himself a quizzical look from said mercenette. His warning tone didn't work very well like that, though.

The sergeant's patience was clearly starting to wear out a bit. "Because I rode in with them both this morning," he said shortly. "I'm milord's *aide-de-camp,* if you know what that is. And I have a ton of paperwork to get through tonight, so we're done here. Out."

He shooed them towards the office door, and they went.

Thony started to breathe a sigh of relief as he and Dae stepped out of that claustrophobic office – *free at last!* But then he realized Sergeant Sterevor was right behind them – to steer them out of the mansion with no further mishaps, he explained, placing a heavy hand on their backs, though he didn't grab the scruffs of their collars again at least.

Dae, of course, began arguing, but Thony cut across her vituperations to ask, "Sir? Is that Captain Fayorn guy *really* in charge here now?"

The sergeant's lips twisted in what looked like an unwilling, wry grin. "Yes. Under milord, of course."

"Of course..." Thony twisted around to look up at the large older man over his shoulder. The sergeant was still marching them down the corridor. "Would it be helpful if we... like, *apologized* to him or something? I mean, helpful to *you*. If he's the kind of guy who holds a grudge or something."

Dae was looking indignant again, and Thony grabbed her arm and squeezed, hoping she'd have the sense to shut up.

At least it won him an approving look from the sergeant. "Won't make a difference for *me*, but that's a mature offer and since you'll likely be seeing a fair bit of him for the next few months... Tell you what, come back around noon and I'll have a soldier watching for you at the gate to take you to the captain. Either or both," he added with amusement, then noted, "Milord seemed to think well of you, lad. Good to see you're confirming that impression. He's a good master – and a poor enemy."

Thony gulped. "Yessir." But inwardly he was very pleased. This had been a complete fail – and he'd managed to turn it around and even give himself, and maybe Dae as well, a totally legit reason to be seen in and around the mansion. Maybe they could parlay this into something even *better*...

Dae was looking thoughtful. Or at least was saving her rant for when they were really free.

They weren't yet twenty paces from the sergeant's office when smelly fumes reached their noses.

"Fire!" a familiar, strident voice called out. *"Fire!"*

Thony couldn't resist a small groan.

Amanita was running towards them.

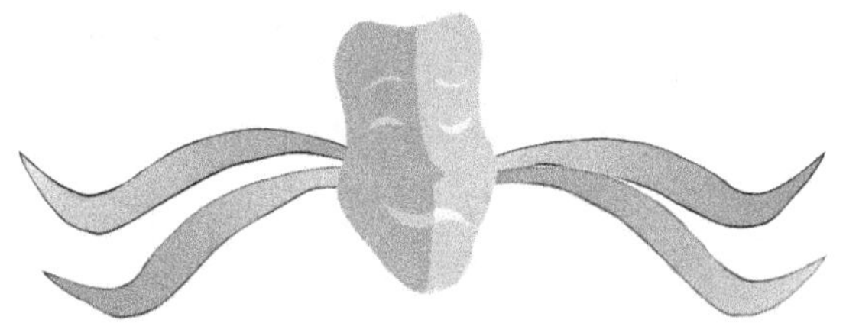

Chapter SEVEN

Go Down in a Blaze of Glory

"*Fire!*" Amanita yelled at the top of her lungs as she sped down the hallway. *"F-i-i-i-i-ire!!!!"*

Thony and Dae stood unmoving in front of that giant sergeant, just staring at her. Idiots.

"Quick!" she told their large captor as she panted to a halt, "Quick! They sent me for help! *Hurry!*"

Sergeant Sterevor gave her a narrow-eyed look, but stinky, thick smoke was undeniably following her up the corridor. He swore softly but rather *colorfully,* and began to run in the direction of the fire, though he called back over his shoulder something about *"you kids get somewhere safe."*

"C'mon you guys," Amanita told her comrades in chaos, "We've gotta get outta here! I don't know how long it'll be before they realize the smoke and the flames are coming from two different places. Thony, will you *move it?*"

Dae was skipping – *skipping,* for the Goddess' sake! – along with her, but Thony seemed stuck.

More voices and shouting were coming from down the hall in the direction they needed to go.

"Amanita, you idiot–" Thony began, as he *finally* started to follow her.

All three of them froze as a certain, all-too-familiar, door opened right in front of them.

Amanita swore under her own breath – if not quite so *colorfully* as the sergeant – as Captain Fayorn and his drooping blonde mustaches appeared in the doorway.

"What's all *this* shouting about?" he demanded of the corridor in general, not yet focusing on the three kids.

"*F-i-i-i-i-i-i-ire!!*" Amanita thrust herself up practically under his nose and hollered as loud as she could. "*FI-I-I-I-IRE!!!!*"

Captain Fayorn clapped his hands over his ears, wincing. Then he seemed to focus – on Thony and Dae – and his eyes narrowed for a different reason.

Amanita broke off in mid-yowl and grabbed Thony's hand.

"*Run, Dae!*" she yelled, and towed the young prince along behind her at the best speed she could make – straight at Captain Fayorn.

The man gave a startled – and unnecessarily *rude* – exclamation, and stepped quickly out of their way. And a couple of Raven-soldiers, seeing their superior officer give way, automatically did the same.

A quick glance behind showed that the mercenette was, indeed, following.

They could hear Captain Fayorn telling one of the men to check on the smoke and the other to "*catch those meddling kids.*"

That sped up all their feet, and there was no way an *adult* could catch up with them, nimble and small as they were. Though, just before they completely lost the guy, they heard a completely incongruous exclamation: "That's *it! Apples!*"

The troublesome trio escaped back to the rooftops via their usual route, and then made their way back more slowly to their rooms at the Inn of the Starred Hoof. Getting past the commotion swirling and boiling in and around the mansion was more than the usual challenge, but thankfully no one was looking up. The courtyard was full of shouting people and confusion that spilled out slightly into the surrounding streets.

Amanita felt quite pleased with herself, all told.

She'd accomplished her mission, obtained valuable new intelligence, made contact with their 'inside man,' and rescued the others from Gods-alone-knew what fate. She was rather looking forwards to giving Thony and Dae a sound – and smug – rebuke for having gotten themselves caught while *she* did all the hard work and covered herself in glory. She had rarely, if ever, managed to so deserve to smirk condescendingly at anyone. It was going to be *great*.

It was, therefore, rather annoying when Thony threw himself onto his bed with a furious glare at her.

"Well, *you* really messed that up," he stated in a sharp tone.

"Ex-*cuse* me?" Amanita retorted, dumbfounded and angry in return. "I just rescued you two morons after *you* got caught playing *mousie!*"

"Yeah, we got caught," Thony agreed, still glaring at her, "but *I'd* managed to talk us out of that – even turn it to our *favor!* And then *you* have to come bulling through, yelling and screaming and drag us off and spoil it all!"

"Listen, *you*–" Amanita began.

"Done's done," Dae cut in from where she stood leaning against the door. "It can't be helped now, any of it." She had a shadowed look in her eyes instead of her usual ebullient good-nature.

"You stay out of this," Amanita told her sharply.

Dae shook her head. "There's more urgent things to deal with just now than fight. I... had a bit of a run-in with some Raven-troops when I visited the Guildhouse yesterday."

"A 'run-in'?" Amanita asked as Thony groaned and threw himself prone on his bed.

The mercenette bit her lip and shifted her eyes around the room. "Um, yeah. You might even call it an 'altercation.' Apples were involved, there was a bit of a public scene – and, anyways, they saw me holding my sword. At the time, they seemed to think it was *funny...*"

Her expression was a weird mix of chagrin and mortal offense, "But I think that last guy who was chasing us recognized me. And with you *shouting my name,* it's entirely possible – if anyone there keeps up with the Guild news – that they'll put two and two together and get *me.*"

She looked at Thony. "And it'll be obvious that you're *not* my brother. Sergeant Sterevor and Captain Fayorn won't be pleased that we managed to pull off a ruse on them."

"Nor will Captain Shalladra or Val– um, the sorcerer-guy," Amanita admitted, remembering not to say his name at the last moment. And Istevan... she winced. He would think they were total screw-ups now and he'd seemed at least open to the idea that they might be allies when she'd talked to him.

Well, maybe they *were* total screw-ups.

"Splendid," Thony grumbled, turning over and burying his face in the pillow.

It annoyed Amanita that he had some justification. She had no doubt the whole mouse/rat thing had been Dae's idea, so arguably *he* was the only one who hadn't totally botched the night's work.

"Yeah, well," Dae gave them a sort of distant nod. "Like I said, done's done. It was going to happen sooner or later."

Thony's head popped up, eyes suddenly alight. "Hey! *I'm* the only one of us who *hasn't* messed up the mission!"

Yeah, he'd have to *notice...*

"*Yet,*" Amanita said darkly, and accepted his glare as her due. "We need a plan. If they know who Dae is and they know Thony is with her, then it won't be too hard to track us down to this inn. And even with the wards Puck left on this room, they'll find us. It's not like there's a lot of people with hair like Thony's in this two-horse town."

"*Again,* with the *hair,*" Thony muttered, but not very loudly, so she ignored it.

"We could move over to the Guildhouse," Dae said a little dubiously. "It's meant to hold up to twenty or so mercenaries at a time – just overnights, nothing fancy – and there's just old Evrien there now, so it's pretty empty."

Thony shook his head as he sat up and gave Dae a *significant* look that Amanita couldn't parse. "If they figure out *who* you are, the Guildhouse is the obvious place to start looking for you."

"Or the *least* obvious," Dae argued. "I'd have to be an idiot to stay there if they're impressing any mercenary who comes through."

"*Right.*" Thony just raised his eyebrows, and Dae looked down.

"I... really don't have enough money to stay anywhere else, Thony," she admitted. "You guys already had to cover the room *here* for me and I have to assume you're going to need your coin yourselves. And there aren't any *cheaper* inns in Flowerdust."

"We should move out to that hidden copse with Davril and the baby," Thony said as Amanita muttered about '*not any inns that are still in business anyways.*' "Twinklestar said the place is naturally warded and he did something to enhance the protections. We'd be at least as safe there as here under Puck's wards – and we can't stay in this room all the time, so we'd probably be *safer.*"

"That's going to make it a pain and a half to get in and out of the mansion to keep working on the mission," Amanita objected.

Dae and Thony exchanged another *look*.

"We'll figure something out," Thony said in a deciding tone. "Safety has to come first until we figure out just how big of a mess we're in. It might be that no one will actually care that much about a couple of kids, even if one *is* a severely underaged mercenary." He gave Dae – *Dae?* – an apologetic look.

"We're going to be right smack dab in the path of Va– the armies when he starts to invade the Fairy Wood," Amanita pointed out. Camping out in the woods when there were civilized accommodations in the city – and with a *baby* – was not high on her list of preferences. "And who put *you* in charge anyways?"

Thony gave her an odd look. "You keep starting to say his name and then stopping yourself. Why?"

Clever lad. He didn't say it himself as he asked her the question. Amanita felt a mite better that Thony would trust her judgment so implicitly.

But... this was another thing they'd really messed up on.

She looked down. "I got my mission done – the papers are back where they belong. And I found out some other disturbing things that I have to tell you about." Which, actually, should make her want to get farther away faster... "And I made contact with Istevan. He pointed out that the... sorcerer-guy might have set up a spell to tell him if people are using his name a lot."

"Oh." Thony's eyes went wide.

"It probably will just tell him someone *is*," Amanita added, knowing that neither Thony nor Dae would have enough understanding of the topic to know this for themselves. Neither of them were magickal types, after all. "It *might* be able to tell him *where* that someone is. It's a lot harder to set it up to tell *who* the someone is, or *what* they're saying."

"He doesn't really need those parts," Dae said dryly, but she was also a little white around the eyes. "He has a whole army of people he can send to go collect anyone with loose lips."

Amanita nodded, deciding not to mention that there was a good chance the spell only told him what *direction* to go in and with buildings and lots of other people in the way, it might not be all that easy to find them anyways. For all she knew, he had set it up to triangulate more effectively. Better to err on the safe side.

Which, dammit, likely meant that they *should* relocate to that little protected copse. If she remembered properly, it had seemed reasonably spacious... but adding three kids, Twinklestar, Silverfoot, and Dae's horse was... going to make it seriously... less spacious.

Not to mention they'd be sleeping on the ground and cooking over a campfire and... ugh. Just – ugh.

Dae was watching her with a considering expression. "Thony," she said, "I need to check in with Evrien Quickfoot and let her know what's happened. And... I'd like Amanita to meet her. She and I can pick up some more supplies on our way out there. Can you take the horses and Twinklestar out on your own if we load everything up?"

He raised an eyebrow. "Because *that* will look normal and inconspicuous. One dude with a unicorn and two horses? Even if I wear the stupid *robe*, that's still going to look pretty weird."

"And *we're* going to *walk* all the way out there?" Amanita complained. "And *that's* not going to be obvious?"

Dae gave her a *hushing* look. "We'll look like a couple of sisters doing some shopping. No one will notice *us*." She frowned at Thony. "Maybe... Twinklestar could take Sandy? And you could ride Silverfoot out?"

"Hmmn." Thony frowned. "I suppose it has to be you to go to the Guildhouse. She wouldn't know *me* from... Jost."

"*You're* the one we have to get out of here fastest," Amanita commented. "You stand out like there's a torch on your head in the dark."

He glared at her. "Me *and* Dae. And you look enough like her that they might pick you up while trying to get *her.*"

"But if there's two of us *together,*" Dae said persuasively, "Then we can't either of us be me. Because *I'm* entirely *singular.*"

Thony rolled his eyes. "They saw the two of you together tonight, Dae."

She shrugged. "There was smoke and confusion. And a lot of *yelling.*" She glanced at Amanita, who winced. "I *really* think it would be useful for Evrien to meet Amanita, Thony."

"Why?" Amanita asked. She hadn't focused on that point before, given the insane idea of *walking* all the way out to the copse.

"Yeah, why?" Thony asked, though he seemed... more inclined to go along with Dae's idea.

The mercenette shrugged a little, but gave Thony another one of those *looks*. Maybe once she got Dae alone, Amanita could make her explain all of that.

"It's... just a feeling I have," Dae said unhelpfully. "I've learned to trust my instincts. It's how I've done as well as I have so far."

Thony looked at Amanita and gave a little shrug himself. "Well, she *is* still alive."

That... was true.

On the other hand, so was Amanita.

On *another* hand, it would delay the inevitable departure to that stupid copse.

"*Fine,*" Amanita said with poor grace. "But we do it in the morning. I want a last night in a *real* bed."

She probably should have distrusted how easily they capitulated to that requirement...

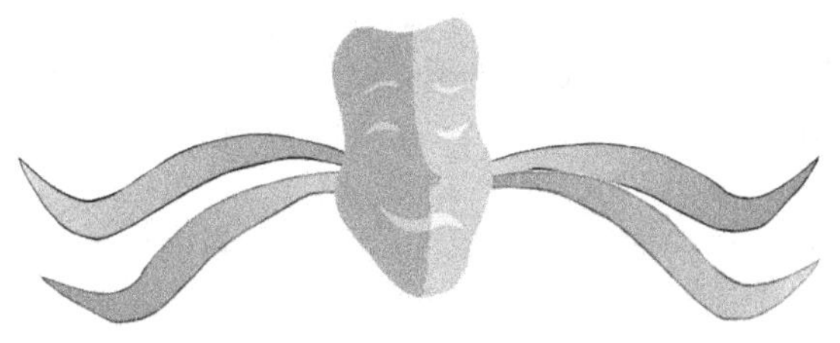

Chapter EIGHT

Long-term Problems

"Ah! It is my little string of garlic!" Evrien Quickfoot said as she opened the door of the Mercenaries' Guildhouse to Dae and Amanita's knock "And you have brought a friend."

"Yeah," Dae agreed, flushing.

"Come in, come in, and have some tea," the old woman made space for them to enter.

"*'String of garlic'*?" Amanita asked in a whisper as they followed the old woman past a vestibule and down the entrance corridor. She tried not to look nervously at the murder-holes on both sides. Dae had said there was no one else here, so there couldn't be anyone in position to shoot them or stab them or pour boiling things on them from those openings. Not that there was any reason why they should want to...

Dae's eyes stayed straight ahead. "When I came before, I rang the bell – that's how the Guildhouse-keeper is supposed to know there's a member outside, not a civilian. But the bell-rope was too high for me to reach. So, I, er, *found* a board lying around nearby and propped it up on the wall so I could walk up it like a ramp and reach the rope."

"Let me guess," Amanita was envisioning the whole thing. "It collapsed while you were on it."

Dae nodded a little sharply. "I'd *braced* the bottom with rocks, it should totally have worked. Anyways, I grabbed for the rope, it rang the bell, Evrien opened the door and saw me dangling there and... well..."

"You had a new nickname." Amanita decided to be sympathetic. "Life is built for tall people out here."

"Yeah," Dae agreed glumly, then gave her a sharp look. "What do you mean *out here?*"

Amanita shrugged, concealing a small smile. She rather liked Dae, and if this piqued her interest enough to get her to come along with them when this, this *Raven War Thing* was all over...

"We're a lot shorter on average in–" she glanced warily at the tall, old woman who was now bustling around a... oh, my Goddess. She was actually swinging a kettle of water in over a *hearthfire*. Who cooked that way for real? "–in my homeland," she finished.

Dae seemed interested. "Really? Because I thought you shared a lot of ancestry with those tall, blonde types in Selavan."

Amanita made a face. "We tossed them out over a thousand years ago, and no one really likes to think about that anymore. It's pretty much a social handicap to be tall."

"Hunh." Dae looked intrigued, but Evrien was gesturing them to sit on giant, leather-upholstered sofas and collecting a pot and tea leaves and cups and such.

Neither of the girls' feet touched the ground once they sat down, even if they didn't try to use the backrest. Amanita gave Dae a knowing look.

Evrien, it might be noted, was sized to fit the furniture, even if she seemed absolutely ancient.

"*Sixty*, you said?" Amanita whispered to Dae.

Dae nodded as the old woman smiled, proving there was nothing wrong with her *ears*. "I have filled a handful of decades, 'tis true, lassie. And am near to completing the next."

Not *quite* sixty, then. She wasn't much older than even Grandmother Reyalla. But she *looked* ten years – or even more – older than she apparently was. The mercenary's life was clearly a hard one.

Dae smiled at the old woman. "Sixty years *young*. I hope I'm in as good shape as you when I'm your age." The quickly hidden look of – *fear?* – in the other girl's eyes suggested that was a real sentiment and not a gratuitous compliment.

Evrien nodded as graciously as if she heard such things on a regular basis. "So, what can an old mercenary do for... Altaba's Eyes, but the two of you could be sisters. Even twins? Is it that you have found your *doppelgänger* and wish my advice on how to handle her, young sister?"

Dae shook her head as Amanita frowned. She'd heard of such things, it seemed, though Evrien made it sound *sinister* and that wasn't what she remembered.

"No..." Dae looked sideways at Amanita. "I wanted you to meet Amanita because... well..."

And she launched into a description of what they'd done and were trying to accomplish even before the other girl could choke on how Dae had so casually given her name to this total stranger. 'Amanita' wasn't common after all, even in Pathremir – though probably the peasants had started giving their daughters the name after it was given to the Princess-Heir-to-be. Though 'Ytheril' still wasn't popular, even though Mama had been the Confirmed Princess-Heir for fourteen years.

Evrien looked... gratifyingly thoughtful and not horrified at the end of Dae's rendition.

"Agree with you, I must," she said after a long moment. "The Guildhouse – I would that I could offer it to you as the place of refuge it is meant to be, but... reality is what it is. And what you seek to do, it may turn the tide of whether we retain our status as an independent entity at all. Like as not, if this – sorcerer-king – manages in his conquests, he will absorb us all."

Amanita felt dismayed. "That's what Thony said Captain Shalladra was advising the, um, sorcerer-guy to do with Bards." She didn't want to give Valderon Raven'sWing the title of 'king.'

Evrien focused on her. "Too much sense in that, though it disobeys all the rules of war that the Guild has promulgated. And... no surprise that such words would come from such as she."

Dae's ears almost visibly pricked up at that comment, and Amanita guessed that she wasn't being any more discreet about her own interest.

"What did you find out?" Dae asked. "And *how?*"

The old woman sighed heavily. "Ah, child – little *Guildsister*–" she corrected herself before Dae could take umbrage. "Would that I need not burden such a fierce young spirit with such a tale. But... the world goes as it will... the *Worlds* go as they will..."

Evrien shook her head. "We are not a major Guildhouse here, and I – *I* was never meant to be a House-keeper. Still, I have had nothing but time on my hands since *That One*–" and now Amanita could hear the capitol letters, "–stole away Tethro and the others. Though I misdoubt me if even he would have had the knowledge straight to hand."

Dae looked more patient than Amanita felt. The woman's odd phrasing and wandering elocution were frustrating to the runaway princess after last night's highs and lows and a restless night in the bed she wasn't going to see again.

The mercenette leaned forwards, elbows on her thighs. "Evrien. What did you learn?"

The woman looked uncomfortable and got up to prepare the tea, though her kettle didn't quite seem to be boiling yet. "The records in this House are old... not so good with recent events, though the records of accounts are kept up-to-date, and the news bulletins are filed, of course."

She shot a quick glance at Dae as if to be sure the girl wasn't going to take her comments as a criticism of the previous administration. Dae nodded equably, and Evrien looked relieved.

"I had not thought to need records of any particular antiquity. *That One* appears no older than thirty. Forty, perhaps. There were rumors in the marketplace that her ears might be pointed – so perhaps it might have made sense to peruse the records so far as an hundred years back, aye?"

"Aye," Dae agreed, and Amanita nodded. There were plenty of kinds of people who might have pointed ears. That time-frame should be a reasonable one for those sorts of people.

"Searching for the recording of *That One* as a new Guildmember, you understand," Evrien explained. "To see if there was some accounting for whence she does hail from, or what exploits she might have been involved with. I expected to find me more of the latter than the former, of course."

Dae nodded, though there was a shadow in her eyes. "The Guild doesn't insist on answers to those questions," she told Amanita. "You can have a fresh start if you want it. No ties to the past."

Thony had quietly mentioned to Amanita what Dae had told him – that she'd been left as a toddler on the doorstep of Sonoro's School for Soldiering and been taken in by the Headmistress. Likely the mercenette didn't *know* 'from whence she hailed.'

Evrien nodded at the description. "Even so. And, aye, there were a great many recordings of *That One*. Never in any prominent role, until now, never in one place for terribly long... never where she was likely to be remarked upon and – methinks – her agelessness and longevity noted."

'Agelessness'... Amanita's lips silently shaped the word in echo, and she saw Dae doing the same.

She cleared her own throat. "So, um... *did* you find record of when she joined the Guild?"

Evrien shook her head. "Nay. Yet as far back as we possess records in this House, there were these brief mentions in the Guild news. And always, she is listed only by her use-name. 'Stillheart.' Rarely, and only in relatively recent times, has the name 'Shalladra' been appended as well."

Amanita frowned at that. It seemed... like something she *should* know...

Dae swallowed and gave Amanita a quick, worried look before turning back to Evrien. "And, um, how far back does this House *have* records of Guild news, Evrien?"

The old woman's faded blue eyes met and held the girl's bright brown ones. "Three hundred years, young sister. *Three hundred years.*"

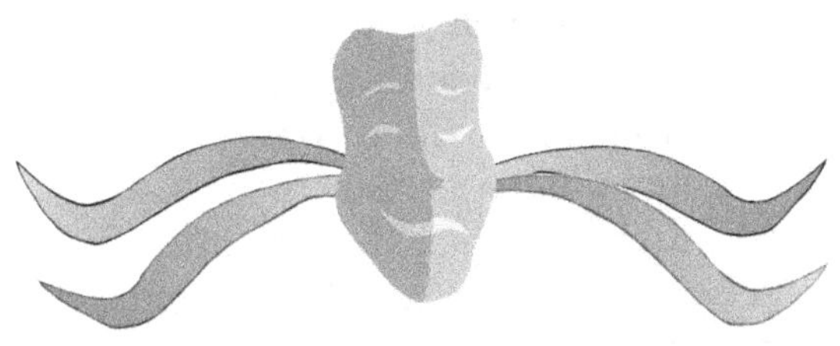

Chapter NINE

Fillies Before Bros

THONY ARRIVED IN THE CAMP practically as the sun set. Alone, on foot, and in a temper.

"You *idiot*," he rounded on Amanita, barely observing the usual courtesies. "You absolutely *slush-headed cuckoo-brain!* You left me to close out the account for Dae's room at the Starred Hoof and you didn't leave me the money to *do* it. The innkeeper wouldn't accept any of *my* coin – too *foreign* for him, apparently."

"So where are the horses?" Dae asked, practically, before Amanita or Davril could say anything.

"He's holding them, along with all our stuff," Thony sat down next to the fire and eased off his boots. "All except Twinklestar. Even *his* moxy doesn't extend to keeping a unicorn against his will." He winced. "Damn, but my feet hurt."

"Didn't you ride Twinklestar?" Dae asked, as Amanita bit out "Prince Tenderfoot can't handle a walk that the two of us managed with heavy baskets."

"Kids..." Davril said in a conciliatory tone as he bounced the baby on his lap, and got a pair of angry glares at him for his trouble.

"There's clearly more to his story," the young man told Amanita. "Just like there was in *yours*," he added pointedly. He was still pale with hearing about what Evrien had figured out.

Dae wasn't, but even though Sonoro's was in the foothills of the Misty Mountains and technically within the borders of Selavan, she hadn't grown up hearing all the old stories.

Davril, to Amanita's intense discomfort, was Selavani himself and *had*. Not that he looked like he had much – or maybe any – *Líonar* blood in his ancestry. He was taller and paler than the average Pathremiri person... the average Pathremiri *nobility,* she admitted a bit unhappily – but barely average for outsiders, if she was any judge of these things.

"*Thank* you," Thony said, also rather pointedly directing his comment to Davril. "*Yes.* Clarick – the innkeeper's kid–"

"I *know* who *Clarick* is," Amanita couldn't quite stop herself from snarking, and got a disappointed look even from Dae. Which was *annoying,* because this was *so totally not her fault.*

And Thony looking vindicated was *not* helping. "Anyways, Clarick couldn't get his dad to listen, so he ran and fetched Jost. Which is why our stuff's being held until we pay for it, rather than confiscated."

"All right," Dae said with remarkable calm for someone all of whose worldly goods were in the keeping of a con-man of an innkeeper. "So, what happened next? And where's Twinklestar?"

Thony gave her an aggrieved look. "Well, he was willing to let Jost come with us, and–"

"Wait, Jost's *here?*" Amanita demanded.

"Not exactly..." Thony mumbled, but he glanced over his shoulder to the entrance to the copse. "I mean, yes he is, but..."

"Spit it out, dude," Dae said. Even Davril was looking pretty wary now.

Thony sighed. "Fine. So... Twinklestar let us both ride. It took longer than it should because, you know, no saddle or stirrups. Or reins. And Jost has never even been on a *horse* before. And Twinklestar's paces are just..." He shook his head. "He's *trying,* but he never had to care about a rider until recently, so it's... pretty hard riding. And like I said, Jost had no clue.

"And I don't think he's ever even been out of the *city* before–"

"That's not a *city,*" Amanita muttered irritably. "It's barely a small *town.*"

Dae shot her another quelling – if understanding – glance, and Davril snorted in amused agreement. They'd established that he was from Dynsfyor which might be the largest port-city on the North Coast.

Thony pursed his lips briefly. "Whatever. Anyways, all of a sudden Twinklestar sped up – he apologized later, but it made Jost lose his balance, and since he was already holding onto me like I was his hope of heaven, we both came off. Twinklestar barely noticed.

"*Apparently,*" Thony said a little too-loudly and with distinct sarcasm, "he scented a filly. Excuse me, a *lady unicorn.*"

There was a sort of apologetic/defiant *whuffling* noise from beyond the screening trees.

And an amused response of the same sort.

What the hell?

Amanita started to get up to go look, but Thony wearily waved her down.

"They'll come in momentarily. They're making some kind of healing elixir with their horns and the stream for Jost."

"Not you?" Dae was looking at Thony's feet. He had removed his stockings and was now staring morosely at his blisters by the lantern-light.

The runaway prince shook his head. "He let go of me when we fell off of Twink. And I know how to fall off a horse properly. And my boots are... better than his." He saw their confused looks. "We walked the rest of the way here. Jost refused to get back up on anything remotely equine-looking."

"Anything..." Dae looked like she was dreading what he was going to say next.

Luckily, Thony didn't have to say anything.

A young woman of about Davril's age stepped into the sphere of light from the lantern, followed by Jost and a somewhat-older young man with the... *fluffiest*-looking hair Amanita had ever seen. It positively poufed up out of a confining headband.

Dae was on her feet, looking ready to flee, but as if she wasn't *quite* sure she wanted to.

"There you are, Dae!" the young woman said with relief as a pair of unicorns – Twinklestar and his lady-friend – and a horse followed the humans into the copse.

"Um, hi," Dae said weakly. "Everyone, these are my friends. Kamauri Spiralspear and Rainsparkle and Daennor Cat'sfoot."

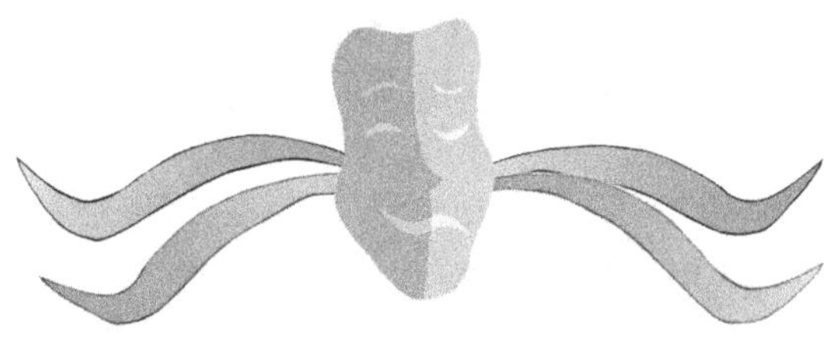

Chapter TEN

Existential Crisis, Part 1
(Why Are We All Here?)

"We only ran across each other by accident," Kamauri explained as they shared out fruit and meat and cheese. "Rainsparkle has been staying out of the city, taking care of Daennor's horse for us while we looked for Dae."

"It's the only way to be discreet," the poufy-haired mercenary commented with a dry look at his friend. "Unicorn-maiden with a sword – anyone with half a brain knows it's Kamauri." He grinned and reached out to tousle Dae's hair out of its neat high ponytail. "Rather like you, munchkin."

"Stop calling me that." Dae gave him a look of mingled irritation and guilt as she checked her hair. He actually hadn't messed it up – just fluffed the tail. Well, if anyone understood hair... "So... you're not mad about the last time I got away from you guys?"

Daennor chuckled. "You're *almost* convincing me it's reasonable to have you out here."

The mercenette felt oddly warmed by that.

Of course, then he had to look at Kamauri and say, "Only *almost.*"

Kamauri didn't look entirely reassured by this backing off, but she gave Daennor that absentminded smile that always made his eyes light up...

"We didn't really finish the introductions," Kamauri said, looking around. "Daennor and Rainsparkle and I know Dae, of course. And we've met Thony and Jost."

Jost waved at Davril, the only person here that *he* hadn't met. His mouth was full, however. That spare, lanky look to him clearly wasn't just his natural body-type. She noticed that Thony was unobtrusively moving food closer to the street-kid-chieftain. So was Kamauri, who was sitting on Jost's other side, and Daennor was handing food over to her so she could.

And, oh, *that* was interesting. Davril was making stuff handy for Thony to pass on.

Wisely, Davril had put himself and the baby between Thony and Amanita, who were still shooting daggered looks at each other.

"I've heard of you," Davril admitted. "Istevan, my..." he hesitated a bit, then went on though his face was rather red, "my *husband*, is in the Guild as well."

He had a slightly defensive look to him, but Kamauri and Daennor just nodded.

"That would be Istevan Highblade?" Daennor asked, and smiled when Davril nodded. "I thought I recognized him in one of those blue uniforms. I knew him slightly at Sonoro's. He tutored me a little in my first year, just before he graduated. The Fox has been trying to get in touch with him for awhile."

Davril looked confused.

"Taridanae Foxheart," Daennor clarified. "The Headmistress. She took over after Sonoro died."

"Yes, I..." Davril hesitated again. "I know whom you mean. Istevan... Well, you'll have to talk to him."

Daennor frowned slightly, but Kamauri set a gentle hand on his arm. "And you are? Besides Istevan's husband?"

The young man gave her a wry look. "Davril Keetering. Of Keetering-and-Salwan in Dynsfyor."

Now even Jost and Amanita looked impressed – the latter rather unwillingly – and *Thony* looked confused.

"That's only the biggest bank on the North Coast," Amanita explained to him. "Maybe..." she slid a look over at Davril, "maybe even on this side of the Misty Mountains?"

Davril shrugged as if he was trying to look humble and wasn't succeeding terribly well. "Probably. We're still small compared to the Metreedi network, but they're mostly located around the Western Ocean."

"And Davril would be..." Amanita looked at him with sudden shock. "You're the *Heir* to Keetering-and-Salwan, aren't you? What in all the worlds beyond the Fairy Wood are they *doing,* letting you wander around and into war-zones like this?"

Thony and Dae looked at each other and both started snickering. Amanita glared at them, and the snickers turned to belly-aching guffaws.

They stopped when they realized that the rest of the group was starting to look annoyed. Well, except for Jost. He had slowed down his eating, but he was staying quiet and just watching and listening hard.

"That's a fair question," Daennor suggested, though he was giving Dae a very stern look.

Davril was bouncing the baby again, and his eyes were only on her. "It's not really all that big a deal. I have three younger sisters. I'm... taking a break from the bank while... while things settle down a bit in Selavan. And my cousin needed to come out here to deal with these things, and she needed Istevan's help. And we didn't think Daphne should have to be weaned too early..." He winced. "Which clearly isn't going all that well."

There was something... *off* about what he was saying. As if it was all *true,* but he was leaving out some humungous part that would set the whole situation in an entirely different context... Dae cocked her head, trying to sort out what that could possibly be.

Kamauri was frowning. "Your cousin needed to be here to 'deal with these things.' What 'things'?"

Davril shrugged again. "You know... *things.*"

The unicorn-maiden-mercenary gave him an irritated look and seemed about to ask more, but Daennor leaned close and began to murmur something into her ear...

...and Amanita's eyes suddenly went super-wide.

"*That's* what she meant!" the runaway princess exclaimed. "When we were, um, exploring the Raven headquarters last night–"

She appeared to catch herself, and eyed the three adults warily, but plowed on to Dae and Thony's combined pride, dismay, and relief. Better Amanita than them, after all...

"Well, anyways, I ended up getting to hear part of a conversation between Julanna Silversea and, um, the sorcerer-guy," Amanita informed the group, and Davril looked up with an expression of worry. "He thought she and Istevan had been dating, and she said, 'no, he's my cousin's husband' or something like that. You! *You're* Julanna Silversea's cousin!"

Davril let out a breath, as if he'd been expecting her to say something else. "Well, yes..."

"Waitaminute," Thony interrupted. "Isn't Julanna Daphne's mother?"

Davril's face got that weird expression again. "Yes."

"Then..." Thony went nearly as red as his hair. "Nevermind. None of my business."

The baby giggled right then and reached out to tug Davril's nose. He was holding her so that she could think she was standing, with some weight on her tiny feet, but all of her balance coming from his arms. Her dark, red curls bounced like little springs as she tried to 'jump.'

The look in the young man's eyes said that she was the center of his heart. He smiled at her, clearly prioritizing her over talking to a bunch of other people.

Dae pulled her knees up and hugged them tight, and turned her head away from looking at them. The Fox – Taridanae – had *tried* to make up for the parents Dae didn't have... But she was still Headmistress of Sonoro's. She simply had too many demands on her time to mother a child who wasn't even hers... who had just been left on her doorstep. Dae had nothing but good things to say about her, but...

A warm arm settled around her shoulders, and she closed her eyes, leaning in to the comfort but not wanting to look up and see Daennor giving Kamauri that *look*. He cared about her, yeah. But she was more of a mean to an *end* in his opinion, and that end was convincing Kamauri to marry him.

And *Kamauri* cared about Dae for her ownself... but Kamauri wanted to put Dae in a box and keep her safe. And right now, she'd be looking away, trying not to meet Daennor's eyes...

Dae wanted a *family,* but not one that had been pressure-fitted together.

"Maybe..." Davril was speaking again, and she opened her eyes to look at him. The Selavani... *banker?*... somehow gave her the impression that he had a good idea what she was feeling. Though surely a man who came from an old and powerful family couldn't possibly have a clue...

"Maybe," Davril said again as everyone looked at him, "this is a good time to figure out why *all* of us are here. Right here. And right now. Then we can organize what we know and put it together in a way that makes sense instead of this... helter-skelter piecemeal thing."

"Makes sense to me," Daennor said from over Dae's head. She imagined the wry look he was giving Kamauri. "Mine is easy. I'm here because Kamauri is." He paused, then sighed with a certain resignation. "I'm being disingenuous. That was true a couple of years ago. Now... I'm here because of Kamauri *and* Dae."

That was a surprise. Dae looked up at him skeptically, and he gave her that wry smile and a small nod. "It sort of crept up on me, munchkin."

"Stop calling me that," she said automatically, and he chuckled.

Kamauri was giving them both a rather odd look. She pulled her long, brown braid over her shoulder to fuss nervously with the tail. "Well... Rainsparkle and I are here because Dae is here. We were friends at Sonoro's School of Soldiering and I thought it was irresponsible of the Fox to let Dae go out into the world and work as a mercenary when she was only twelve. I've spent most of the last two years following her around and trying to extract her from trouble."

"With me," Daennor added, and Kamauri gave him another unsettled look, but nodded.

"She – the Fox, Taridanae Foxheart – she, ah... didn't exactly *let* me go," Dae said in a tiny voice. "I... kind of ran away. And then wrote her a letter saying that I was going to tell people I graduated and she could either go along with it and give me a letter for the Guild or not, but I was going to do it either way."

She actually *felt* Daennor's chuckle, snuggled up against his shoulder as she was. "We know, munchkin. She told us one of the times we stopped in. After Kamauri," he grinned over at the woman, "was telling her off. Again."

"Oh, no..." Dae covered her mouth with both hands.

"Oh, it was beautiful," Daennor told them. "The Fox is... well, have any of the rest of you met her?"

Even Davril shook his head 'no,' though he looked as fascinated as everyone else.

"Well, she's a very elegant, sophisticated sort," Daennor described. "Tall, slender, always well-put together. Hair sort of somewhere between yours," he gestured at Thony, "and hers." The baby. "Nothing ruffles her – or at least it didn't during the years I was a student there. And no one *ever* talks back to her–"

"*Please* tell me this was in private," Dae begged, horrified.

Kamauri gave Daennor, and then Dae, an irritated look. "Of course, it was. Though, if she's willing to *let* the whole world believe she let you graduate and go off, maybe she deserves some embarrassment."

"I didn't give her a choice–"

"The woman has contacts with most of the elite mercenaries in the *world,* Dae. If she'd wanted to, she could have put out the word and we'd have rounded you up and brought you home."

"I'd just have escaped again," Dae retorted, "it wasn't *home,* not after *you* left, and–"

She shut herself up, suddenly hyper-aware of their rather interested audience. "Nevermind."

It seemed to be her turn to explain why she was in Flowerdust, though.

"I'm here because..." Dae sighed. "Because I'd run out of money from my last job and it was the only place that was close enough to get to. There's usually a ton of traffic going through Brelsin at this time of year, so I figured I could pick up another job... hopefully before Kamauri and Daennor caught up with me. Again."

"There's tons of *armies* going through Brelsin at this time of year," Kamauri said in a horrified voice. "You're a *bodyguard,* and they want *soldier-recruits.* It's just a miracle you weren't impressed into the Raven-troops before we got here."

"Yeah, well I wasn't, *Mom*," Dae retorted. "Instead, I ran into Thony and Amanita and – ooops."

The three adults all suddenly focused on Amanita.

Who rolled her eyes and said *"Dae..."* in that tone that really only adults should ever use...

"Well, now I get what all the laughing was about earlier," Davril said lightly.

Jost was frowning though. "I don't."

Davril gave him a very... *not*-condescending smile, Dae decided it was. She liked this guy. He was taking them seriously, even if he was worried because they were kids. "Amanita is the only daughter of the Princess-Heir of Pathremir. Her mother is going to be the next Queen, and she'll be the Queen after that. She disappeared about two years ago... Just about the time that..." He looked at the baby again and sighed.

Amanita gave him a rather pained look. "That... didn't cause trouble between Pathremir and Selavan, did it?"

"You mean because your trail led straight down into Selavan?" Davril gave her a wry look. "It very nearly did. If Julanna's song hadn't more or less forced King Mithral to accept Lochea as Disciple of the Goddess of Light and Darkness – *and* his co-Disciple of the Lord of Light..." He shook his head. "The Goddess of Light and Darkness took a rather direct hand in the whole thing. My understanding is that She informed Queen Namarina that you were not in Selavan, and that, when the time was right, you would return."

"Oh," Amanita said in a rather small voice. "Good. I guess. I didn't mean to start a war."

"Well, you didn't," Davril said sternly, if kindly. "But it was a near thing. I hope you'll be a bit more careful when you're Queen – or even Princess-Heir yourself." He paused. "Except, you sort of *are*, aren't you. At least there's been rumors that Princess Ytheril was going to step aside for you. Or that she's being pressured to do so."

Amanita nodded, looking rather miserable. "That was why I... it's not *fair*," she burst out. "*Môthir* should have her turn before I have to be Queen."

Davril looked sympathetic, but not particularly yielding. "From all accounts the Queen is in excellent health and should rule for a good long time. But your absence has pushed Eldest-Princess Reyalla's agenda to get one of your aunts considered for the throne. There's even been a movement to require fal-Princess Falmyra to bring her daughters back from Ilseador."

Amanita looked horrified. "She can't do *that*. Aunt Fala is *Bound* to Elaarwen province across the sea in Ilseador."

"But she has five daughters," Davril pointed out. "All of them getting training in how to rule. And *you weren't there.*"

Amanita wilted a bit. And Thony looked very uncomfortable.

"Anyways," Dae broke in, hoping to smooth over some of the tension. "I ran into Amanita and Thony—"

"*Literally,*" Thony muttered, and *that* broke the tension as Jost chuckled and leaned over to whisper in the young prince's ear while Daennor laughed and fluffed Dae's ponytail again and said "I'll bet."

Dae rolled her eyes, but there was a much less fraught feeling to the group now.

"—and they brought me in on their plan to stop the invasion—"

Oh, whoops. There went the tension again.

But Daennor's arm tightening around her felt rather good, even if it was really *too* tight now.

"You kids were going to do *what?*"

Thony lifted his chin slightly. "We *are* going to do. It's our worlds, too."

"That's exactly what I told Istevan last night," Amanita agreed. "*He* seemed to think we had a right." She tried glare at Davril, who had tried to talk them all out of it at least twice, but she was clearly still feeling a bit... squished by the discussion of what had happened when she ran away from home.

The Selavani banker gave her a mild look back. "I assume – from other things you've said – that this was in the middle of the night, in the middle of their headquarters, and he had no real way to get you out without causing a ruckus."

"Um, yeah." Amanita wilted again a bit. "And he was going up to see the... sorcerer-guy right then. He'd been summoned. He's the one who told me not to use the guy's name in case he's spelled it so he knows where people are talking about him. And, um," she looked a little sideways at Davril, clearly having forgotten to convey this part. "He said to tell you that they're all right and that they're sticking to The Plan."

Davril looked like he was torn between relief and terror. And chose to cling to the baby to avoid giving in to either.

"Thank you," he said quietly. Then mumbled, *"Dammit,"* into Daphne's curls.

There was a moment of silence.

"I'm here a-cause it's my town bein' invaded and ta'en o'er," Jost volunteered after a moment. "An'..." He looked at Thony for a moment, which would have been *fine,* except for Thony deciding to blush a very bright red for no reason at all. "An' I'm a-plannin' t'help these others wit' their plan as well. Me an' my gang o' street-kids," he clarified.

"Lovely," Kamauri muttered. *"More* children to worry about."

Surprisingly, it was Davril who had a different viewpoint.

"They've already proven themselves to be capable spies, Miss Spiralspear. Whereas my darling *husband,"* and *he* flushed unaccountably for a moment, "and my overconfident cousin have managed to get themselves... in a pickle."

The wry look on Davril's face suggested he was thinking about how the girls had told him Julanna had been confined in a pickle cellar, so it was more or less literal.

He nodded at Amanita. "Do you want to tell them what you reasoned out today, or shall I?"

The runaway princess gave him a small nod and took a deep breath.

"Shalladra Stillheart – who seems to be the sorcerer-guy's chief advisor and was in charge of this town until yesterday – is a *Dökkálfar.* A Dark-elf," she translated as everyone gave her blank looks.

"Okay..." Daennor said.

Thony was frowning. "You mean, like Lady Opalsinger?"

Amanita nodded, focusing on him. "Yes. And that should help. If Puck can bring her out of the Wood or... something. Lady Opalsinger is the ruling princess of the Dark-elves. Stillheart – that would be Shalladra's elf-name, I imagine – would have to listen to her." She hesitated. "I hope."

The rest, other than Davril, still didn't seem to grasp the gravity of the situation.

Of course, Dae only understood because Amanita and Davril had explained it to her. More Amanita than Davril. The Selavani man's knowledge of the *Dökkálfar* (Dae liked using the more exotic-seeming word) seemed to be entirely based on legends and stories. Amanita had actually met the princess of the Dark-elves. And the Fairy Queen.

And so had Thony, it appeared.

"You *'hope'?*" Thony was asking. "If Lady Opalsinger rules the Dark-elves, shouldn't that be the end of it? I mean, Shalladra – Stillheart – is pretty scary… but as I recall, so was Lady Opalsinger."

Amanita's brown eyes were almost black with fear. "You don't understand, Thony. None of you do – except maybe Davril, some. *Dökkálfar* aren't like other elves – just people with some extra skills and longer lives. They – and the Light-elves – are more or less forces of Nature. The next thing to Gods themselves… and their ruling princess might just as well be a demi-Goddess.

"I spent some time in the Fairy Queen's Court. Not long, but… I heard stories. The Dark-elves and the Light-elves have been at war for longer than we can comprehend. Lady Opalsinger's dad – Lord Nightcreeper – and Lord Aspenheart – he's the Light-elf prince, but his dad, Lord Oakfire – they killed each other. About three hundred years ago. And even Queen Lilysong hadn't been able to stop them… or *save* them…

"And then Lord Aspenheart and Lady Opalsinger have been trying to end the war. But their people don't like that, and they sneak around behind their rulers' backs trying to do dirty things to get it restarted and approved and all."

The Princess of Pathremir looked around at everyone. "It was at least three hundred years ago that Shalladra Stillheart began to appear in the records of the Mercenaries' Guild."

After a moments' pause where everyone thought about that, Kamauri said, "Fine, so she's a *rogue* Dark-elf who won't come to heel when her princess whistles. She's still just one person." The unicorn-maiden-mercenary frowned. "Unless you have reason to believe that she's actually the power behind Valde– behind this sorcerer," she corrected herself as Dae and Thony and Amanita and Davril all made choking noises. "Do you?"

"No, she's not," Thony said slowly, thoughtfully. Dae recalled that this was all new information to him, too. "No, I got pretty up-close and personal with both of them, and *he is* definitely controlling *her.* With some sort of *spell.*"

Thony's expression suggested he found the whole idea repulsive.

Amanita nodded, still looking pretty freaked out. "He's strong enough to control a *Dökkálfar.*"

And she turned and looked at Davril. "And he has your cousin and your husband in her power. I'm so sorry."

She looked faintly surprised, Dae thought, when Davril just heaved a sigh.

"My turn..."

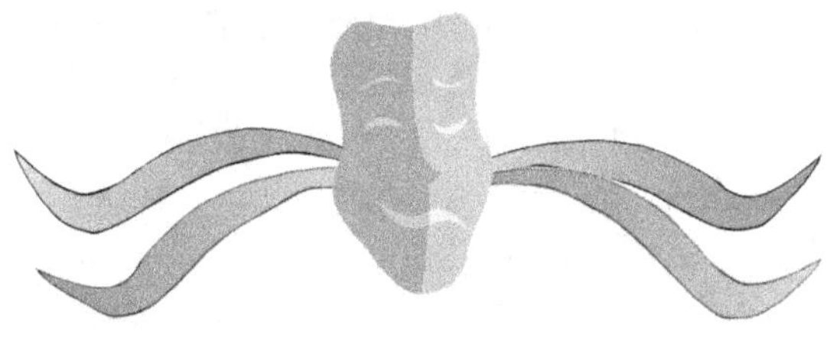

Chapter ELEVEN

Existential Crisis, Part 2
(Love is Dumb)

"I... SUPPOSE I SHOULD TELL you *our* end of the story. And why we had to be here." He stopped to smile faintly. "Well, Julanna. The rest of us are... more or less support staff for her."

"We overheard you guys saying that someone else sent you or you report to them or something," Dae volunteered, and Davril's eyebrows went up.

"We had the adjoining room in the inn," Thony muttered, looking at his feet. "And there was a loose floorboard in our room that opened up right above where she sat when she was playing."

Davril's expression was... a treat.

He went through a range, but settled on amused. "Well, I guess I'd wondered how you knew Daphne and I would need help when Julanna was arrested."

Daennor was chuckling almost soundlessly – Dae only knew because he still had an arm around her.

"All right then," Davril appeared to be recalculating what he was going to say. "I'll start from the beginning. Or rather, where we came into it.

"About two years ago – right before Her Royal Highness here got the border shutdown between Selavan and Pathremir," he grinned at Amanita's discomfort, "Julanna went up to the University at White Crystal Dome to do some research."

Jost and Thony both looked blank, but the rest nodded. Dae tried to mouth *'I'll show you a map later'* to the two boys, but wasn't sure if they got the message.

"While she was up there," Davril went on, "she met... a man. An *older* man. Julanna was about twenty and this gentleman appeared to be close to forty. My sister was studying up there as well, and she watched what seemed to begin as the... *gentleman* offering himself to show Julanna how to use the university's libraries and archives, and then began to turn into a romance. It... made Jess nervous for our cousin for reasons that she still has trouble explaining.

"So, she – my sister Jessina – wrote to me for help and I asked Istevan to go see what he could do."

And now he looked abashed. "I probably should have gone myself, but there were some, ah, touchy things I was working on and..." Davril shook his head. "It doesn't matter for this. Istevan went up – it's a ride of about two weeks in good weather and this was nearly Winter–"

He nodded at Amanita, who was wincing. Presumably she was familiar with the conditions. You had to go up into the Misty Mountains to Pathremir, then across the Pathremiri plateau, and then over *another* set of mountain passes to get to the university from Selavan. Dae had looked into it extensively before setting out from school – the university had been a potentially promising option, except for the cost.

"Anyways," Davril was going on, "Istevan more or less agreed with Jess that Julanna was getting herself in over her head. And he... sort of strong-armed her into coming back to Dynsfyor with him."

"The sorcerer-guy mentioned that she left without saying goodbye," Amanita commented. "At least I assume that *he* was her 'gentleman friend'."

Davril nodded. "He was."

"*She* told *him* that she hadn't wanted to say 'goodbye' at all," Amanita added. "That was all *before* I ran into Istevan and he talked to them. So, I don't know how *that* went. All I heard was that much and them sorting out that she hadn't been dating Istevan."

Davril winced. "I... was feeling better about things before you said that."

"Sorry..." Amanita looked almost ashamed.

He sighed again. "Not your fault. They're both just... too convinced they can save the world. I suppose it's why they're both dear to me, but..." Davril shook his head. "Well, it took them about three *months* to get home, and the delays they ran into gave Julanna what she needed to write the song that turned Selavan upside-down... Which took another couple of months. We were all worried that the song was going to end her up in jail or worse—"

"King Mithral would jail a *Bard?*" Amanita was shocked. As shocked as Dae had felt when Captain Shalladra Stillheart – the *Dökkálfar* – had actually done it.

Davril gave her a small grin. "No. And the idea upsets me – all of my family – as much as it does you. As it would all of Selavan – so that's our shared *Líonar* heritage, I suppose." He held up a hand as she looked ready to take umbrage. "*My* ancestors were conquered by them when *yours* drove them out of Pathremir. I have all sympathy – but *we've* spent the last thousand years integrating our society with theirs, and it's silly not to admit that there's been some good of it. Nor that we're all descended from them."

"*I'm* not," Amanita said as if it were a point of religion with her. "Varella was the first Queen of free Pathremir and she was of pure *Mistling* stock."

Davril gave her an... understanding but uncompromising look. "Wasn't Queen Varella's husband the *Líonar* king? And wouldn't that make her daughters half-*Líonar?* And then all of their descendants – which would include you?"

Amanita looked like she'd... swallowed a slug. A live one.

"Anyways," Davril went on, letting that point rest, "No, I don't think King Mithral would have jailed her. But his closest advisor was a man of... few scruples, let's say." There was something hard in Davril's eyes now. "But by the time the song was ready, Julanna had something else going for her besides her protected status as a Bard."

He smiled down at the baby, who had gone to sleep in his arms. "She was heavily pregnant. And the protection of a pregnant woman is deeply ingrained in our culture."

Amanita looked like she wanted to say something, but didn't really want to argue against that point.

"So... the baby's father is... the sorcerer?" Kamauri asked.

Davril looked up sharply at that. "No. *I'm* Daphne's father. And Istevan is her *other* father. Julanna gave birth to her, but we've adopted her. She's *ours*."

His tone was fierce and possessive.

Dae approved entirely.

Daennor tugged her a little closer, and Dae looked up at him, wondering if that could possibly mean... anything. The poufy-haired mercenary gave her a slight smile and a nod – which could mean *anything,* really – and directed his attention back to Davril.

"But the baby's *sire* is... this sorcerer who's taken over Flowerdust." Daennor didn't so much ask it as state it.

Davril's head drooped. "Yes."

"Ah..." Daennor's breath whooshed out softly in understanding.

Surprisingly, it was Jost who spoke up, his tone skeptical. "Don' see what diff'rence it makes. A kid ain't all that 'mport'nt."

Davril's head shot up, his eyes briefly sharp... and then they went soft and...

But Thony had already looped an arm around the street-kid. "Come on, Jost. You know there's families where kids *are* important. Clarick's, for example. And we spent the afternoon talking about mine."

Jost folded his arms and looked truculent. "Seems a long shot t' b'lieve a man as'd send armies hither an' yon'd care. Or 'e'd already 'ave 'is own kids setup t' follow 'im on the throne 'e's settin' 'is cap for. Wouldn't need nor want a nother'un."

Davril winced. "I could actually wish that, lad. But our not-so-favorite sorcerer spent a great deal of effort trying to find my cousin. If she and Istevan *hadn't* vanished into the Misty Mountains for three months... I don't know. I met him briefly – he'd tracked her down to her family in Selavan, though not to my Uncle Ryan out in the Western Ocean, I *think*. And Jess wrote to warn me that he was in a black rage when he realized she was gone with... he'd gotten the impression she was *betrothed* to Istevan."

He shivered. "When he made it to Dynsfyor, he was the perfect gentleman again, but there was something... *implacable* about him. And he said..."

Davril closed his eyes, and held Daphne close, as if for comfort.

"He said, 'when your cousin returns, tell her that I *will* come back for her. And I will *win* her love, no matter whom else she's chosen to give it to. Because when I lay all the world at her feet, she will have to be mine.'"

"Was... *is* she in love with him?" Thony asked.

"She sounded like she might be," Amanita said thoughtfully. Then shivered. "But Captain Shalladra was listening in on their conversation from the next room also – a different next room than me. And she looked absolutely *scary* when I got a peek at her. I don't think she's too happy about the idea."

"Well, if he's controlling Shalladra with a *love spell,*" Thony said dryly, "that might be par for the course. Is there a single story on *any* world where using a love spell turns out well?"

"On *'any'* world?" Daennor always had been observant. "Her Highness here said she'd spent time in the Fairy Queen's Court, and you said the same thing, Thony. You knew that Dark-elf princess. What's your story?"

Thony winced. "So... it sounds insane to say it, but I'm from one of those 'worlds beyond the Fairy Wood' that you all keep referring to."

"And he's Crown Prince of *his* country," Amanita put in as the rest all stared at him as if he might suddenly have two heads or a bushy, black tail or something. Jost looked particularly floored.

Thony winced again. "Yeah... and we strongly suspect – no, we *know,*" he corrected himself, his eyes checking with Dae and Amanita, "that the sorcerer-guy is going to use the armies that he's collected to invade the Fairy Wood. Though whether he plans to go to other worlds or just use it to travel around on this one – which I gather is also possible – we couldn't tell."

He looked intently at Davril. "Is there any chance you can remember whether he said he'd lay all the *'world,'* singular, at Julanna's feet, or all the *'worlds,'* plural?"

Davril gave him a baffled look. "I have no idea. At the time – well, we know there are other worlds, since the *Lionar* came from one of them and so did most of the other peoples, if my reading of the oldest legends is right... I did a minor in Comparative Mythology at the university," he said, looking a little abashed. "So, I'm familiar with– nevermind. No. I'm afraid it wouldn't have occurred to me to even think about that possibility at the time."

Thony sighed, and leaned back again. "Well, that doesn't change anything either way, then."

Davril gave him an awkward nod. "No, I don't suppose it does. Anyways, Julanna turned things topsy-turvy in Selavan in... a great many ways. We now have a Goddess to go with our God, and She is much more... hmmmn, interested in making sure we follow Her directives than the Lord of Light had been for the last few hundred years. It's... good for us as a people, I think.

"Good for *Istevan and me,* in particular... which was apparently why Julanna had gone up to research at the university in the first place." He smiled faintly. "She wanted to find a way to help *us* before *we* had even really decided there *was* an *us.*"

Just about everyone looked baffled at that, except for Amanita.

"Selavan is – or I guess, *was* – super-picky about guys marrying women," she said.

"*Was,*" Davril said with a happy smile. "Most definitely *was.*"

Amanita looked deeply disgruntled about that, but didn't say anything.

"That only gets you about halfway through the story," Dae pointed out. "We still don't know how you guys ended up *here.* Or *why.*"

"Or who you're working with," Thony added.

Davril gave them both a short nod.

"I was getting to that.

"Things had got too... *hot* for us in Selavan. No one was going to harm Julanna – she's a Bard and was pregnant. But then Istevan and I got married." His smile went soft and dreamy again, and Amanita had to poke him to get him to start speaking again. "Oh, sorry. It's *legal* for us to be married now, and my whole family was supportive... but there's still a great deal of... negative public sentiment. We kept the ceremony small and private, but Word got out..."

"*Word* always does," Thony said with the world-weary tone of One Who Knows.

Davril gave him a startled look and nodded. "Things got... *more* contentious when *Word* got out that we were going to adopt Julanna's baby.

"She's not interested in being a mother," he said, a little defensively, and cuddling his sleeping daughter. "She's doing a great job at all the things she *has* to do for Daphne – she didn't even want us to hire a wet-nurse. But she's just started her career as a Bard. She doesn't want to be tied down and..."

Kamauri was giving Daennor a wry look and Amanita was waving Davril to go on with the *story* rather impatiently.

Davril chuckled. "Sorry, wrong audience. I've just had to have *that* conversation so many times. It sort of comes out automatically now.

"Anyways, we figured that getting all three of us out of Selavan for awhile might be a good thing. We thought about Dawil or some other part of the Western Ocean, since Julanna wanted to see her parents – but the travel seemed too chancy with an infant. Then possibly Canador... though there was some question of the political instability..."

"*That's* all fixed," Dae said blithely. "*I* did that."

"Sort of," Kamauri muttered, and Dae stuck her tongue out at her while Daennor chuckled nearly silently again.

Davril raised his eyebrows. "Well, we hadn't quite decided before we were asked by... a certain group of people... to come down here. Because of Istevan's expertise as, um,"

"He's a professional spy," Dae said brightly. "Everyone in the Guild knows now."

Kamauri and Daennor nodded.

Davril sighed. "Well, he used to be. He was done with that. After all, it's rather ineffective to try to work as a spy if everyone knows that's what you do. He chose that work for reasons that... aren't applicable anymore, so...

"But, yes, that's why. And Julanna because... this situation is the work of her 'gentleman-friend.'"

"And *who* were these people?" Amanita wanted to know.

Davril went a little pale. "I was told – *we* were told – not to share that information with anyone. I'm not sure if just knowing that there *were* people involved is going to get me – or you – in trouble."

"Hmmn." Amanita looked very thoughtful. "These 'people' wouldn't happen to have the job of dealing with Evil Wizards *elsewhere* in the world, would they?"

Davril shook his head. "I don't know. I don't *want* to know." He hesitated. "All right, that's not really true. It drives me crazy not to have all the pieces of a puzzle. But in this case... I'm telling myself that the less I know is probably the better."

The three mercenaries exchanged speculative looks. Dae had heard the rumors of a secret society of spies, thieves, and assassins that worked behind the politics of the Western Ocean, and Kamauri and Daennor probably had as well. On the other hand, no one had ever suggested it had anything to do with *this* side of the Misty Mountains.

Amanita looked dissatisfied with the answer, and Thony was clearly impatient as well.

"So, what's your Grand Plan?" the runaway prince asked. "The one that Istevan told Amanita they were still sticking to?"

Davril winced. "Julanna... is convinced this – the invasion – is all her fault. She was going to come and try this on her own if we didn't help... And knowing Julanna, *try* isn't really the operative term."

From Davril's expression, *try* wasn't really an operative term for *him*, either. And Istevan hadn't earned a reputation as one of the Guild's most successful spies *ever* for no reason.

Not to mention that it sounded like the three of them had already managed to turn *one* kingdom upside-down.

"That didn't really answer anything, you know," Thony pointed out. He had the look of a guy used to giving others the runaround, rather than getting it himself.

Davril sighed. "It's just... it seems *stupid* now. It seemed stupid when she *proposed* it, but neither of us had any better ideas, and Julanna was convinced this was *her* problem to fix... And like I said, she was going to go without us. We... hoped we could at least see she got a chance to *try*. And that maybe we could get her out when it didn't work."

Except he'd said *trying* wasn't what Julanna Silversea *did*...

"Davril, spit it out," Amanita told him sternly.

Dae noticed Kamauri and Daennor giving each other rather alarmed looks, as if *they* had figured something out from what he *hadn't* said already. Thony and Jost looked as blank as Dae felt herself.

What possible solution could the most famous Bard in the world have come up with to stop a war that she had decided was happening because an evil sorcerer fell in love with her?

Something grown-ups would understand, but not *kids*...

"Davril," Kamauri said softly, in that concerned tone that Dae had gotten all-too-used to hearing from her these last two years, "Julanna – your cousin – she didn't decide to *give herself up* to the sorcerer? To try to convince him to stop his war... because he loves her?"

The young banker from Selavan just looked at her for a moment, holding the sleeping baby. His worried eyes answered the question before he even gave the confirming nod.

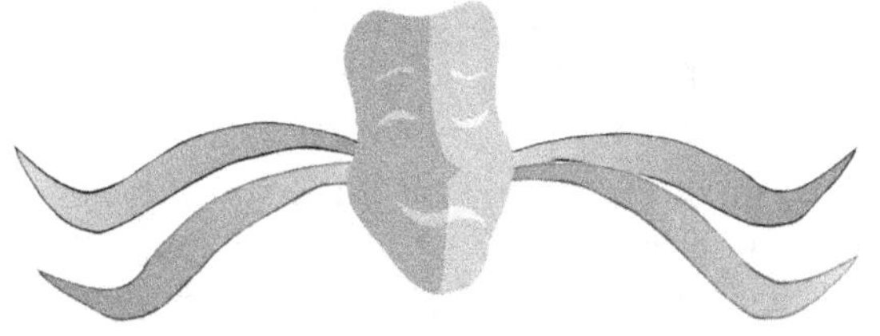

Chapter TWELVE

Existential Crisis, Part 3
(So, Why Are We *Really* Here?)

"WELL, WHAT GOOD WOULD THAT do?" Jost demanded after a moment of horrified silence descended on the group. "So's this Bard turns herself o'er to the sorcerer. Does she really think 'e's gonna call it a day an' let ever'un go back t' what they was a-doin' afore 'e was involved? Like this army o' 'is 'll jes' disappear inta the woodwork? Doesn' she know that unemployed so'jers are th' worst kind fer th' rest o' us?"

He spoke with the kind of authority on the subject that only a boy who'd grown up in a town that was regularly overrun from all directions could possibly manage.

Kamauri and Daennor winced at that, but didn't disagree, and Davril looked dismayed and grim and unsurprised. Amanita and Thony looked sick.

"Not to mention that if it's only the sorcerer-dude holding Shalladra Stillheart back," Thony shivered. "That is one *scary* lady. Did I mention that I think she has *pointy teeth?*"

"*Dökkálfar* do," Amanita said with her own shiver. "It's said they'll eat people. And she'll know how to navigate the Fairy Wood."

Thony's fists clenched. "And there's all those other armies we saw on that map. All over to the east and south. If she's been his second, they might just follow her for a chance at... at loot and conquest and... the other things that go with that. Even if he's not involved."

"And that zombie army he's bringing up from Darjil," Amanita added glumly. "The one that consists of the whole population right down to the newborn babies and old and sick... but likely can't be stopped by any normal means."

Even Jost looked unnerved at that.

Dae straightened up. Daennor had kept that very nice arm around her shoulders the whole time, but she was pleased to note that he didn't try to stop her. She sort of missed that sense of being protected and cared for as his arm fell away... but there was the feeling like he still had her back, and that was almost as good.

"So," the mercenette began in a business-like tone, "We have a sorcerer who controls vast armies, including a zombie army. And who may or may not stop because he's in love – or was in love, or thought he was in love – with Julanna Silversea and might have been doing all this to get her back. That really doesn't sound likely," she told Davril. "I mean, this is way too complex an operation for him to have put it all together just in the last two years."

"Less than two years," Davril agreed. "At least if he didn't get started seriously until after he discovered she hadn't made it back to Dynsfyor and left his message with me. I told Julanna that, and Istevan told her that. And she should know for herself how long it takes to get large numbers of people doing anything. But, well..."

Amanita frowned. "Why would she know for herself? Bards have all those songs, but they usually don't get into the details of logistics." She made a face. "Rather the opposite, if anything. That's the kind of thing that mercenaries or royalty would know."

"Or merchants, or bankers," Davril agreed mildly. "She *is* my cousin." Though there was something just the slightest bit evasive about his comment.

"Later," Dae decreed. "Why Julanna Silversea does or doesn't, or should or shouldn't understand military logistics is not relevant right now.

"We have sorcerer – and his possible motivations, though we have to believe we don't know them all. And we don't know how long ago he started working on all this, though that might or might not matter.

"We know he can cast compulsion spells on masses of people – and strong enough ones to control a Dark-elf on individuals. And that he has lots of armies, including an enspelled army that is due to arrive here in the next week.

"And that he has designs on the Fairy Wood, either to invade other worlds or to achieve total world-domination on this one by using it to move his armies around faster. And he has some reason – possibly having to do with the Dark-elf Shalladra Stillheart – that gives him reason to believe he'll be able to do that... even though the Great Goddess of All guards the Fairy Wood in Her Aspect as the Waywalker."

"Lilysong, Queen of the Fairies, is the Guardian of the Ways Between the Worlds," Amanita clarified.

"That seems like a pretty good summary of the situation," Davril agreed. "And the resources we have are the seven of us–"

Twinklestar whinnied indignantly and Rainsparkle stomped a forehoof.

Davril made a sort of abbreviated sitting-bow in their direction, his movement hampered by the baby in his arms. "My pardon. The *nine* of us. You've both been so quiet, I'd almost forgotten you were paying attention. The *nine* of us and Istevan and Julanna on the inside."

"I can organize th' street-kids in Flowerdust," Jost offered. "Cain't think we can do much 'gainst armies, though."

"And... we have liabilities," Kamauri put in. "Rainsparkle agrees with me. There's no good reason to have the Lost Princess of Pathremir, and the Crown Prince of one of those countries beyond the Fairy Wood in this war-zone. Or..." she sighed, "or the only child – so far as we know it – of the sorcerer-king."

"Or the Heir to the largest bank on the North Coast," Daennor added. "Even if this sorcerer-king fellow doesn't already know the power of money, he soon will. You're as much of a liability here as the children, Davril, and that's even without the fact that you could be used as a lever to compel the Bard and Istevan."

Davril looked stubborn... but possibly also scared.

"Rainsparkle wants for her and Twinklestar to get all four of you to safety," Kamauri went on after a nod to Daennor. She hesitated, looking at Dae with troubled eyes, then went on. "She says the rest of us should stay and see what we can do – leave war to the professionals."

Dae looked up at the unicorn-filly her best-friend had bonded to and got a wink.

Or maybe that wink was for Daennor, who was looking rather stunned.

"Well, *I'm* not going anywhere." Thony folded his arms. "I'm the only person here with a real stake in defending the Fairy Wood. And there isn't a heck of a lot that three or five of you can do that wouldn't be better off with a few more of us."

He glanced at Amanita and got a nod back. "Amanita and Dae and I have already been running a campaign to actually *do* something to hinder the Raven-troops. What have the rest of *you* done?'

Kamauri frowned at him.

"*And* I agreed that Jost could come with us when we left," Thony added, looking at the street-kid. "So, he could start fresh somewhere else. I'm not going back on that promise, and I don't think Jost is going to want to leave his friends right before they get run over by an army of zombies."

Jost... looked both relieved and somewhat torn over that.

"After all, the sorcerer who enchanted those poor folks to be zombies is still *right here,*" Thony pointed out, his eyes on the other boy. "Who's to say he won't decide to add the population of Flowerdust to his army? I can see what your cousin saw in him," the runaway prince told Davril, "he seems to have a... compelling personality even before he turns on the *compulsion* spells. His regular troops seem to respect him. But I read the letters that he sent to Captain Stillheart. That might be *her* name, but I'm not sure *he* has any heart at all. He referred to how his enchantment zombified the babies and old and sick as *inconvenient. To him. And his plans.*"

Thony looked around the whole group, not excluding the unicorns.

"We need to do more than stop his armies – and with as few of us as there are, I can't see any way to do this *other* than using pranks. But we need to do *more* than that. We need to figure out how to break his *power.* His secular power *and* his magickal Power. And how to break that spell on the people of Darjil.

"Because if we don't do *both* of those things, this war is *never* going to end."

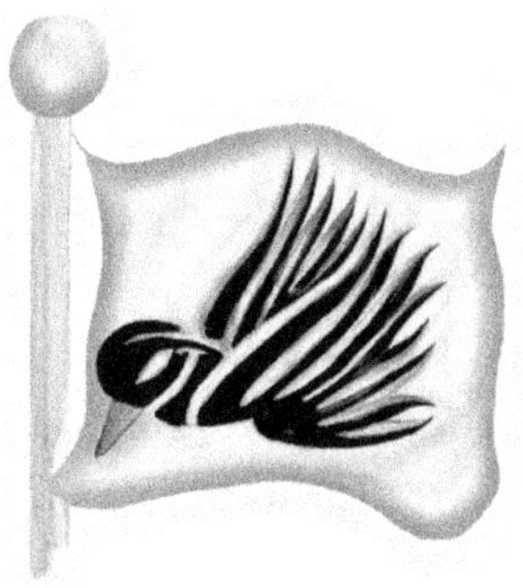

Chapter THIRTEEN

Bros Before Fillies?

IT WAS A GREAT RELIEF when everyone else absorbed that and was willing to get down to cases.

In Thony's opinion, the session had been useful – because all of them who were working together were now on the same page. It was also vindicating when the adults all deferred to Jost's knowledge of the city and to Thony's and Amanita's – and Dae's – expertise in pranks.

Amanita still had the copy of the map that she had copied showing Raven'sWing's troop-emplacements. She turned it over to the three mercenaries to mutter over and discuss. Kamauri and Daennor took Dae reasonably seriously, Thony noted, though he suspected there would still be a row when theory turned into practicum. And Kamauri's unicorn-friend seemed to be part of that team.

Davril offered Thony enough money to get his and the girls' stuff – and horses – out of hock at the Inn of the Starred Hoof. It wasn't a huge amount – and Thony felt like an idiot after Amanita had snarkily pointed out that she'd shown him where her share of the money that he'd needed had been hidden in her saddlebags... and that if he'd only *remembered* to get it out before losing possession of said-saddlebags he would have had a much easier day of it.

Of course, his and Jost's *hard day* had landed them a couple of more allies.

Davril engaged Jost in a discussion regarding the economy of Flowerdust. Based on the banker's comments and questions, and the alert sparkle in his eyes, the young father had some ideas about how *his* expertise could be used to help The Cause.

Bank pranks were rather beyond Thony's fairly rudimentary understanding of economics, he quickly realized. Aldyrwald's economy was just too *small*. They didn't properly even have banking, though Papa made loans to the nobility from the Royal Treasury, and even to the peasants of the home-villages on occasion. He didn't charge them this thing called *interest* that Davril seemed to think would be a major lever.

It was a bit lowering to realize that *Jost* was following along far better than *Thony* with his 'royal' education. The street-kid even had some ideas that Davril appeared to consider good ones.

Amanita had joined the group over the map... but she at least knew something about the territory over here.

Twinklestar seemed to have disappeared.

Thony decided to step out of the copse for a moment himself.

After taking a moment for himself and nature, the young prince wandered somewhat randomly around, not really wanting to go back in and be useless. Eventually the discussion would have to get back to what pranks would actually work, but until then...

He found Twinklestar standing on the rise that hid the tiny valley. The unicorn was more or less silhouetted against the sky – a darker blob against the darkness.

Thony was informed that it wasn't really all *that* dark, and invited to join him.

"I didn't think horses could see all that well in the dark," the young prince commented as he came up beside his unicorn-friend.

Twinklestar informed him that he was not a *horse*, thank you very much. And that he could use his magick to see whatever he liked. To demonstrate, he shared his vision with Thony and the whole plain almost seemed to glow under the brilliant moonlight and the fainter, but still distinct starlight.

The dark bulk of the Fairy Wood filled up one side of the horizon. The orangey-glow of Flowerdust filled up the other side.

"Can you see magick as well as use magick to see?" Thony asked after a moment.

He was informed that Twinklestar would rather *not*, given that the Fairy Wood was so close. There was so much magick there that he would practically be blinded unless he took some specific precautions.

Thony thought about that, scratching absently at Twinklestar's itchy spots and idly planning to give the unicorn a proper grooming once he had their supplies back. Twinklestar liked that idea and showed his appreciation by 'grooming' Thony to the prince's distinct *lack* of appreciation.

"So..." Thony said after he gave up on getting unicorn-saliva out of his hair. Again. "This filly, Rainsparkle. You like her. Does she like you?"

Twinklestar sounded fairly confident that she did. Thony couldn't tell if it was typical stallion/guy bluster, though.

"Does that change anything with *us?*" he asked. "I mean... if you and she got... *close.* And decided to make some baby unicorns or something."

Twinklestar didn't see how that was any of Thony's business.

"You're the one who said we were going to be 'best bros,'" Thony pointed out.

Bros didn't talk about stuff like that, Twinklestar told him a bit loftily.

Thony rolled his eyes. "Sure. Whatever. But you seem to have decided whether *I* like someone is *your* business. It only seems fair if it goes the other way."

Twinklestar gave him a sly look from his nearer eye and wanted to know if *someone* was *Jost.*

"Don't be silly. I have a duty to Aldyrwald to find a princess."

Presumably Davril also had a duty to provide an Heir to his bank. And *he'd* figured out a solution to *that.*

"It's not the same thing at all," Thony disagreed. "Besides, Jost and his army of street-kids can't defend Aldyrwald from the neighbors. Even if I *were* thinking like that. Which I'm not."

You weren't willing to leave him behind and go to safety.

"I made a promise, and I keep my promises. And he's a nice kid who's had a tough life. And I wasn't willing to go 'someplace safe' either way. Even if there is such a thing." Thony sighed and leaned on Twinklestar. "Look, dude, you saw the way Dae's friends looked at each other. Is that ever going to work out? Because that looked... super sad."

Rainsparkle says she's almost finished training Kamauri. Once that is done, they can adjust their relationship.

"So, *you're* training *me?*" Thony snorted.

I just taught you how to see in the dark, didn't I?

The unicorn sounded distracted, though.

And that was about when Thony realized that he was actually receiving Twinklestar's comments as *actual words*. Which suggested they had reached a new level of bonding... didn't it?

He was about to ask, when Twinklestar shook his head violently and Thony had to duck backwards for fear of that sharp horn. The unicorn's shake continued in a skin-twitch all the way from neck to hocks, and he stamped his feet restlessly as well.

"What's wrong?" Thony asked, hanging back a little bit to avoid personal damage.

Twinklestar was looking rather fixedly to the west. The southwest.

Someone is coming... an Elder. And... others. I need to talk to Rainsparkle.

The unicorn turned abruptly and went back into the copse, leaving Thony standing, somewhat bewildered, on the hilltop.

Could *he* see or sense whatever it was that had startled Twinklestar? The young prince tried to remember what had felt different when his unicorn had shown him how to see in the dark. It had been a very *small* difference...

To his right, the Fairy Wood suddenly began to blaze up, and he quickly looked back in the direction that Twinklestar had been looking. Very, *very* far away, there was a soft glow that was nonetheless somehow *deep* and *powerful* and reminded him of Twinklestar and Rainsparkle. A unicorn Elder, Twinklestar had said.

Well, doubtless they'd find out shortly. And surely more unicorns would be a good thing. Thony couldn't imagine a creature as *good* as a unicorn as having any truck with an evil sorcerer, so the newcomer would certainly be on their side.

The young prince turned himself around to go back into the copse and see if they were talking about pranks yet – but he took care to turn himself towards the left so as not to face the Fairy Wood again...

Flowerdust caught his eye as he did so.

There was far more of a blaze than he would have expected – the whole plain had an ambient glow that had intensified under this new kind of sight, but Flowerdust seemed to be scattered with small, bright stars set in almost an *absence* of light by comparison to the plains. And there were a handful of much, much *brighter* stars that all seemed distinct, but to be emanating from the same spot.

Valderon Raven'sWing was one, he guessed. And Shalladra Stillheart – given all that he'd heard about those Dark-elf-types – was probably another. But there were more than *two*...

Actually, there seemed to be four or five distinctly different kinds of *brightness* at that spot. One made him think of vast quantities of water. Another, of wind. A third... of the silence of the night and the darkness between stars. The last couple were... mixed up together and he couldn't get a firm impression – his best guess was sort of what Twinklestar had smelled like when they hadn't had a chance to groom him for a couple of days. Soured old unicorn-sweat.

Weird. And icky. But still somehow alluring.

And not at all useful, any of this.

Thony tried to figure out how to *stop* seeing all this and ended up losing the night-vision Twinklestar had started him out with. He stumbled blindly back down the hill and into the copse, cursing under his breath until he entered the little sphere of lanternlight again.

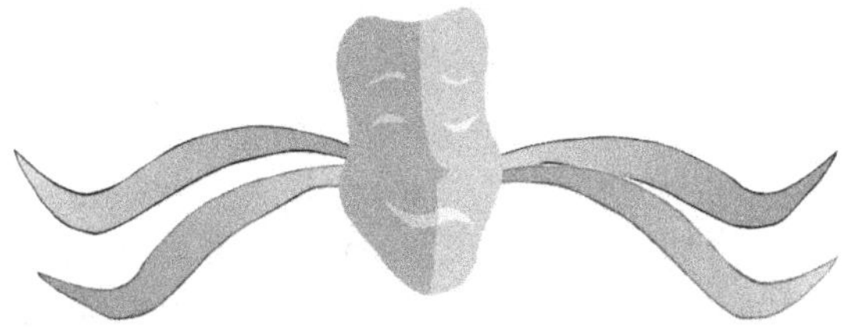

Chapter FOURTEEN

Clearing Things Up?

THE GROUP – *SANS* DAVRIL, the baby, and the unicorns – trickled back into Flowerdust the next morning by ones and twos.

Kamauri had pulled some very feminine clothes out of her saddlebags and insisted that she and the girls wear them. There had been a great deal of expostulation and vituperation *(none of it particularly aided by Thony's sarcastic comments about the unicorn-maiden* **robe** *that he* had to wear... *but he was rather put out that Kamauri didn't feel a need to wear* **her** *'robe.' She* **had** *one, he saw a bit of it when she'd been looking for the dresses and skirts.)*

In the end, however, the unicorn-maiden-mercenary's argument that the Raven-soldiers would be looking for a young girl who was a *mercenary,* and carrying a bunch of *large weapons,* not a couple of girls in dresses, had won the day.

It had helped that *she* was wearing a dress as well, and leaving *her* weapons behind.

Or maybe not *helped,* but sort of cut out Dae's complaints from under her.

When it was clear that Kamauri and Daennor were going back in as a courting couple, Dae's objections vanished rather abruptly. Although she did cast several suspicious looks at Kamauri's unicorn-friend.

Thony got stuck wearing his unicorn-maiden *robe,* and it was decided that using some dye on his hair to tone down the color a bit might be helpful. Daennor offered to help him with that after Thony and Jost got the horses and packs – including the packet of hair-dye Amanita had purchased a couple of days earlier. Daennor Cat'sfoot had turned out to be the only member of the group who had experience with hair-dye, though he wryly noted that his previous experience was with colors usually reserved for exotic festival-garb, not trying to adjust more natural-looking colors.

Thony had thought the idea of turning his hair purple was brilliant, but no one else agreed. Amanita pointed out that the idea wasn't just to make him less recognizable, but also less conspicuous, and the idea was tabled.

From everyone else's perspective anyways. Thony had a notion to revisit it sometime in the future. Hair wasn't permanent after all, so why not?

He ended up walking back up with Jost. He carried the stupid *robe* under one arm so he didn't have to trip on the thing while cutting through the grassy prairie-land *en route.*

"When d'ye plan t'put that thing on?" Jost asked as they made it to the road and Thony resolutely set out for the town without pause.

"Never, if I could get away with it," Thony muttered under his breath. But Jost didn't deserve his bad temper over the thing. "When we get to the outskirts? I can't walk as fast with all that fabric around my knees and toes."

Jost eyed him. "I'll slow down an ye do need it. Ye're quite fetching in that dress, y'know."

"I'd rather get this errand done as quickly as possible," Thony ignored the second half of the comment. Amanita and Dae had each taken him aside to remind him that they needed Jost's help to give The New Plan half a chance of working. And that that meant he probably *shouldn't* explain to the street-kid-chieftain that he wasn't *interested.*

Jost snorted, sounding not at all fooled. "Ye're quite fetching w'ou' the dress as well." But he stretched, loudly unkinking his back. "Niver thought I'd say't, but sleepin' out there on th' ground was a tad sight better'n in town. Freer, y'know, fer all that I have me a sweet li'l spot in an abandoned house. 'Course the food didn' 'urt neither."

Thony glanced sideways at him with a small smile. Watching Jost get as much as he wanted to eat hadn't been a pleasure for himself alone, given how Kamauri and Daennor had helped. But it *had* been a distinctly satisfying touch to the evening.

He'd never been chronically hungry like that himself. And the last year or so, he'd been *hungry* all the time, though he hadn't seemed to grow terribly heavier *or* taller to his personal dismay. But it had made it entirely easy to sympathize with Jost, who was, after all, very close to his own age.

"Ye kin stay wit' me in th' 'ouse," Jost added nonchalantly, "an it seems more convenient than that bit o' valley there. Fer all th' schemin' and mischief-makin'."

Awww, geez.

The girls were right, but... darnit, it wasn't Proper Princely Behavior to let Jost go on thinking...

Thony stopped in the dusty lane, and caught Jost's sleeve to make him halt as well. They were in sight of town now, the crest of a low hill blocking off all but the highest roofs ahead.

"Jost..." he began, not really sure how to say this.

The street-kid-chieftain gave him a wry look. "Ye're goin' t'say ye don' lean that way. I'm offerin' ye a place t'sleep an' rest, Thony. Nothin' more, less ye're interested."

Thony looked down. "I... just don't want to mislead you. I think you're a good friend. And we need your help. But... I'm not *interested* in anyone. And... well, you heard who I am last night. My land is under threat – even without all *this.*"

He gestured in the direction of Flowerdust. "I need to find a princess with a fath   er who'll lend me troops to defend my home. I... don't have the *right* to be interested in anyone who can't help me with that."

Jost tilted his head. "Sad, that."

Thony shrugged. "It's the way it is. It's always been that way for me, so I don't suppose I'd know what to do with something else."

"But ye swore ye wouldn't leave Flowerdust wit'ou' *me,*" Jost reminded him. "So's *I* could 'ave a fresh start."

"One of us should be able to," the young prince replied. "And... I promised."

"An' I s'ppose ye *promised* t'return home wit' that princess and 'er army."

Thony looked out over the endless sea of grass. "Not exactly."

He'd implied it. And... he wouldn't really abandon Aldyrwald. It was *home*. His parents were there. And his sisters. And...

Well, his parents and his sisters. And Roger and Jeremy, his brothers-in-law. And his friend Wes. And maybe the stablemaster, Tad.

And a host of other people he didn't really *miss,* but who didn't deserve to have their homes destroyed by an invading force just because Thony went off to please himself.

"Ye said... 'twas not like here, yer home," Jost said quietly. "Nor like Davril there described Selavan."

Thony looked back at him in confusion. "What? What are you talking about?" It seemed like a *non sequitur.*

"Ye said it didna matter if lads fancied each other, there in yer home," Jost clarified, though his face was red.

"Oh, that." Thony shook his head. "No. It doesn't. Not except for royalty."

"Which ye are."

Thony nodded.

Jost looked at him for a long moment, then started walking towards Flowerdust again. Thony had to stretch his legs to catch up.

"So, th' girl. Amanita," Jost said as they ate up the distance. "She's another o' yer ilk. Armies to 'er name an' all, jes' th' way ye want."

"*Need,*" Thony corrected automatically. "And – *Gods,* no. I mean, yes, she probably does, but she's the Heir to her own land, so she couldn't come home with me anyways. Not to stay. And – have you *heard* her? She makes jackals look like friendly lap-dogs when she gets her dander up."

They had passed a pack of jackals feasting on something dead in their somewhat-unintentional perambulations yesterday. It had been shortly after they recovered from Twinklestar dumping them – the unicorn had vanished into the distance in search of true love *(or whatever)* – and they had been trying to follow his trail. The jackals and their prey had mightily impressed both boys and they'd circled wide around although the animals hadn't even bothered to snarl at them, being too busy eating.

They came in between some sheds and shacks about then, and Jost chose a back-alley for Thony to put the unicorn-maiden robe on over his other clothes. The perfectly white fabric had lost none of its gleaming cleanliness nor developed any unsightly creases from the rather unenthusiastic care Thony had given it.

With a sigh, he pulled it on, dragging the cloth-of-gold sash out from a pocket to tie around his waist.

Jost watched all of this, also keeping an eye out for anyone on the streets. It was mid-morning by now, and the day-laborers would all either be off at work or sleeping off hangovers, he had said. Goodwives would be at market, their little ones slung on their backs or in baskets or tailing around their feet, and older ones would be seeking to earn their own coin or two or perhaps score a piece of fruit that fell from a cart.

He turned back as Thony finished with the sash and sucked in his breath for a moment. Then he stepped close and put his hands on Thony's face. His calluses from years of street-living were rough against the young prince's cheeks.

"Jost..." Thony said uncomfortably. "I told you..."

"How can ye know an ye don' gi' it a chance?" Jost said reasonably. "Ye're young to know such things about yerself anyhoo. Not even down on yer cheeks yet, aye." His thumb rubbed Thony's cheek.

Thony looked up at him. Jost was an inch or two taller, though the hollowness of his cheeks and a certain ranginess to his body made it clear that he'd be taller still if he were properly fed.

"That's why I ran away from home, Jost. I'm *too young*. Papa was going to have me wed shortly after my fifteenth birthday which would be..." He frowned. "Another couple weeks, I think."

Jost looked startled. "*Wed?* But ye said ye had to find yerself yer own princess?" He frowned, but put his hands down. "And if ye're too young t' *shave,* then surely..."

Thony sighed. "The neighboring kings are going to invade Aldyrwald – my home. Papa was going to let one of them give me a sister – or even an aunt as my bride. An old woman, whose instructions would be to kill me and Papa both off so that her brother – or nephew – would inherit Aldyrwald. Because there wouldn't be any other Heir."

"Couldn' she take it fer 'er ownself?" Jost asked. "Cain't think o' a woman *here* as would give up sumthin' o' 'er own."

"Girls can't *rule*," Thony said a little more sharply than he intended. "Girls... women... *ladies* are supposed to stay home and take care of the castle."

There was Amanita and her country, of course. But Dae had said that was an anomaly even here.

Jost snorted. "I'm thinkin' 'tis not merely *Amanita's* attitudes that make ye poorly suited."

Thony glared at him.

Jost chuckled and reached up to ruffle his hair. "Aye, ye're still a li'l lad. P'rhaps I'll try yer opinions 'gain when there's summat on yer cheeks t'say ye've grown." He turned back to the main road they'd been following into town. "C'mon now. Ye've horses to free from that conniving innkeeper. I swear, if 'twerent for Clarick bein' such a good li'l lad..."

Thony followed him, not sure if he should be relieved – or fuming for being treated like a little kid himself.

The horses were soon freed. The only complication – with Jost standing at Thony's back with folded arms, anyways – came when the innkeeper wanted to know what to tell the gentleman who had arranged the room for them if he should return. Thony made up a story on the spot about his unicorn suddenly insisting on moving on. He wasn't sure if it was *more* or *less* believable without Twinklestar there with him.

Not that it mattered, since Jost was and the innkeeper looked sour, but seemed disinclined to argue. Clarick helped them load up Silverfoot and Dae's horse Sandy, and gave them to know that he'd made sure their bags hadn't been disturbed.

Thony pulled off the stupid white robe as soon as they were out of sight of the inn and stuffed it in a saddlebag before pulling his hood up to cover his hair. Sandy was attached on a lead to Silverfoot's saddle.

He said goodbye to Jost – who had a long list of his own things to accomplish, apparently after that chat with Davril – and headed back to the copse. He'd come back tonight for another shot at pranking the Raven headquarters.

A long morning just to fix the screw-up of yesterday... but it was a relief to be back on a proper saddle, with a horse that had good paces.

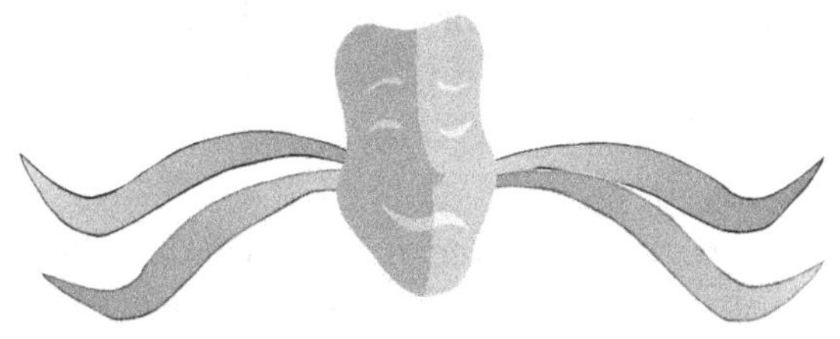

Chapter FIFTEEN

Au Pears and Potatoes

AMANITA AND DAE HAD SEPARATED as soon as they got into town. Part of The New Plan was to confuse people by making them think the two girls were actually one person – which required them to not be seen together.

Today's main job was to meet with Jost's crew of street-kids to scout out locations where they could set up pranks in the city most effectively. Jost thought that some of his kids would have ideas once they understood what was going on and the stakes involved. It had been his idea for Amanita and Dae to pretend to be one person.

"Ev'ry sojer's come through here's been superstitious-like," he'd said wisely. "Makes a ton o' money, sellin' 'em lucky charms an' wardin' bracelets an' whatnot. Fakes, most o' 'em, but th' sojers feel better havin' 'em, and we'll niver see th' most of 'em again," he added with brutal practicality. "So's there's none to call us out on th' useless things.

"But we've added to the market by revivin' – or inventin' – plen'y o' stories 'bout ev'ry last li'l critter and kind as might cause ill-luck if they're offended."

And he'd gone on with a long, long list of touchy minor Elementals and other magickal beings, each of which had specific things they were known for being offended by and specific ways of being placated. Kobolds, gremlins, tsukumogami, lutins, brownies, pixies, duende, dokkaebi, clurichauns... and more. The sheer variety was a bit mind-boggling.

The idea that battle-hardened troops could be demoralized and frightened off if they were convinced that their army was haunted by pesky boogey-men seemed... more like wishful thinking than reality. But Jost was sort of an expert, and it was something to work with.

Secondary jobs included Dae checking on Evrien Quickfoot at the Guildhouse, and Amanita doing some shopping in the marketplace. Jost knew where they were each going and said he'd send for them once he'd talked to his crew.

He himself wouldn't be part of this. He had other things to do.

Exactly what those 'other things' were, Amanita had no clue. It probably had something to do with the very *(very)* long conversation he'd had with Davril last night. The two of them had still been talking long after everyone else had gone to sleep.

The marketplace was its usual bustle, and Amanita moved around it happily. Being able to wander around on her own in a city was one of the greater pleasures of the wandering life in her opinion. She'd never have been allowed to do that at home.

Flowerdust was pretty small – she'd spent time in Dynsfyor, among other places – but it was huge compared to Aldyrwald and its tiny villages.

While she was waiting, the Lost Princess of Pathremir browsed over stacks of last year's apples, new potatoes, and some early pears. The pear-seller eyed her suspiciously, given that she'd been hanging out next to his stall a couple of days earlier while she was waiting to meet Jost.

Who had arrived late, talked in circles, and generally been rather useless. She was entirely of two minds about including another *boy* – and one who was clearly so *flighty*-minded – in their plans. Her grandmother – Eldest-Princess Reyalla – had always insisted that men simply didn't have it in them to think deep thoughts or stick to plans.

Her *other* grandmother, Queen Namarina, had a better opinion of men than that, but still didn't award them positions in her *government*.

And the idea that two men might want to *marry* each other... well... It was against Pathremiri law because clearly there had to be *someone* in the family who was qualified to make decisions.

Legally qualified, since men in Pathremir needed a woman to sign certain documents and could not hold property or run businesses without a female conservator to supervise their transactions and review their records. An attorney or accountant was often hired to serve that purpose for families that were unfortunate enough not to have daughters, as well as sons... or for those who sued to be freed of overbearing female relatives.

Amanita had a fair amount of sympathy for that last situation, and she'd met a fair number of sensible boys and men since she left home. She thought of herself as fairly open-minded at this point...

But she'd had to consciously hold her tongue when Davril had proudly declared himself *married* to Istevan. He'd been serving a husband's proper place, certainly, looking after the baby, and the girl hadn't really thought about how the trio of spies was connected.

If she *had* considered the question... well, in Pathremir it was permissible for a woman to take on a second husband to sire children or provide manual labor. Men who were good with babies weren't always stellar at other things, or so she'd been told. And a man who was good with physical things wasn't always very good at running a household while the woman of the house managed their business and property. Grandparents and brothers and such could help, but sometimes you just needed another adult around.

It hadn't made a great deal of sense to Amanita personally. Her grandmother the Queen had never married at all and seemed to do fine. And her own father, Prince-Consort Naeel was a good, quiet man who loved his wife and children and spent as much time as possible playing music for his flock of sheep.

Mama was often to be found out there with him, with her paints and easel, which was probably why a good portion of their people thought she wasn't quite clever. A woman was supposed to be more... *driven* and *ambitious,* as Grandmother Eldest-Princess Reyalla always commented.

But Princess-Heir Ytheril was already going to be Queen someday. What possible other ambitions – besides taking time to paint – she could have, had never been made clear to Amanita. Her parents were intelligent and well-aware of the political currents they were swimming in. They simply chose to handle them differently than, well, Eldest-Princess Reyalla expected. Or wanted. Or...

Amanita shook her head. Not having to fulminate on her grandmothers and her parents and the *entire messed-up situation in Pathremir* was a big part of why she'd runaw– *left home* in the first place.

Well, that and because Grandmother Eldest-Princess Reyalla had been begun stirring up the noble classes about seeing that *Amanita* be wedded off soon to secure the succession. Just as though she hadn't gone on and on and *on* forever about how neither Grandmother Namarina nor Mama had managed more than one daughter because *they'd* started too young.

Amanita had only been twelve... so likely it would have been a few more years, but...

She understood Thony's situation all too well. Not that she had an invasion hanging on it.

Probably.

Though with Selavan and Dawil – or rather *Mountainmeadow* – both looking friendlier...

Not that she really approved of *that,* but no one had asked *her...*

Darnit, she was doing it again.

And really, she was just looking for reasons to think better of these new acquaintances and allies.

The pear-seller was giving her dirty looks, so she hastily purchased a bunch of pears, then moved off a little to a basket-seller and purchased a market-basket. Some of the other girls that she saw around the shopping area were using their aprons or even their skirts to store purchases. But Kamauri hadn't offered her an apron to go with this commoner's dress, and hoisting her skirts high enough to keep her produce from escaping seemed chancy.

Amanita was sensibly wearing pants underneath the skirt, of course, but still. Most of the other girls using their skirts seemed to be trying to show off their skinny, Winter-pale legs to the passing Raven-soldiers... which just – *eewww.*

And it didn't seem terribly *safe,* either, given that the troops weren't just guys and most of those girls looked old enough to be impressed into the army.

Amanita wondered if Clarick's fifteen-year-old sister, Magritte, had been let out of the inn's backroom and was out here somewhere. Or if it was really a good idea that Kamauri had come back into town on her own mission for The New Plan.

And speaking of whom...

She spotted Kamauri and Daennor at the other side of the market. The unicorn-maiden-mercenary was... not really behaving like a unicorn-maiden, Amanita thought disapprovingly. Rather, she was acting like one of the silly girls in the marketplace, though at least she was using a basket. At least Daennor was deferring to her as a man ought...

"You going to buy anything, lassie?"

Amanita realized she'd stopped in front of someone selling... broccoli. And Brussels sprouts. She tried not to wince at the thought. Greens were *probably* a good idea... though it appeared that the only members of their entire group who could actually *cook* were the pair over there, though Davril had mentioned passingly that Istevan was quite a chef when he felt like it, and...

The pair over there, who were now being detained by a four-man patrol of Raven-soldiers.

Who were possibly saying something rather *rude* to Kamauri, because Daennor was looking grim and stepping in front of her...

"Friends of yours, miss?" the greengrocer's tone had gone quiet and sympathetic as she saw where Amanita's attention had gone.

"No," but Amanita couldn't draw her eyes away as Daennor's arms were tied behind him before the patrol forced him out of the marketplace, and Kamauri was dragged after with a strong hand on her upper arm.

They hadn't even *tried* to resist, not really. Was this a part of The New Plan? Amanita hadn't paid a great deal of attention to what the two adults were planning to do. Neither one of them were pranksters, so whatever they did wouldn't have a great deal to do with what *she* was going to be working on after all.

And, admit it, she'd been distracted by watching Davril and Jost. Because they were only *guys* and surely needed some help.

How was she going to explain this to Dae...?

"Shoulda known better than to walk abroad at this time-a day." The elderly woman's tongue clicked in disapproval. "Young folks like that, just old enough to make perfect draftees. I suppose they're new to the area, though, so they wouldn't know. And young love does make one stupid."

She chuckled at Amanita's blank look. "You've a ways to go yerself, dearie, but you'll see."

Silver Goddess, but Amanita certainly hoped not.

She started working her way carefully towards the edge of the market. Another patrol was entering the area, and it was better to be safe than sorry. Jost's people could just... find her somewhere else.

The obvious way to unobtrusively escape was to finish her marketing while getting closer to one of the exits from the area. Carrots, potatoes, onions, and apples all found their way into her basket. Davril had assured her that he could trap rabbits for meat, or shoot prairie-dogs, or something.

That last had sounded... *wrong* until Dae had explained that prairie-dogs were not dogs at all. Of course, then they'd explained that prairie-dogs were basically giant rats, and then it had all sounded *wrong* again.

Amanita was almost to her target exit when she turned away from a stall selling leafy bundles of early Spring greens, like dandelions and clover, and literally walked into a blue-tunicked chest...

And found herself grabbed and hustled out of that same exit that she thought would be her place of safety...

She reached into her basket to find something to throw in the guy's face – a pear or a potato or something...

...and then realized it was just Istevan.

"You almost got a faceful of potato," Amanita informed the tall man tartly. "Or maybe pear."

He chuckled. "Never come between a woman and her grocery shopping. I'll remember."

That sounded... hmmn. More like a joke than condescending. And he had called her a *'woman,'* not a girl, which had a nice ring to it. She decided to let it slide this time.

"What's up?"

The famous *(if oxymoronic)* mercenary-spy looked much better than the last time she'd seen him. The dark circles under his eyes were all but gone, even in the bright light of day, his hair was combed and looked freshly washed, there was healthy color in his cheeks, his uniform looked like it had been recently pressed and starched, and there was energy in his posture. Amanita hadn't actually realized how *bad* he'd looked the other night until she was presented with this comparison.

Just as well. If she'd had to describe him to Davril last night with the words that were now coming to mind – greasy, lackluster, and hopeless – she had the feeling the young banker would have found a way to ditch the baby on her and the others and come here on his own. And *he* clearly had the wrong skillset for clandestine activities.

An *accountant,* by the Goddess!

A *male, Selavani* accountant!

"Made a bit of a fuss the other night after we parted ways, I heard," Istevan told her with a grin. "I must admit, you've restored my faith in the Old Man's granddaughter. I thought the Fox was insane for letting you graduate at age twelve, but you do seem to have... flair."

Oh.

He thought she was *Dae.*

Well, that *was* the impression they were trying to foster, right? And the fewer people who knew for certain that the Lost Princess of Pathremir *(Dae had called her that, and Amanita had decided she liked it)* was wandering around here the better. And the less Istevan knew – stuck in close quarters with the enemy as he was – the better as well.

"Um, thanks," she responded.

"It'll take more than *flair* in this situation, though," Istevan warned her. "Though you seem to have a talent in this arena. Though how you knew Captain Fayorn would have a particular reason to fear large rodents, I can't imagine."

Amanita buffed her nails on the shoulder of her dress and inspected them coolly – and so that she didn't have to meet his eyes. "We have our ways."

"Mmm-hmmmn." That amused tone suggested he'd seen right through her. Like her father or Tad could do. Who *was* this guy?

"You'll have to be on the lookout now, of course," Istevan pointed out unnecessarily. "The sergeant and Fayorn both identified that boy you were with as the one who helped them navigate the city. Val liked him, so they were willing to give the boy some leeway – and they'd still rather not have to chance Val's reaction was my impression – but it's obvious he's one of your confederates now. Likely he should do something about that blazing red hair."

"Yeah, we have it under control," Amanita hoped to – ah, *blazes* – that Thony made it out of the town without trouble. He was supposed to be dressed as the unicorn-maiden, which meant he had to have the hair showing, but she knew how he hated the dress. He'd planned to cover it and put the dress away once he had the horses, but there would probably be a short span of time where he was obviously a *boy* with *bright red hair...*

And with Daennor taken by the Raven-soldiers, any attempt at a dye-job was going to be pretty... messy.

Istevan nodded. "You're being pretty professional about it all. And you clearly have each other's back. But they've figured out who you are, Dae. They've already gone back and questioned the old woman who got stuck taking care of the Guildhouse..." He had a sort of grim smirk. "Neither Fayorn nor Shalladra has a clue who Evrien Quickfoot is and what a mistake they made in leaving *her* there, old as she is. I'd've expected that of Fayorn – he's clearly a back-country rube with no *real* training. Not like you and I have, but Shalladra is – or was – a proper mercenary."

Wait, did he not know?

"Evrien said the Guild records show Shalladra Stillheart showing up as long ago as three hundred years," Amanita told him. "We think she's a Dark-elf."

The man winced. "Yes, I know. And her association with Val goes back at least that far. What I've gathered – mostly from them snarking at each other in my presence, I'll admit, and I'm reading between the lines – is that *she's* responsible for his long life. There's something she needs him to do... and she was willing to tie her life to his somehow. Possibly because of that love spell he's cast on her, though ... I have the impression there's more to it than that.

"But that suggests, at least, that he hasn't needed to do all the sorts of awful things an Evil Wizard *usually* has to do to extend their life." He frowned. "Though... he didn't have that white in his hair when I met him two years ago."

Amanita swallowed hard, trying to *not-remember* the stories she'd heard about just what sorts of magick it took to make Evil Wizards more or less immortal. Rather less than more, thank the Goddess, since a hero would inevitably arise to do something about them... eventually. Not that that did a great deal for all the innocent people they victimized on their path to attempted immortality.

Actually, the runaway princess had been trying to *not-think* about exactly what that entailed ever since she'd realized that they really *were* dealing with an honest-to-badness Evil Wizard, and had assumed the others were doing the same.

Except maybe Thony. He wouldn't know the same stories and she hadn't been in Aldyrwald long enough to really guess what he might know or might not know. His sisters were Goddesses, and there seemed to be a lot of magick in the region – though a great deal of it seemed to be spent rather frivolously on exotic Quests to match up princesses and princes.

A cultural thing, she supposed. Culture-stuff often didn't make a great deal of sense.

"So... you think he's not as evil as other Evil Wizards?" Amanita asked.

Istevan sighed. "I... could almost wish. For Julanna's sake, if nothing else..." He gave Amanita a sharp look.

She waved it off. "Davril explained your Grand Plan."

"*Julanna's* plan, anyways," the man muttered with a certain frustration. "And it's not working as well as she'd... hoped."

"Wishful thinking rarely does," Amanita tried not to sound too severe – or like one of her grandmothers. Because – just, *no*. "But you're finding out useful things... even if we don't really know how to *use* them yet."

He gave her a wry nod. "Let's *hope* they're useful. But to answer your other question... I don't think he's done more than dabble until recently. He's more of a... theoretician when it comes to magick. A researcher. His main focus was apparently in building up this massive military force that he has spread out all over the southern central plains–"

"We know about that," Amanita cut him off. "We got a copy of the deployment map. There's like twelve thousand people altogether."

Istevan's eyebrows went up. "Impressive. I hadn't managed to get hold of those numbers yet. Not that our backers don't have most of that independently..."

"About those backers," Amanita began, but he was already shaking his head.

"They can't intervene – yet – for one reason or another. They wouldn't give us details, or even a way to contact them. And we have only the haziest idea of who they might be." He winced. "Actually, they said that if *I* wasn't involved, they wouldn't be able to do even this much, and they tried to talk me out of coming here. But they wouldn't tell me *why.*"

Weird... irrelevant, but weird.

"That must be frustrating," Amanita commiserated. "So, you say the sorcerer-dude is more of a military leader than a magician?"

Istevan shook his head. "No. But he's able to generate a ... great deal of loyalty. Even without spells. And when he uses his spells – it's a devastating combination. Shalladra is the military mind, but as you said, she's a Dark-elf. People would rather flee her than follow her. It's a visceral thing." He shuddered.

One might imagine so. Pointy teeth, after all, generally suggested a rather... *assertive* approach.

"But they're at odds *now,* aren't they?" Amanita asked. "Because of Julanna and you. So, you *are* doing something good."

"It's... less of an issue than you might think," the man told her. "They've been working together for so long, and they're apparently quite close to their goals. This – Val's interest in Julanna – may just be a hiccup." He frowned. "I'm still not sure *what* their goals are. They don't really need to *talk* about them anymore, so again, it's all reading between the lines..."

He sighed. "The Fairy Wood is involved. They are definitely planning to use the enchanted army that Val is bringing up from Darjil, and taking it into the Fairy Wood. Exactly what they plan to do *then,* I don't know. I've heard some things that make no sense..." He shook his head again. "They can't *really* be planning to assault the Fairy Queen's Court."

Amanita went very still. "Actually... maybe they could." She looked up into his eyes. "I spent some time in the Fairy Queen's Court. Enough to pick up a few old stories. It's... totally possible."

Istevan frowned at her. "When would *you* have had a chance to 'spend time' in the Fairy Queen's Court, Dae Goldeneyes?"

As Amanita tried to figure out how to weasel her way out of that one, he looked up sharply. He was looking out of the side-street he'd pulled her into, back at the marketplace.

"Damn. They've noticed I'm missing. I really just wanted to let you know that you've been ruled a local problem, so it's Fayorn and not Shalladra dealing with 'rat-control.' That and..."

His eyes were on the market, but he looked unhappy. "I need you to tell Davril to come in. Val still seems to think *I'm* in love with Julanna. And vice-versa. He's not willing to get rid of me – he's still decent enough somewhere inside to realize that wouldn't do much for him – but her plan can't go any farther unless she can prove otherwise."

His expression was very... taut. Clearly, he didn't like this idea.

Neither did Amanita.

"You want him to take poor little Daphne into the sorcerer's lair?"

Istevan glanced at her and shook his head, before returning his gaze to the market. "No. We want to keep Daphne out from under Val's eye entirely, if possible. And Julanna has managed to avoid letting Val realize she's had a child."

Amanita narrowed her eyes at him. "So, what is Davril supposed to – *oh, no.*" Her eyes went wide. "No. You are *not* sticking us with looking after a baby."

He gave her an anguished look. "If I had any other choice, no. I want Davril in danger about as much as I'd like to cut off my right arm. Or to leave our child in the hands of strangers. But if we don't get Dav in here it's all for naught and I still have to somehow get Julanna out – but with Val chasing after us. And..."

"And 'all for naught' means that the sorcerer's plans have that much less hindrance." Amanita pinched the bridge of her nose with her hand. Grandmother Queen Namarina did that a lot and it had never made sense before. But now it sort of felt like she was squeezing her brain back into place while the whole world spiraled out of control and she was going to left holding the...

...holding the *baby.*

Damn.

She'd done that, once or twice, with her younger cousins – Papa's sisters were as nice as their mother was awful – but she'd always been happy to give them *back.*

"All right," she said reluctantly.

Istevan gave her a look that was both grateful and regretful. "Thank you. At least..." his lips tipped up wryly, "at least we can keep from bringing 'poor little Daphne into the sorcerer's lair.'"

Her own words thrown back at her.

No chance to reply, though, because he was striding back out and greeting his patrol with some sort of prevarication.

What a morning. Two of their allies taken by the enemy and in addition to that bad news they were going to have to take care of the baby in order to send the last adult in their group into danger.

Ugh.

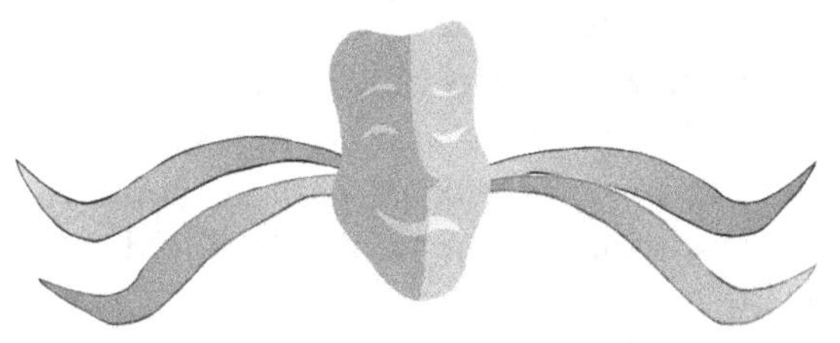

Chapter SIXTEEN

An Explosive Situation

WHERE THE HELL IS PUCK? Thony wondered as he watched Dae nonchalantly pack more of their homemade *(and entirely unmagickal)* explosive mixture into a package that looked a great deal like a sock.

Actually, it *was* a sock.

The pair of them were ensconced in a long forgotten sub-cellar, the entrance to which was hidden behind the pickle cellar where Julanna Silversea had once been confined. They had discovered the tiny space through another one of Dae's accidents, but it was a perfect place to hide out during the day so that they didn't have to travel back and forth between the copse and the town every night. Even lines of ants coming and going eventually got enough attention to get squished, after all. Better not to have such regular habits.

And if it meant they smelled a bit... *pickly* at times, well, it was nothing that a good airing out didn't cure, right?

And at least it was cool down here. Spring was starting to segue into Summer, and it was getting entirely too hot in the daytime for mountain-bred Thony's sensibilities.

Too hot for the also-mountain-bred Amanita, judging by her grouchy complaints. Which was another reason to avoid the copse as much as possible. Jost was making sure she had supplies and occasionally getting a baby-break so that they could run the 'double-trouble' scheme and make people think 'Dae Goldeneyes' was in two places at once.

Unfortunately for Amanita, everyone – meaning Thony, Dae, and Jost – agreed that the Lost Princess of Pathremir and the Sorcerer-King's Secret Baby should be kept as far away from danger as possible.

Even more unfortunately for her, they had been making this situation work out for some *ten days*. Amanita looked about ready to run away again, and Thony couldn't blame her. He'd done some baby-duty himself, and while Daphne was a cute kid, she clearly missed her family, so she cried. A lot.

And then there were the diapers.

They made Thony glad that once he had his own kid, he'd have a wife and servants to take care of things like that.

He wondered if Mama had ever changed a diaper when he or Priscilla or Joanna were babies. She tended to faint rather a lot at relatively normal things like frogs, so he supposed the smell of a full diaper would have taken her out before it ever became an issue.

He was sure *Papa* had never even gotten *close* to a full diaper.

Well, at least there was *one* good thing about eventually being King of Aldyrwald.

Though... Thony had to admit that when Daphne was happy, she was a lot of fun. And when she fell asleep in his arms, with that trusting expression... he felt like he was ten feet tall.

Of course, then he'd remember that the reason she was falling asleep in *his* arms was because her mother and her fathers were trying to convince an evil sorcerer to stop a war because her mother was in love with him.

Which... was not going terribly well.

It wasn't going terribly *poorly,* either, but that was mostly because there was so little that they were actually able to do.

Thony and Dae *(and occasionally Amanita)* were continuing their campaign of pranks inside the Raven-HQ. Jost's street-kids – and, by now, he'd recruited most of the other gangs to help – were doing the same to the patrols out in the city. And they were rigging real booby-traps that could be sprung when the enchanted army finally showed up.

The troops were buying good-luck charms and warding bracelets like crazy, and you could hardly walk through the barracks-levels of the mansion at night without tripping over bowls of milk left out for brownies or dealing with other spirit-pacification and/or -traps that they were trying. It wasn't helping their morale when different patrols both came in simultaneously reporting Dae Goldeneyes sightings.

Istevan and Davril seemed to have more or less convinced Raven'sWing that they were married – and given how entirely ooey-gooey they were together, Thony could see how. Istevan was still working as a lieutenant, and Davril was free to move about the city, though it was clear that they didn't dare try to *leave*.

This situation seemed to please the young banker, so long as he got regular updates on his daughter. He and Jost were working on something, though they weren't sharing details with anyone else.

Davril was the only person who seemed fairly happy about their progress.

It turned out that Kamauri and Daennor had gotten themselves caught and impressed into the Raven-troops *on purpose*. Which *Dae* had known, but no one else had. They were pretending to be a couple of country-people so that they could blend in with the lower levels of Raven'sWing's army.

Istevan had approved, once he'd been told... though he warned Thony *not* to give him such details in the future, given how close he was to Raven'sWing and Shalladra. And he thought it was a little foolish of Kamauri and Daennor to be using their real names, even though neither one was a particularly *uncommon* name in this area and they *weren't* using their mercenary surnames.

Trying not to let Istevan in on all the other details – despite his preferences – had actually proven quite pointless. The first few days had worked all right, but as days stretched into a week and then beyond, nearly to a fortnight, things slipped out. And Istevan was a pretty clever guy and sort of *exuded* that sincerity that made all the kids trust him. He knew who Amanita was, for instance, before the first week was out.

The unicorns were keeping an eye on the other equines and Amanita and the baby, as well as taking turns scouting for the approach of the hostile forces. The enchanted army coming up from Darjil should 'only' be about seven thousand, assuming the number on the map was correct, but Raven'sWing's other forces – some five thousand *more* – might be converging on Flowerdust as well.

Twinklestar and Rainsparkle could each communicate mentally with their bonded unicorn-maidens, so Kamauri and Thony could pass things to each other without being seen to be in contact.

Puck, however, had not yet returned. And it was long past when he had said he'd be back.

The tiny cold-room behind the pickle-cellar had precisely enough space for Thony to pace two steps in one direction before he had to turn and go the other way. It wasn't terribly satisfying.

"Sit down," Dae ordered peremptorily. "You're making me nervous."

Well, she *was* working with the explosive.

He sat.

"What are you working on?" he asked. It was getting harder and harder to come up with *new* pranks. They were re-visiting some of the ones that had been most effective more and more often... but this looked new.

Dae was seated at the makeshift workshop they'd assembled to create the props for their more involved pranks. Lanterns were set in the corners of the room and as far away from the supplies as they could be while still providing adequate lighting.

"Oh, just a little something for Private Hent," she smirked.

"Isn't he the guy who has all the singed toes on his socks?" Thony asked.

Dae nodded. "Yup! I found out why, the last time we were scouting. We knew he smokes in his room – against regulation – based on the smell. Apparently, his sergeant – and his roommates – will ignore it if the sergeant doesn't actually *see* him doing it, though. And she has to make bed-checks. *Irregularly.* I overheard her complaining about that, but apparently Sergeant Sterevor has been getting on everyone else's case ever since he got here.

"So that means Hent has to hide his smoking gear on pretty short notice sometimes, and the way his room is set up, his underwear drawer is in easy reach."

Thony was impressed. Personalized pranks took a great deal of extra effort, since you had to learn a person's habits well enough to know what would drive them bat-crazy. (*Not that Thony had yet figured out who would freak out with bats... nor had he figured out where to obtain bats.)*

Most recently he'd been reduced to messing with the minds of the more obsessively systematic people by moving their stuff around – randomly, but to other perfectly logical places so that they thought they going a bit nuts – and doing other minor things, like shortening everyone's laces an inch every night. Granted that last thing had started to really make a difference about three days ago...

But this scheme was rather more involved than he'd come to expect of Dae, who seemed to have a sort of helter-skelter bull-it-through approach to strategy and whose logic was often upended by those inevitable and innumerable accidents. He was half-convinced she was thoroughly scatterbrained and survived on luck alone.

Whomever had let her into the Mercenaries' Guild should either be cursed... or blessed for helping Dae end up in a position where her rather... *extraordinary existence* had actual potential to be useful.

He was also convinced that once this affair was over, he wanted to stay as far away from her as possible. For the sake of his personal safety.

"Anyways," Dae was continuing her explanation, "this time when the private tosses in his pipe with his, ah, *unmentionables* like always, he'll be in for a *bit* of a surprise."

She grinned and judiciously packed in another scoop of the explosive mix. "Best of all, once this stuff goes, Evrien says there shouldn't be hardly anything left to connect it with the supplies Jost stole for us last week."

The aging mercenary had turned out to be an expert in mining fortifications and had a wealth of knowledge that was turning out useful to the young rapscallions. Her use-name – Quickfoot – was apparently a reference to a rather hairy situation that had arisen when she was studying her specialty as a young woman.

Evrien also knew every detail of military operations. And she adored the idea of using her lifetime's worth of wisdom to defeat the sorcerer. Some of Jost's crew had taken to hanging out at the Guildhouse to help her mix things up and draw up plans for the booby-traps around the city. She was very helpful at pointing out where something else might be more effective, and managed to shoot down a *(likely **highly** effective)* plan to explode the city sewer system once the enchanted army was here on the grounds that they were still hoping to *free* the enchanted army from the spell... not to mention how many of the local population might be killed.

Thony had a feeling that at least some of Jost's crew – or the other, ah, *disenchanted* street-kids he'd recruited – had gone ahead with the sewer plan anyways, as a last resort. Since that was the sort of thing that could easily get out of control if *anyone* panicked, he sort of hoped he was wrong.

To his utter humiliation, Thony had needed to have the concept of a sewer system explained to him. Which Dae and Jost had done. In graphic detail.

"Hmmn," he said in response to Dae now.

Untraceability had also become important to them, given that they were trying to impersonate angry pixies and kobolds.

And, erm, not *actually* anger the local spirits. Twinklestar and Rainsparkle had assured him there wasn't an issue – that the locals had all evacuated because of Raven'sWing's aura.

Apparently, all Evil Wizards more or less *reeked* magickally, based on the nasty stuff they did. Death-magick and demon-summoning and stuff were apparently enough to drive off most magickal beings. But Raven'sWing's was... nasty in a different way, the unicorns reported, though they seemed unable to explain *why*.

Actually, they seemed a bit baffled by the reports of the brownies and such. They said he didn't smell nearly so bad to *them*. Though, granted, they hadn't gotten terribly *close* to him.

They were more concerned about Shalladra. Though it seemed pretty much *every* thinking creature – and a great many of the ones that reacted on instinct alone – were wary of Dark-elves. And Light-elves, too, Amanita had explained at one point when they were trading off baby-duty in the copse. There were other kinds of elves, but these two groups – who hated each other – were the Fairy Queen's armies.

All of that sort of backed up what Istevan had told Amanita about Raven'sWing not having done the usual nasty Evil Wizard stuff. Or not until recently anyways. Presumably enchanting an entire town into zombie soldiers counted big wherever that sort of thing was accounted for.

But it left a great deal unanswered.

"That's an awful lot of the explosive," Thony commented. "We haven't really been able to test this latest batch. Are you sure it's *all* going to vanish?"

Dae gave him a dark look and pointedly added another small scoop before tying off the sock.

They were both spared an incipient bickering session by a stirring at their concealed exit.

Their *only* exit.

Tensely, they both stood, weapons to hand, until Istevan squeezed himself though the opening and they could sigh with relief.

"That's a *very* small opening," the tall mercenary-spy commented, checking himself over as if worried that he'd left bits behind.

Dae bristled immediately.

"It is *not*," she corrected. "*You're* just oversized."

Thony rolled his eyes as Istevan held up his hands in a gesture of surrender. "Whoa there, Goldeneyes. No offense meant. This is a perfect spot. I had trouble finding it, and *I* knew it was here. You did well in finding it."

"Well, then." Dae settled down immediately at the compliment, and Thony looked at her wryly.

Istevan had a way with kids. All three of them – and Jost, Skylir, any of the other street-kids he'd been introduced to – all felt comfortable with the tall man. Part of it was that he took them seriously, never dismissing their observations or suggestions or concerns. Part of it... who knew. They liked him.

Even Dae. Even after Amanita had finally relayed Istevan's comments about thinking Taridanae Foxheart shouldn't have graduated her from Sonoro's School of Soldiering.

And she'd only looked sheepish when she'd admitted to him – as she had to the rest of them that night in the copse – how she'd kind of forced the Headmistress' hand.

Though he'd told her that Sonoro himself wouldn't have let her get away with such a thing – he'd apparently known the Old Man *(as Istevan had called him with a sad look in his eyes)* rather well.

"I can't stay," Istevan told them now. "And you'll need to leave, too. The Word has come."

"The unicorns have spotted the army?" Thony tried to tell himself this was a *good* thing. That they'd played out the pranks as far as they could really go and were at their peak of readiness for the Grand Finale.

It didn't help the sinking feeling in his stomach.

Istevan nodded. "Kamauri slipped me word at morning review." He rolled his eyes. "Val was going on at breakfast about how this is taking too long and costing more than he planned for. Shalladra told him to take some more loans."

Thony tried to smile. "Over cost and past schedule. This guy's setting up a government all right. Sounds just like home."

Dae snorted, but Istevan chuckled.

"I've got to go," he said. "Shalladra called for a noon assembly, so I'm guessing that she and Val have also figured out the army is approaching, though I don't know how. Likely this will be about organizing their arrival."

He looked at each of them for a moment. "You kids have done great at raising dissatisfaction among the rank-and-file. The insurrection that Kamauri and Daennor are planning should go off without a hitch, though I'm not sure when they'll actually get it started. The enchanted troops shouldn't arrive until early afternoon tomorrow..."

His lips compressed. "Along with the troops who are, ah, *guiding* them along."

The saboteurs had been having a rather long-running and disconnected argument about the *un*-enchanted troops. Word had been coming back about what was being done to move the zombified townsfolk along – and it was pretty dark.

The zombies couldn't be killed, it seemed. Nor did they need food nor rest.

But they had no volition. They could be started moving in a direction and would continue for awhile, but eventually run down like a wind-up clock and need to be re-started. And while the enchanted army appeared to be *mostly* adults between the ages of fifteen and fifty, there was a significant fraction that were... not able to easily keep up.

The *un*-enchanted troops were using whips and clubs to 'motivate' the zombies and keep them on track.

Istevan was of the opinion that anyone who had participated in this atrocity was just as guilty as Raven'sWing and Shalladra and deserved the same fate that would hopefully be theirs. He was the one who seemed to be acquiring the details – Shalladra had kept him on as her aide – and from the tight expression on his face when he spoke about this, it was clear that even worse things were going on than he was telling the kids.

Dae gave him an anxious look. "Our Guild-brothers and -sisters who've been spelled to do this..."

The tall man's face softened slightly. "If we can *determine* that they've been enspelled, young sister... But that may not be so easy if the *compulsion* spells all fade when Val is... dealt with. As we all hope they will be. Though any man or woman in that army with half a brain will *claim* they were enspelled and avoid the consequences of their actions."

Yes, they had to hope that the Evil Wizard's spells would fade with his demise.

(Though Thony still had to think around that likely part of the solution. Despite it being nearly two weeks since his personal encounter with the man, and all of the terrible things he'd learned since then, the young prince still couldn't help some lingering fond feelings for Raven's Wing. When they spied on the man in the course of their pranking, he still seemed... awfully nice to the people he knew.

*It was always a shock to hear Raven's Wing casually throw out a comment regarding the masses of people he **didn't** have a personal connection with that was so far beyond callous and heartless that it made the pranksters actually sick to their stomachs. The orders he was sending out to his troops on how to treat the enchanted army. He seemed somewhat more solicitous of the people inhabiting the surrounding countryside, it was more in the nature of how a shepherd viewed his sheep than a person viewed his peers... and after all, shepherds were known to eat a great deal of mutton.*

Thony knew he'd be having nightmares for months, if not years, just recalling some of those statements.)

But if Raven's Wing's spells *didn't* just up and vanish on their own... The other option was that they would have *several thousand people* needing to have their *compulsion* spells individually broken. Which apparently the unicorns *could* do, but it would take... a very long time.

After all, it wasn't just the townspeople of Darjil who'd been enspelled, as Dae had just pointed out.

Nor was it clear that what was affecting the people of Darjil was a *compulsion* spell such as the mercenaries – and Amanita and Davril – were familiar with. Normal *compulsion* spells didn't make people invulnerable to harm or personal needs. The mercenaries were speculating that the descriptions were exaggerated and the people were merely *oblivious,* not *unaffected...*

...which made their treatment by their... *herders* all that more atrocious.

Dae looked miserable, but nodded. There wasn't really anything else they could do.

Istevan had been about to press himself back out the door. Instead, he stopped and turned around. In the tiny space, he could reach his long arms out and pull both younger people into a warm embrace.

"Life... doesn't always work out," he said quietly. "Sometimes terrible things happen and all you can do is your best to make them *less* terrible. We've done everything within our power to prepare and to salvage whom and what we can – once we win."

And he didn't need to remind them that *that* was a far from inevitable end.

"You should be proud that you didn't just stand in the sidelines and watch as the catastrophe took place," he went on. "I wish I could ask you to get out of here..."

Dae closed her eyes and leaned her head into Istevan's shoulder. "I *can't.* Everybody I care about in the whole *world* is *here.* You guys and... and Kamauri and Daennor..."

Maybe Thony *wouldn't* try to get as far away from her after this as he could. Dangerously accident-prone though she was.

"And... *I* can't," Thony added, also feeling unreasonably reassured by the hug. "You guys and... everyone at home."

Istevan – all of them – had taken to the idea that Thony was from another world rather more *easily* than he would have expected, personally.

Istevan nodded heavily. "I know. And... Kamauri said that the unicorns will get Amanita and the baby out before that copse gets swarmed – given that it's right in the path to the Fairy Wood. And... she *should* be able to rally help..."

They all knew that was pretty iffy.

Who, after all, could help against a force that had been designed to assault the Great Goddess Who Was the Guardian of the Ways Between the Worlds?

"I've got to go," Istevan said again. "Tomorrow is when it's all going to happen. Good luck."

And then he spent the next couple of minutes getting out of their exit.

Dae and Thony looked at each other once he was gone.

"One more night of pranks," Dae said, trying for her usual chipper, nonchalant tone. She reached over and hefted the explosives-filled sock, then seemed to think better of it and set it carefully down.

"Yep." Thony agreed, and started pawing through their supplies for ideas.

They worked side-by-side in silence, neither really having anything left to say.

But Thony's mind was wandering... Rainsparkle had told Kamauri, who had told Istevan who had told them. Why hadn't *Twinklestar* told him directly? Even if it had been Rainsparkle who had spotted the enemy approach on a scouting run, the unicorns communicated with each other even better than with their bonded unicorn-maidens. Or so Thony had *thought*.

He tried *reaching* for Twinklestar with his mind, the way he'd been doing. They hadn't had any contact since early this morning, when Thony had come in from a hard night of pranking to grab a couple hours of shut-eye.

That weird sour-unicorn-sweat smell was there when Thony extended his senses, as it always was. It seemed incredibly pervasive when he was in the mansion – not directional at all. And it was thick enough that the young prince was only willing to do this for very brief periods. It was usually worth it to wait until he was out in the open air.

None of it made a difference now, though, no matter how Thony ignored the reek to try to focus on making contact.

There was a sense that his unicorn-friend was *somewhere*... A vague feeling of reassurance *did* come back to Thony. But it was as if he was too far away to really be felt.

Weird... Maybe this being underground was interfering – or that funky smell – though it hadn't before...

"I'll go out tonight and make sure Jost and Evrien know what's going on," Thony told Dae. "Since you and Private Hent have a date."

She made a face at him. "I have to get the sock in there this afternoon. Maybe we should both go. Stretch out a bit, get some fresh air. Maybe even sleep at the Guildhouse or Jost's place to be ready for tomorrow."

"Instead of pranking tonight?" Thony looked at the half-baked props he'd been assembling. He really was out of ideas.

Dae was looking as wrung out as he was. "Yeah. We'll need to be awake in the daytime tomorrow anyways, right?"

Thony nodded. "All right. Let's go deliver your 'package' and get out of here."

Chapter SEVENTEEN

When the Zombies Come Marching In

THE NEXT MORNING STARTED OUT with a literal bang, since Private Hent had apparently skipped his evening smoke for a morning one.

Thony, Dae, and Jost had decided to keep watch from a nearby rooftop starting at dawn. Evrien and the street-kids would be positioned by traps and trip-lines all over the city by noon, since the best estimate they'd been able to get from Rainsparkle was that the enchanted troops would be arriving an hour or so after that.

The rest of their team was inside the Raven-HQ, of course.

Except for Amanita, who was presumably seething in the copse as she packed their camp up. She and the baby were supposed to be a-horse before the enchanted army arrived– on Silverfoot, most likely, since he had a saddle and reins, but Dae's horse and Daennor's horse were there as well. And the pack-donkey.

She'd doubtless have an earful for them later about how she'd missed out on everything.

At least, Thony hoped so.

Thony still hadn't heard from Twinklestar, and Puck was still MIA.

The first sign of excitement – besides the flames shooting out of one of the top-story windows and broken glass raining down on the mansion's courtyard – was Davril backing out of the main entrance with Raven-troops who were *not* Istevan, Daennor or Kamauri escorting him as he continued to answer someone who didn't follow him out.

The kids were just close enough to hear the young banker calling back apologetically to someone inside. It appeared to be something about how he'd *try,* but without *collateral* that he could vouch for, his hands were probably tied. He looked serious and worried as the Raven-troops to his sides grabbed his arms and marched him out of the mansion's courtyard.

But Jost was snickering. "Well, that'un worked better'n I thought 'twould."

Thony and Dae looked at him curiously.

"Think I might try m'hand at bankin' after this," the street-kid-chieftain told them. "'At there Davril's a dab hand at teachin' me a passel o' things. Got them bankers on Goldsmith Street lookin' *at* me, not *past* me wit' 'is letter in m'hand. And then they was all bowin' an' scrapin' t'get me a drink an' a seat an' did messir want anythin' else? Fine life, bankin'."

"Doubtless," Dae said crossly. "But what did you *do* that worked so well?"

Jost grinned. "'Tweren't me. 'Twere all Davril, an' I was jes' 'is 'ands an' feet. Well, t'get it started. "'E's let me be a mouse on 'is shoulder since that there sorc'rer started givin' 'im th' run o' th' town."

"*Jost...*" Thony said threateningly, and the other boy laughed again.

"Ah, jes' wave those pretty eyes at me 'gain, an' I'll tell ye anythin' ye want t'know, laddy."

"*Jost..!?*" Thony buried his face in his arms.

They were all lying flat and peeking at the mansion over the peak of the roof to avoid being noticed as silhouettes against the brightening sky. People rarely look *up,* Thony knew, but you could never be sure.

"'Twas a fair lot of bankin' stuff," Jost finally explained. "Word sent *here* and word sent *there*. I didn' get the whole story on all o' it, but th' long and the short is that apparently the sorc'rer's armies are like th' rest that come through here in one big way. They're paid for on loans."

Thony lifted his head to frown. "You don't need to pay enchanted – or enspelled – troops, I wouldn't think."

"Nah," Jost agreed, "but there's all th' rest o' them, righ'? And 'tis more'n pay fer th' troops. The rest need *food* bought an' cooked, an' *weapons* made or mended. Laundry done, 'orses tended and shod. Barbers an' herbalists – not a great many 'Ealers as'll work fer an Evil Wizard – an' oh, all manner o' jobs an' supplies. An army is a great deal like a small, movin' city, says Davril. An' milor' sor'crer don't bother to enchant th' support staff."

"So, they can't buy stuff and pay people," Dae mused. "Even if they're 'requisitioning' their supplies by stealing them from the population, all their support staff would have to be compelled – which takes more manpower, and once the troops know that it's because there isn't pay to *go around...*"

She grinned, fiercely and maliciously.

"Oh, 'tis worse'n 'at," Jost was actually rubbing his hands together with glee. "A good 'alf their bigger ticket items – 'orses an' tack an' tents an' whatnot – that was all bought on loan. They've been *repossessed.*"

He said the unfamiliar word carefully, then proceeded to define it for the other two.

Dae nodded, but it was a new idea to Thony.

"So, it sounds like milor' sorc'rer 'as jes' found out," Jost was snickerin' again. "'E's clever enough t'send our lad Davril out t'try t'fix the situation – bein' as 'ow 'e's such an *expert* at bankin' an' all. Don't know as t'sorc'rer's clever enough t'figure out 'twas our lad Davril set it all in motion, though."

"How could he not?" Dae frowned.

Jost shrugged. "Davril said t' 'ole thing was an 'ouse o' cards anyways. Loans built on loans in some way I don't quite get. Not yet," he corrected himself with an eager light in his eyes. "There was summat abou' how 'Is Sorc'rousness didna 'ire th' brightest lads on the block as accountants. Or p'rhaps 'twas that they were a little *too* bright, an ye take my meanin'."

He winked at Dae.

"Getting it to come out today was incredible timing," Thony commented, his eyes back on the mansion where Raven-soldiers were setting up for their morning review.

He reflected that whomever had the moxy to repossess essential items from an army – let alone an *evil sorcerer's army* – was... someone to be either feared or admired. Or both.

Jost waved that one off, though. "Ah, that was jes' plain ol' dumb luck. Davril's been waitin' for word these last three days or so. T' problem bein'," he confided, "'At there's no messengers 'tall goin' north. Ever'thin' had t'be sent south, farther inta milor's territory and then out from there, bein' that th' Keetering bank's up on th' North Coast. But *Davril* says there's a big bank down south in Vel-Gash as'd 'andle things for 'im, most like."

The street-kid sighed like he'd just finished a satisfying meal. "Must be nice t' 'ave th' 'ole world 'op on yer say so."

Sewers and repossession, the young prince mused. City-people's lives were certainly... different.

They settled down to watch some more.

The fun didn't take terribly long to start.

Valderon Raven'sWing came out at Shalladra Stillheart's side as he did every day, but there was something about his stride that made his frustration and distraction clear. He followed Captain Fayorn along the line of at-attention soldiers, nodding and likely saying things the kids on the rooftop couldn't hear.

The troops looked rather more ragged than they had a week ago.

More than one fellow's pants were looking precarious, among other things.

The bright early sunshine didn't reflect off an array of polished buttons – Dae had gotten into the polish a few days ago and what the soldiers possessed now made their silver and brass turn black instead of shining them up. One could shine up the metal bits using elbow grease alone, but it was... a great deal more work and after a few days of forcing the soldiers to do that, even the officers seemed to have given up.

A closer examination would have shown uniforms raveling at every hem and seams gaping as weakened threads gave way unexpectedly – which was more of the mercenette's nocturnal efforts proving out.

And a number of them belched (and farted) rather continuously – fairly noxious fumes, to judge by the greenish complexions of the fellows unlucky enough to be standing near them... the kitchens had remained Thony's mainstay and his addition of beans and broccoli to pretty much every food prepared was having the predictable effects.

The yawns that had marred that first review – because people had been yanked out of bed unexpectedly – had been as discreet as possible and the soldiers yawning had looked embarrassed. There had been a sense that the troops wished to present themselves as professionals, and it was only the early arrival of their superior that had them presenting in such disarray.

This time the yawns were egregious and luxurious and two hairs off of insubordinate.

That wave of almost fanatical seeming loyalty that Thony had noted that first day when Raven'sWing had arrived didn't seem to be subsuming the troops this time as the sorcerer passed them by.

Rather the other way, if anything. They slumped visibly once his eye – and Shalladra's – was no longer on them, and looked resentful.

Clearly Kamauri, Daennor, and Istevan had added the necessary finishing touches to the misery that Dae and Thony had made of the troops' lives.

Julanna Silversea leaned against the doorframe of the main entrance to the mansion, not stepping out, her eye following Raven'sWing. The three adult mercenaries on the sabotage team were probably mixed in somewhere with the blue-tunicked masses.

Davril returned in the middle of the review, artistically wringing his hands.

Raven'sWing dropped the pretense of paying attention to his troops and hustled the young banker inside. Julanna vanished after them.

Captain Shalladra followed more slowly, not looking pleased. She took her time, stopping to run a hand over the chest of a soldier who *might* have poufy hair, though he was behind a taller man from Thony's perspective and he couldn't tell if it was Daennor.

She turned away to look back over her shoulder and make some sort of a gesture before she went up into the mansion. The tall, black-haired soldier who broke ranks to follow her was almost certainly Istevan.

Captain Fayorn finished the review alone, then dismissed the troops and everyone slouched off.

Even up on the rooftops, the kids could hear the disgruntled mutter of the soldiers.

The sun began to get quite hot, and first Thony, and finally the other two, moved into the shade of a chimney pot. They shared some food and had sips from the water-bottles they'd brought along to their vigil.

"Looks like things might be done for now," Dae commented. "At least what we can *see.*"

"No, wait." Thony had caught movement in the mansion's courtyard. "Something *else* is happening. And isn't that–"

"That's *Daennor,*" Dae whispered, her tone worried. The man's pale, poufy hair was unmistakable now that he was clearly visible, even though he was dressed in the same blue tunic as everyone else.

Daennor was being hustled along by another couple of Raven-troops. He was clearly unhappy and trying to shake them off.

Another figure in blue, this one with a long, dark-brown braid came dashing into view, and Daennor's... guards?... held her off.

"*Kamauri...*" Dae whispered, eyes gone wide and white-ringed. "*No...* Did the sorcerer and Stillheart figure out what they were doing? Who they *are?*"

Thony quickly put an arm around her. To reassure Dae... but also to keep the headstrong mercenette from trying to go down there, either on-purpose or – knowing Dae's proclivities – accidentally. "Jost, do *you* have any idea what's going on?"

The street-kid-chieftain shook his head, his eyes nearly as worried as Dae's.

Daennor had quit fighting his captors when Kamauri appeared, but the two of them were being kept apart. He seemed to be trying to calm her down with words, but it didn't appear to be doing a great deal of good... though finally she slumped, clearly in tears. The guards hustled them both inside.

"It can't be that anyone figured out what they were doing to stir up the lower ranks," Thony tried to sound reassuring. "If that were the case, surely they'd both have been summoned. Even if they only thought *Daennor* was doing stuff, he and Kamauri were obviously a pair. And it was obvious they only took her in just now because she was causing such a fuss."

Dae glared up at him. *"Not helping."*

"Sorry..." Thony whispered, and she nodded her thanks for the attempt.

"Keep yer pants on," Jost said absently. "D'ye see that cloud o' dust from t' south? That's our expected guests arrivin', I'll bet." He looked at the other two. "Think I'll jes' head down an' make sure things're on track, aye? Keep an eye on that place for me, will ye?"

Thony gave their friend a nod and a worried smile. The plan had been for all three of them to check in with all the different groups of street-kids *(and Evrien Quickfoot)* but it was obvious Dae needed to stay here now... and someone would need to be with her. It even made sense for it to be Jost to go down, rather than Thony – he knew the city better and the street-kids knew *him* better.

And it wasn't like they didn't all know the plan.

Dae was whispering under her breath and as tense as a bowstring. She pressed her hands to her stomach as if it hurt.

"Now, I understand why Kamauri didn't want me doing dangerous stuff," she said just loudly enough for Thony to hear her. "Oh, I promise, I promise, I *promise* I'll be more careful. Just please, please, *please* let them be okay."

It seemed to be a prayer, though she wasn't calling on any particular deity... which seemed an odd omission in a world as rife with divinity as this one seemed to be.

"Dae," he said softly, "Are you okay?"

She shook her head almost violently, brushing tears away with an angry hand. "NO, of course not. How could I be? They've spent the last two years trying to take care of me and I just... I never... Daennor said... And finally, we could..."

She threw herself on Thony's startled shoulder in a thoroughly uncharacteristic burst of tears.

"I'm sorry," Dae said after a moment, sitting back up and dashing the tears away again. "That was... I think I'm done. I'm good. Or... good enough to cope." She took a deep breath. "It's just... Daennor said we could be a *family.* He even said maybe we were *meant* to be family, the way our names are so similar, his and mine. And... and I always thought he was only saying that stuff because of Kamauri. But... I don't know. That night in the copse. It sounded like he wanted me for *me.* Like he was my... my *big brother* or something. More than just my *Guild*-brother, I mean."

"Or like a *dad*," Thony said softly, and Dae nodded, tearing up again.

"I don't think I could handle it if... if..." She shook her head hard again. "Thanks, Thony. I needed that hug."

"Your turn may come," he told her seriously. "If we don't stop them from getting to the Fairy Wood..."

The young prince's eyes were drawn to the smudge of dark green just in sight past the roofs of the city and the intervening grassy hills.

"...I might need a hug myself," he finished. Dae squeezed his hand.

They settled back in to wait as the sun climbed higher and their shady spot got smaller.

Jost came back at last with more food and water and the news that there had been some small problems with one of the explosives, but Evrien had been summoned and it was being fixed. The trip-lines were being prepared and the other booby-traps were ready to go.

"And the kids know not to stick around and watch, right?" Thony said for the umpteenth time. If Skylir or Clarick – who'd joined their efforts, despite not properly being a street-kid – or anyone should get hurt when it was avoidable...

Jost shrugged. "'Tis outta our 'ands now. Gotta believe they 'ave th' sense th' Gods gave li'l green apples."

Which was not at all reassuring.

Even if Thony's worries were basically the same ones that Kamauri and Davril had tried to use to get him and Dae and Amanita to leave Flowerdust entirely.

Damn. Dae was right. He *did* understand now.

The dust-cloud was filling up the entire southern horizon. And there were crashing noises coming from that end of town. People in blue tunics started running in and out of the mansion from that direction.

And Skylir popped up on the roof beside them.

"Workin' well, Jost," they said as they flopped down carelessly on the hot shingles. "Focusin' on th' live ones now and turnin' th' herd, like we planned. First trip-wire took down th' spelled folk like dominoes, so th' live ones started searchin' ahead."

"Course, we only had that couple o' trips up front there," Jost agreed.

Skylir shrugged. "Rema thought it'd be a good idea to add a few more later – jes' t'give the live'uns sumpin' t'find. Make 'em feel like they's earnin' their pay, see."

"Nice," Thony commented as Jost started to look dubious at this last-minute ingenuity. "They won't be able to stop looking for trip-lines – just in case. We should have thought of that straight off."

Dae nodded absently. Most of her attention was still on the mansion.

Jost reluctantly agreed. "And ye're turnin' 'em, aye?"

Skylir nodded. "Fellas as are herdin' 'em ain't got the slightest idea of 'ow to get 'round th' streets 'ere. An' all those buildin's 'at 'Is Sorc'rousness 'ad pulled down t'make a straighter path in – an' out – somehow those spelled lads and lassies keep veerin' off onta th' side-streets where there's a split."

The co-option and destruction of those privately owned buildings – homes and businesses that just happened to be unlucky enough to be on the path Raven'sWing had determined his enchanted troops would need to use – had become sore-point for much of the local populace. There had, Thony gathered, been a weird sort of 'gentleman's agreement' with the armies that usually passed through that their young people might be drafted and their livestock eaten or driven off, but the infrastructure would be left alone and the permanent population – children, older folks and disabled veterans of previous wars – would remain unmolested.

Skylir was snickering. "Drivin' their keepers fair wild, 'tis. Cain't keep a straight line in th' streets here nanyways, an' seems they was promised'un."

"Everyone's staying safe?" Thony asked, trying to sound curious instead of anxious, and Skylir waved that consideration off.

"Leave be, laddy. We don' need a nanny-goat nibblin' at us t'blow our noses an' wipe our asses. We knows these streets. An what'll they see nanyways? Buncha street-kids runnin' off like street-kids do. Nothin' t'say we 'ad aught t'do wit' any."

Thony nodded reluctantly as Jost gave him a warning look.

Skylir waited for a moment, their expression challenging, then nodded appreciatively when Thony didn't pursue the matter besides pursing his lips. "Got th' live'uns fair turned around, too. Seein' as 'ow they ain't niver been here a-fore it ain't even *hard*. Th' messengers they keep sendin' back and forth t' th' mayor's mansion are startin' t' catch a clue, but they're rankers an' no'un is listenin' t'*them* 'tall."

"Good work, Sky," Jost told the youngling approvingly. "Off wit' ye now. Give us an update an anything new 'appens."

"Oh, sumpin' new'll *'appen* a'right," Skylir said as they scampered off. "We ain't even tried out Evrien's latest batch o' sparklies yet."

"Cheeky," Jost called after with a fond look. He caught Thony's expression as he turned back. "What?"

"Nothing." Thony smiled back, worried though he was.

Jost had reminded him a great deal of his brother-in-law Roger right then. Who'd more or less been his big brother for a lot longer than he'd officially been married to Joanna, having lived in Aldyrwald since Thony was a baby while he'd earned his knighthood in the Aldyrwald Court.

"You're a good big brother, that's all," he added.

Jost gave him a curious look. "*That's* what catches yer eye?"

Thony shrugged a little self-consciously. "I come from people with a lot of responsibilities. I... guess I appreciate someone who can do it right."

"Hunh." Jost looked very thoughtful as they all settled back to focus on the mansion.

They were sort of anticipating that at least *some* of the enchanted troops would make it to the headquarters. Or some of the 'live'uns' as Skylir had put it, the free-willed troopers who were herding the enchanted ones so cruelly.

Flowerdust wasn't *that* big of a town after all. It wasn't really possible to get *that* lost in it.

And, indeed, some rather exhausted and careworn-looking troopers on horses were beginning to appear at the edges of the marketplace square. Vendors were pulling back as the dusty and odd-looking people on foot arrived... Pulling back and hurriedly packing up.

Thony didn't blame the farmers and crafters. There was something distinctly *wrong* with the straggle of people filtering in. And it was more than that they were stopping and needing to be prodded – with the ends of short horse-whips, the butts of spears, even the ends of unstrung bows, Thony noted disapprovingly.

They didn't seem to stand properly erect. They didn't look to their sides to see the new place they were in or check on their neighbors.... but they didn't slump and stare dispiritedly at the ground like one would expect of people who were thoroughly beaten.

They just... stood there, swaying slightly like tall grass in a light breeze, their heads moving semi-randomly and out of synch with their other movements. They all seemed to be *searching* for something...

...but when one of those strangely weaving, *searching* faces randomly – or so it seemed – tipped upwards, Thony found himself shivering back behind the chimney-pot and hoping the enchanted person hadn't seen him.

It was the *eyes* that were the worst. The face was slack, unaware, but the eyes weren't eyes the way Thony knew such things. They were lambent orbs of a glowing, pale green, the shade of new pine needles or the surge of grass that grows after a mowing and good rain. And they almost seemed to *glow*.

"Gross," Dae said succinctly, and Thony thought she'd seen the same thing. But instead, she was pointing to how the enchanted troops were just sloshing into the market square without regard – or seeming awareness – of their surroundings. Though fresh horse poop, over fallen fruit, unnoticing of brooms or water buckets or...

... or of the water fountain in the middle of the square with the great pool surrounding it.

Some of the troops were attempting to walk into it, or were simply tipping in...

Jost was chuckling.

Others were walking straight through the vendors' carts and stands and getting insults and food – and worse – thrown at them in response as those worthies hurriedly packed up and departed. Or in some cases simply abandoned their goods and fled. There were some unfortunate altercations between the mounted troopers in charge of the enchanted troops and the local vendors, but there were too many enchanted people and insufficient 'live ones' managing them to also deal effectively with angry farmers and crafters.

Their 'herders' certainly had their work cut out for them, Thony thought.

And it looked like there had been some idea of setting up a review of the new arrivals, but getting them to line up was an utter loss. Simply getting them *into* the market square was a challenge... and then *keeping* them in there was another one, as they tended to wander out when not prevented.

The Raven-troops guarding the entrance in the wall around the headquarters mansion looked entirely unnerved and were of no aid in anything besides shoving enchanted people away from themselves and the gate with the butts of their spears. The mounted troops were at the end of their energy and patience and clearly put out that they weren't getting any help from their 'brother- and sister- soldiers.' A great deal of shouting was involved.

"Something else is happening," Dae said suddenly. "In the mansion."

She, of course, had kept her focus on where her... incipient family was located.

Thony and Jost tore their unwillingly fascinated eyes from the milling mob of enchanted people and their keepers.

Frustratingly, the boys had missed some transition and there was no way to tell how all the principles had arrived in their current positions.

It was, however, undeniable that *Kamauri Spiralspear* was in the middle of the cobbled courtyard holding a naked blade pointed at *Captain Shalladra Stillheart*. A ring of Raven-troops surrounded the two women.

Istevan and Daennor were at the top of the steps leading down from the main entrance to the mansion. The older man was holding Daennor back from trying to get through the thicket of armed soldiers to get to Kamauri.

And... an old man with hair streaked black and white was hobbling out of the mansion supported by Julanna Silversea and... *Davril?*

"I *have* to know what's going on!" Dae all but wailed, starting to scramble across the roof.

Jost caught her and dragged her back down by the chimney-pot, clapping a hand over her mouth as the enchanted troops all suddenly looked up and in their direction. Even the mounted troopers 'managing' them seemed unnerved by that, and glanced upwards automatically.

"Calm yerself. They're a-keyin' on strong emotions," Jost hissed urgently. "Did ye not ken how they oriented on th' farmers as were angriest? Or how they all follow th' trooper as seems t' 'ave most lost 'is cool?"

Thony hadn't – and Dae hadn't been watching the enchanted troops. But she subsided, and was crying again, this time tears of frustration though she kept them quiet.

"I can't – I have to *know*," she was saying.

"I'm sorry, lass," Jost whispered. "But keep yerself cool a moment and... aye, there they go. There's emotion enough t'draw them t' th' mansion an we do stay quiet and cool up here. There's naught ye can do e'en could ye see an' hear better, Dae," the street-kid-chieftain added, though his tone was sympathetic. "An' nowhere near time t' get o'er there in person. Nor a thing ye could do an ye did."

Thony could agree...

...but not being able to tell was nearly as painful to him as to Dae, since this might be the end of all their plans...

...and Twinklestar had done this for *him*, though maybe it had worked because they were bonded...

No way to know, but to try...

"–n't need help to handle one overwrought girl." Shalladra's cool, amused, musical voice was suddenly loud in Thony's ears. By the small, gasps he heard from Jost and Dae he knew what he'd tried to do had worked.

He opened eyes he didn't remember having closed, and suddenly he could focus much more closely on the interior of the courtyard. He was abruptly immersed in that weird, sour 'smell' of stale unicorn sweat that had assaulted him the last time he had tried this.

Shalladra had gestured her troops back, and was pacing forwards... like a predator.

Kamauri held her sword firmly, competently... she was an experienced warrior, Thony knew. Two years in the Mercenaries' Guild before she'd begun chasing around after Dae, he'd been told, and she had taken on a number of mercenary-soldier jobs even while she did *that*.

But she looked utterly terrified.

And she was backing up as Shalladra paced forward and then began circling her.

"You were one of the ones who dared the Plains of Gavenor, weren't you, little girl?" Shalladra purred. "I thought I remembered that name – though *Kamauri* is such a *common* name that I nearly didn't pay you any attention. Did you imagine you'd learned a little about *magick* there? Did that experience give you a taste for the *dark* side of Power? You *failed*, you know, *all* of you.

"They'd have done better to hire me. *Alone.*" The Dark-elf-woman sneered. "The only *un*common thing about any of you fools was your unicorn. A unicorn-maiden as a mercenary – a novel idea even to me. Not that it did you or your friends any good, did it? How many of them *died* in Gavenor, little girl?"

Tears were rolling down Kamauri's cheeks as she faced the Dark-elf captain. Even with his magickally-enhanced hearing, Thony lip-read more than heard the response. "Too many."

"Leave her alone, Stillheart," Daennor called out. "I'll do what you want."

Shalladra spared him a glance. "Oh, *that* is true regardless, darling. You – and dear Istevan – will be my pets as I reclaim my proper place. But *this* child... needs to be taught a *lesson.*"

"Shalladra..." the old man croaked. Julanna and Davril had lowered him to the wide, marble steps. His hair seemed to have barely any black in it at all now and he seemed to be collapsing before their eyes. "This is *not* how..."

"Oh, shut up, Raven'sWing," the Dark-elf said dismissively. "You're useless to me now."

*(The white-haired old man was **Valderon Raven'sWing**?)*

Shalladra paused to glance at Julanna and Davril. "I may have a couple of others to make examples of, though. *That...* promises to be a distinct *pleasure.*"

Istevan let go of Daennor at that comment, and both men drew their own swords.

"You'll have to go through us first, Stillheart," Istevan said firmly. "To touch any of them."

Daennor took a step towards Kamauri...

Shalladra snorted. "My men will slay you all if either of you takes one more step."

"They're *my* men, not yours," the old man croaked.

The Dark-elf-woman gave a... darkly musical laugh. "Oh, my dear Raven'sWing. I don't *need* you to control people anymore. You've gathered them together for me and humans are most easily controlled by *money,* once they've been gathered, I shall have as much of *that* at my disposal as I wish, shall I not, Davril Keetering? In return for Istevan's life?"

Davril's look of hate should have been able to set the woman's hair on fire. His hands clenched...

...and he bent his head.

Shalladra's laugh rang out again. "Don't worry, little boy. I shan't try your *morals* for too long. I only need *you* until I claim my throne. I'll keep Istevan around – but *you're* far too ugly to grace my Court."

She glanced around the courtyard. "What say you, men? I'll double what the sorcerer promised you and you swear to *me?*"

She smiled that predatory smile again. "Or you can *leave,* and see if you can outrun my vengeance. Go now, if you wish. I'll even give you a headstart, while I deal with more pressing matters."

That sweet malicious smile... "Though I'd stay in well-lit places for the rest of your lives, were I you. And away from old-growth forests. Not that my people have trouble moving about in the light – night is merely our *preference.*"

No one moved so much as a muscle amongst the troops encircling the courtyard.

Thony swore under his breath. The whole time they'd seen Raven'sWing as the threat and Shalladra Stillheart merely as his accomplice and underling.

"You still have to get through *me,* Stillheart," Kamauri's voice was steady. "I may not have *defeated* the demon on the Plains of Gavenor, but I gave it a damn good fight. I can give you one, too. If you dare."

The Dark-elf laughed again. "Ah, but you are so *ordinary,* Kamauri *Spiralspear.* On your *own* anyways. And you *are* on your own, aren't you, love? Can't really be a unicorn-*maiden* anymore, can you? And really, that was the only thing that gave as *common* a mercenary as yourself even a chance against a demon."

She paused. "Or against a Dark-elf. I don't think I'll even bother with a sword to take care of you, little girl. I think I'll use my bare hands."

She took off her uniform jacket, folded it, and handed it backwards without a glance. "Wouldn't want to get that dirty. Blood – and other bodily fluids – are so difficult to get out without ruining that shade of blue."

A Raven-trooper scuttled forwards to take the jacket. The man was visibly shaking.

Shalladra Stillheart smiled and *stretched...*

... and suddenly her hands sported claws and she was... several inches *taller.*

Or perhaps that was only the terrifying ambiance that she now seemed to exude from her very pores. It was almost as if she had been *restraining* herself and this was her more natural state. Almost more disturbing than her obviously predatory aspect was how she was still so insanely and unearthly *beautiful*.

The humans surrounding her – and the three kids on the rooftop – all shivered.

"Put up or shut up, Captain Stillheart," Kamauri blustered, though she had shivered along with everyone else. Thony admired her moxy... he rather felt that if all that *ambiance* had been focused on *him*, he'd have been curled up on the ground waiting to die.

"That would be *Lady* Stillheart," Shalladra smiled viciously. "Soon to be *Queen* Stillheart."

She took another predatory pace forwards...

... and Daennor took two steps *back* and away from the women.

He grabbed a spear out of one of the Raven-guards' hands, shouted "Ho, Kamauri!" and hefted it like a javelin and *straight at her.*

Thony gasped in horror, but Dae was laughing through her tears. "Yes! Yes, Daennor!"

The young woman discarded the sword she was holding, seemingly without a second thought, and actually pulled the flying spear out of the air. She looked a great deal more confident as she re-settled herself to face the Dark-elf.

"Spear is Kamauri's primary weapon," Dae explained as the two boys gaped. "She's a genius with it."

It still seemed like a bad idea to *Thony*, but Kamauri was doing a pretty good job fending off Shalladra's first attacks. She used the shaft like a staff to block and strike and the spearhead to slash. She was strong and lithe and agile...

And she was faced by someone who was more of all of those things. And who had her own, *natural* weaponry, and therefore wasn't hampered by the inertia of the long piece of hardened wood.

Thony tried to put an arm around Dae, but she shook it off – though she had all of her fingers crammed into her mouth and her eyes were wide. He exchanged a look with Jost, who gave him a grim nod and brandished the butt-end of his all-purpose knife where Dae couldn't see it.

Thony blinked, then realized Jost was planning to knock the girl out to prevent her from doing anything foolish... and possibly giving them a chance to save her life.

A look of question in Jost's eye suggested that perhaps they should just do it now and begin their own retreat. Their own hopes and plans were obviously irretrievably shattered.

While it appeared that some portion of the enchanted army might have been diverted off, more of them were still shuffling into the market square, drawn – if Jost was right – by the powerful emotions emanating from the courtyard. They still had no way to break the spell – even if the unicorns' magick would do it, they hadn't thought it could be done quickly or on the move.

Shalladra had gained the loyalty – or at least the fear – of the independent troops.

Kamauri and Davril and Julanna would shortly be dead – and Istevan and Daennor would be... *pets?* After Shalladra overthrew the *Fairy Queen?*

All that was left was to hope that Stillheart wouldn't care about anything else once she had what she wanted – to rule her own kin and kind, it seemed, and possibly the Fairy Wood and the Fairy Queen's Court. Perhaps mere mortals and their worlds wouldn't be of interest to her. Though Thony would probably never get to go home again – even if she didn't know who he was and how he'd tried to oppose her, travel between worlds would become far too dangerous.

Aldyrwald was doomed either way... but hopefully just doomed to be conquered by the neighbors, not *consumed* by bloodthirsty Dark-elves...

Thony was about to nod in agreement. Jost could knock Dae out and they could try to make their own escape...

...Kamauri was still fighting, though she had ribbons of blood dripping from her here and there – slashes along her shoulder and her thigh. And a long gash across her lower back that Thony hadn't seen happen and couldn't imagine how she'd gotten away so lightly if she'd been touched at all like that...

"She's *playing* with her," Dae whispered tonelessly. "Like a cat plays with a mouse. Oh, I can't watch."

The mercenette's hands covered her face, but she was peeking out between her fingers as if she also couldn't bear *not* to watch.

Istevan was holding Daennor back again, Thony noticed. The younger mercenary was fighting to get free. But there were far too many sharp objects pointed at the two of them... and at Davril; apparently the Raven-troops had taken Shalladra at her word.

Julanna... had the old man's head on her lap. He seemed all but dead. She seemed to be crying.

"Let me go, damn you!" Daennor was shouting. "Do you think I care what happens to me, if she–"

Istevan's arms tightened, and he whispered something in Daennor's ear.

And the poufy-haired mercenary froze, his eyes going higher... until he spotted the kids on the rooftop.

No, until he spotted *Dae*.

And he instantly stopped fighting to go to Kamauri's side. Though he fell to his knees, out of Istevan's grip. The tall, older man knelt beside him, a hand on his back... and his own eyes going first to Davril and then to the kids on the rooftop.

To *him*, Thony somehow knew. Istevan was asking – for himself and Davril and Daennor and Kamauri – that Thony would get their children away. Daphne... and Dae.

Kamauri, Thony had come to understand from random comments during all those hours in the pickle-cellar, had been Dae's best-friend since the moment they had met. She'd come to fill in, in some ways, for the mother that had abandoned Dae as a toddler at the mercenary school. I

t wasn't that their teachers – including the Headmistress, whom Dae half-seemed to resent, half-seemed to adore – it wasn't that they had *ignored* her or anything. They simply... hadn't had the time for a toddler. And Kamauri *had*.

And over these last two years... Daennor had made her his own as well. Little sister, foster-daughter... *friend,* for all that he'd found her as exasperating as Thony did.

Both of them... but the young mercenary could do nothing for Kamauri, though it broke his heart.

And the only thing he could do for Dae was to not get killed in front of her at Kamauri's side.

We're going to spend the rest of our lives trying to figure out how to rescue Daennor from the new Evil Queen of Fairyland, Thony thought to himself.

But what else could he do?

Kamauri's strength was waning. Her swings of the heavy spear-shaft were slowing, and each encounter was ending with another gash. She surely couldn't hold out much longer...

The young prince nodded at Istevan, and was again, about to give the nod to Jost to knock Dae out. The girl shouldn't have to see her best-friend die in front of her eyes...

A commotion in the marketplace square distracted Thony momentarily.

A troop of mounted people was forging their way through the green-eyed enchanted troops.

Thony started to turn away – more Raven-troops wouldn't change anything for the better – when he realized that the newcomers were...

Unicorns.

Chapter EIGHTEEN

When Push Comes to Shove

U*NICORNS.*

Three of them, making a wedge that somehow repelled anyone from coming near them, and with several horses behind them. Three of the horses carried riders, two more followed behind, unburdened save for packs, with a small, swaybacked donkey trailing after all the rest.

The riders were a woman and a man whom Thony had never seen before... and *Amanita* with *baby Daphne* in a sling on her chest.

What the **hell***? Those two were supposed to be heading someplace safe... that was the only part of The New Plan that* **should** *still have been working...*

And following close behind *them* was a small troupe of mounted warriors – all rather short, dark-skinned women – with a young man in the middle. All of the women looked very unhappy... and *fierce*...

It might have been encouraging... if they weren't all surrounded by several *thousand* enemy troops.

The unicorns were clearly in charge – especially the one taking point. Rainsparkle and Twinklestar seemed to be following the other one's directions.

And the unicorns were taking no guff from anyone. Whomever their *magickal siege engine of repulsion* didn't disperse, their sharp, pointy horns were eliminating. Apparently, unicorns weren't as sweet and gentle as Thony had believed.

They forced their way through the mansion's gate just as Kamauri sagged to her knees.

Shalladra had no chance to stand over her and gloat, however, since the unicorns forced her back. Twinklestar and Rainsparkle took up stances to either side of the exhausted mercenary, and the strange unicorn bulled her way in between the opponents.

The troop of women warriors guarded the back end of what was becoming a protective circle around Kamauri's sagging, wavering form. They looked grim and fierce. The young man nudged his way up between the other riders to take a place next to Amanita who... gave him a look of mingled annoyance and fear and incredible relief.

Relief? Who *was* this guy?

Istevan and Davril were both looking rather horrified to see Daphne brought into the arena of danger. Davril began trying to get Julanna's attention...

"Dae, look," Thony couldn't find a voice above a whisper. Jost looked in utter bafflement at the altered scene as the mercenette uncovered her face.

Shalladra, unfortunately, looked more amused than discommoded by all the changes.

"Thinkest thou to stand against me, Quellarie Unicorn-Born?" she asked in her amused, musical voice. "Thee hast not the Power. *Thy* kind are meant to *serve* mine, not *rebuke* such as I."

There was a *shimmer* and the lead unicorn disappeared to be replaced by a slender woman of average height with incredibly long, pale hair. Her very feminine gown was a soft shade of lavender.

She looked, in other words, entirely non-threatening.

Though her name... sounded familiar to Thony for some reason.

"Should I seek to stand against thee *alone*, that might be true, Stillheart," the woman – Quellarie – said quietly. "Or had I spent my years as do most of my kin, in silence and reflection and the tending of innocence and wisdom. But curiosity hath ever been both my curse and my blessing – as thee wouldst have known hadst thou bothered to ever *talk* to young Valderon."

The unicorn-woman's gaze flickered over to the man who was breathing raspily and shallowly with the sudden onset of advanced age.

"Poor lad," she said with absolutely no irony.

"Princess–" the unicorn-woman called over her shoulder. "Do thou take the child to her parents."

"Yes, Quellarie," Amanita replied in a more docile tone than Thony had ever heard from her.

The young man helped her dismount from Silverfoot with the baby, and the women warriors also dismounted and kept the pair of them surrounded as Amanita followed the unicorn-woman's orders. The women warriors abandoned Kamauri – who was now entirely prone – to keep Amanita and the young man surrounded as they moved, arrogantly brushing past the Raven-troops separating the people on the stairs from those in the courtyard.

Shalladra watched all of this with narrowed eyes, then suddenly laughed that dark laugh again.

"So, the boy actually managed sire a babe at last. I wondered why the flower had started to brown – he'd found light-o'-loves in the past and it hadn't disturbed my spell. But that would have done it. I suppose that *human need* finally overwhelmed *good sense.*"

"To reproduce is a *living need,* Stillheart," Quellarie corrected gently. "As thy brother knew."

"Speak not to me of Nightcreeper," Shalladra's cool was finally disrupted. "He was *weak* in the end, and a fool. He let himself be blinded to how his own *daughter* would betray us all and abandon his plans."

The unicorn-woman shrugged. "Perhaps."

"And *thou* hast been a fool and given me more hostages." The Dark-elf lifted her head with a confident smile. "Thou shouldst have minded thine own business, Unicorn-Born."

Quellarie tilted her head. "But this *is* my business, Stillheart. *My* mistake, and therefore *my* business to mend it."

Shalladra frowned at that, as if the words made as little sense to her as to Thony.

The unicorn-woman was already looking away to... Julanna?

"Bard," she called. "Art thou ready to Sing to Summon a Goddess?"

Julanna gently laid down Valderon Raven's Wing's head – he appeared to be gone entirely now – and stood. She looked... very pale. Daphne was in Davril's arms again, at last.

"We're too far away," the Bard said shakily. "This land doesn't belong to the Gods I know. How can I begin to Call Them?"

"What is distance to a Goddess?" Quellarie asked, making it sound as though she were asking a rhetorical question of a stubborn student. "There is One who will always Bless thee with Her Answer, Bard. As did She Bless thy parents most fulsomely in the reaches of time. As She will Bless also the tall stallion beside thee, for that She has long Blessed his Line." The unicorn-woman smiled slightly. "As will Another also give Answer for the sake of these other children, should She be asked."

The young man with Amanita wrapped his arms around the girl, protectively, as more than Julanna's attention was drawn to them.

Shalladra folded her arms and settled her weight on her heels. She still seemed supremely confident – as, indeed, made sense – but Thony noted that she wasn't just immediately eliminating these new challengers. There must be some Power here that was giving the ruthless Dark-elf pause.

Or perhaps, as Dae had said earlier, she merely preferred to toy with her food.

"I am all but a Goddess myself," the Dark-elf claimed. "And this is a wasteland for deities. And loyalty is to the highest bidder. Which is *me*. There are none that will challenge me, here."

Quellarie tilted her head again. "Is it so? Shall we see? Sing, Bard."

Julanna looked confused, but started to draw a breath...

And Shalladra cast out a hand...

...and the Bard choked and gasped, attempting to draw air.

Davril cursed and shoved the baby at his husband, freeing his hands to help his cousin keep her feet. "Let her breathe, damn you!" he cried out.

Shalladra, however, was looking at Quellarie. "So much for thy 'plan,' little half-breed." She waved dismissively. "Get thee hence. Take thy comrade's former unicorn-maiden with thee an thee dost wish. I have an invasion to set upon and a couple of thrones to overthrow."

Julanna was still choking for air, twisting on the hard marble at the top of the steps... but...

Thony cast a confused look at Jost. "Is she really *backing down* by letting Kamauri go?"

"Aye," Jost agreed, frowning. "No need for it, an she does 'ave such control o'er things as she claims."

"Does it *matter?*" Dae was choking as well, but on tears, not for lack of air. "Kamauri isn't going to *survive.* She's lost too much blood *already.*"

Indeed, red trails were filling the gaps between the cobblestones like some horrific new grouting, spreading out from the collapsed form of the brave mercenary.

"Amanita," Quellarie called out. "Daffyd. We talked about this. Ask your Grandmother to send to us Her Son."

Wasn't *Daffyd* the name of Amanita's *brother?*

Thony and his friends watched as Amanita – and her brother – held hands and seemed to... *pray?*

Shalladra glanced over with amused unconcern. "Not even a Goddess, Quellarie? What *demi-God* could stand against me, here?"

Quellarie Unicorn-Born smiled. "Why, one whose followers have been building him a base of beliefs here. A very *sturdy belief-base,*" she added. "Possibly a sturdier one than he's ever had before."

Neither of them seemed to notice the most famous Bard in the world turning purple and going limp... and Davril crying...

And then, suddenly, *Puck* was standing there next to Amanita and her brother.

He looked briefly rattled, but *he* didn't ignore the unconscious woman practically at his feet.

"*Aleri!*" he shouted, after briefly kneeling to touch Julanna's shoulder. "We need you, cousin!"

Shalladra didn't look terribly impressed.

"*This* demi-God, Quellarie?" she sneered. "Or even this one *and* the other? Couldst even thou *find* a weaker pair?"

The unicorn-woman smiled as another male figure appeared at the top of the stairs and began doing... something... to Julanna. Her color was improving, though Thony couldn't tell if that was because she'd actually died and was no longer struggling for breath, or if she was actually breathing under the newcomer's ministrations.

Puck had straightened up and was stalking down the stairs, pushing aside the Raven-troops as if they were nothing. A few of them tried to stop him, but he didn't seem to be physically there when they tried to touch him – though it was clear he was entirely solid when he shoved one aside and they went flying.

"*Power,* my dear Lady Stillheart," Quellarie Unicorn-Born said as Puck approached, "Is always a matter of *belief.*"

She turned back into a unicorn with that strange *shimmer* and headed out of the courtyard. Twinklestar and Rainsparkle followed her.

"*Rainsparkle!*" Daennor bellowed. He had followed Puck closely, using the corridor made by his passing to escape both Istevan and the Raven-soldiers who had been guarding them from the courtyard.

He dashed over to the young woman, who was as still and pale as Julanna had been, as soon as he was able and he now cried out in anguish and desperation to the unicorn to which Kamauri had been bonded to for so many years. Unicorns, after all, could Heal many injuries.

Rainsparkle looked at him for a moment, then swished her tail and followed the others out of the courtyard.

Daennor stared after the unicorn's departure in disbelief, then hunched over Kamauri's body. He started picking her up.

Shalladra gestured at him, and Daennor was flung into the legs of some of the other soldiers.

"It isn't polite for the Fairy Queen's pet to fuss over another woman," the ambitious Dark-elf told him smugly as he picked himself up and began trying to get back to Kamauri. "Isn't that how this whole little fracas started in the first place, darling?"

"Hold him," Shalladra said casually, and some of the Raven- no, *her* troops took Daennor's arms. Though they seemed hesitant. Or maybe that was Thony's wishful thinking.

Puck placed himself in front of the Dark-elf-woman, blocking off her view of both of the young mercenaries.

He looked just the way Thony had first seen him – though noticeably taller. He was every inch a prince of the Fairy Court, accoutered elegantly in a frock-coat and hose of lavender and green and with his silver-gold locks in fashionable curls. Gone were the dusty traveling leathers that Thony had seen on him last.

150

His expression, however, was the entirely familiar look of pure mischief.

"Stillheart," he said in the tone of one renewing an acquaintance. "We wondered where you'd gotten to. You missed Nightcreeper's funeral. And Oakfire's."

Hadn't Amanita said those names – the princes of the Dark- and Light-elves who had killed each other out of spite some three or four hundred years ago? Puck referred to them as if it had all happened recently.

Shalladra lifted her chin slightly. "Neither of them were worth my time, Prankster."

She seemed to be trying to give the impression that *Puck* wasn't worth her time either, but she couldn't seem to ignore him.

Thony wondered if anyone else could see the towering rage hidden beneath Puck's genteel exterior and mischievous grin.

"Perhaps not," Puck said nonchalantly, "but you've mortally offended a number of people with that cavalier attitude. Your niece, just to begin with."

"*Opalsinger's* preferences are shortly to become entirely *irrelevant,*" Shalladra said dismissively as her phrasing slid back into the common vernacular to match Puck's. "And I don't care about *mortals* at all. Now, if you don't mind, I'm rather busy. Run along and play your little pranks, why don't you. And leave the *important* matters to those whose minds can handle them."

Puck took that... rather better than Thony would have.

"All right," he said affably. "Giving people what they ask for is often the better part of a good prank."

He clapped once. Twice. Three times.

Nothing happened.

Shalladra frowned at him, then shook her head and took a stride away.

There was the faint faraway sound of bells, though Thony didn't remember seeing a belltower. Flowerdust's people had seemed refreshingly uninterested in marking the hours, actually, but it had never made sense to him why precise measurements of time mattered to anyone in Aldyrwald.

And then... Shalladra stopped.

And went... well, on someone else it would have been pale. On the already-pale Dark-elf, it was more of a turning slightly green.

"What have you *done?*" she demanded, rounding on Puck.

The fairy-prince – *or should that be* **demi-God?** – tucked his thumbs into his wide, silver belt and rocked back on his heels with a smirk. "Wouldn't you like to know?"

"*Puck!*" Shalladra Stillheart raged... but now Thony rather thought there was fear in her eyes.

"You screwed up, Stillheart," he told her, patently enjoying the moment.

The other male figure who had arrived was now moving from Julanna down to Kamauri. He looked up at that comment with a look of dark humor. "Shall *I* tell her, cousin? She owes *me* even more than she owes *you,* I think."

Puck looked thoughtful. "You have a point. Sure, Aleri, old son. It's the joy of watching things unfold that amuses me. I don't have to be the one who delivers the denouement."

Aleri glared at Shalladra, then turned his attention back to Kamauri's still, wan figure.

"Your niece is coming for you, Stillheart." The... *other* demi-God spoke without so much as turning to look at her. "To deliver you the punishment you so justly deserve after all you've done these last few centuries."

"As if I'd believe the God of *Liars!*" Shalladra glared at them both, but she was clearly unsettled. "*Lies* and *pranks*. I've had enough of *both* of you!"

She raised her hand dramatically, just as she had before stealing Julanna's breath and tossing Daennor away from Kamauri, and – nothing happened.

"A-a-ah," Puck waggled a finger at her as he smirked. "Air is a *secondary* Element for Dark-elves, even if it *is* your own strongest. With the Sons of two Wind-Goddesses here you can't imagine we'd let you play with what rightfully belongs to our sweet Mothers, can you?"

Thony had idly wondered once or twice over the last few weeks if it was possible to grind pointed teeth. Apparently, it was.

"Start running *now,* and maybe you'll have enough of a headstart," Puck taunted her. "Stay in lighted areas and – well, you know the drill, don't you? *You've* been on the run for three hundred years."

Thony could see the Raven-soldiers exchanging looks. That was what she had threatened *them* with... and *she'd* been on the run?

"You might as well, Stillheart," Aleri said from behind Puck and still without looking up from whatever he was doing to Kamauri.

Thony wondered if he really was the God of Lies, and why on the world – any world – Puck had summoned the God of *Lies* when there was an injured person. There must be some reason, but there was still that faint ringing in his ears, making it hard to concentrate.

"The unicorns are breaking the enchantment Valderon cast upon the Darjeeling people," Aleri went on. "Puck and I aren't going to let you hurt any of these people anymore."

"And without being able to threaten any of my nieces and nephews," Puck added, "you really won't have the money to pay these poor fellows. Our dear Aunt in the Fairy Wood isn't going to let you overthrow Her simply so that you can use Her treasury to fulfill your debts and promissory notes... and that's assuming that any of them would take faery-gold anyways."

It was easy to see that none of the soldiers relished *that* idea.

Thony didn't blame them. At least not if the tales of faery-gold from his own world were anything close to true.

"And now..." Puck's eyes turned towards the mansion's gaping gateway as the sound of chiming bells that had been gradually getting louder suddenly became distinct. His expression was one of interested anticipation.

Shalladra Stillheart turned towards the gate herself. Though *her* expression was still cool, a tendril of dread seemed to underlie it.

The hunting party that began to arrive was like none other Thony had ever seen.

The leader was a woman as like unto Shalladra as... Dae was to Amanita. Weirdly similar, but entirely distinct.

They had the same pale skin, the same dark hair, though the captain's was short and straight and the huntress' was long and wild and free. Where Shalladra was trim and straightlaced in the blue jacket she'd retrieved, every stitch neat and perfect... the newcomer was dressed in flowing silks, soft leathers, and luxurious furs still hung about with the paws and tails and *heads* of the animals who had once lived in them.

It was the eyes that distinguished them the most, however.

Shalladra's were a bright, cold blue. The huntress' were pale, almost white, reflecting sheens of green or gold, purple or pink or blue depending on how she shifted her head.

The remainder of her hunting party entered after her, each of them clad similarly and uniquely. Each pale with dark hair and eyes that spoke of ages gone by.

Their mounts were lovely – clearly kin to Chillabiaen, the fairy-horse that Puck had ridden out of the Fairy Wood. They were dainty of foot, tall at the shoulder, proud in the neck, and with tails like flags and manes like spun silk. The leader's mount was a wild-looking stallion whose coat matched his rider's multi-colored eyes, and the rest were a veritable spectrum of horses.

And the last member of the party stayed just beyond the gate.

He was as wildly dressed as all the rest... but his face was shaded by the massive deer skull-robe that draped his head and neck with the huge double-rack of antlers still attached to it that seemed to practically grow out of the hunter's head. Thony counted, automatically, and had to rub his eyes and count again – deer simply didn't *grow* seven points. Though this one clearly had.

This rider's horse was more skittish than the rest, nor was he decked out in bells and caparisoned in bright silks. This Hunter, and somehow Thony felt the title should be capitalized, was something different.

Dogs that were as different from the half-starved city curs as the fairy-horses were distinct from such plebeian mounts as Silverfoot and Sandy curvetted around the skittish horse and its rider. Sleek, wild, more wolf than dog... Thony caught a glimpse of dark-golden skin as the silent, final rider stretched forth a hand to settle a small dispute between two of the canines.

"Stillheart," the huntress in the lead said. Her voice was... filled with the living forest, was the only thing Thony could think to describe it. Not that that was a particularly good description. She didn't sound like birds or rustling leaves or anything. She just... seemed to carry the whole forest with her. The whole *Fairy Wood*.

Thank goodness he had no pretensions at being any kind of writer. He'd clearly fail.

"Opalsinger." The woman they had known as Captain Shalladra acknowledged. The usual sneer was still there – but it seemed toned down, as if she didn't quite dare.

Another fail on Thony's part. How could he not have immediately recognized the terrifying woman who had stood to the side of Queen Lilysong's throne?

"We thought you dead, Aunt," Lady Opalsinger stated dispassionately. "A mortal's Age has gone by since last you graced our halls."

Stillheart snorted. "Hardly. Though apparently 'tis been long enow to turn thy speech to *common* patterns, niece. Tell, me hast thou so corrupted all of our people? And is't to pander to the Light-elves or for some other lowly purpose that thou dost so debase thyself?"

Opalsinger's expression didn't vary. Nor did she bother explaining herself.

"You stand charged with high crimes, Stillheart. Will you submit to our justice or shall we take you to the Fairy Queen?"

Stillheart sneered more visibly. "*Crimes,* Niece? For playing with mortal creatures? Since when does *our* kind concern ourselves with such as these?"

Lady Opalsinger's eyes flickered to the two demi-Gods. Puck was still standing to one side. Aleri was half-kneeling beside Kamauri's body. Both of them wore deeply ironic looks upon their faces.

"Not often," Opalsinger agreed. "And no. Though Queen Lilysong sees things differently. Should you face Her, *She* will doubtless take you to task for what you have wrought here."

She paused. "No, Aunt. The Puck has brought us evidence that it was you behind the abduction of Lord Aspenheart's baby daughter, Sweetrowan. Your accomplices have been identified. They have given up what they knew and received their punishments."

Stillheart looked rather green, but she forced another sneer. "*You* would have made *peace* with those damned Light-elves. Even after they killed my *brother.* Your own *father.* And now *you* would take *me* to task for seeking some vengeance against one of *them?*"

"*Children* have always been off-limits in our wars," Lady Opalsinger had no forgiveness in her voice. "And Sweetrowan was barely of age to toddle. But you might have gained yourself sympathy amongst our own people had you not *also* taken my own young sister, Moonsray. Your accomplices were quite clear, Stillheart, that both abductions were at your instigation.

"And they one and all," the Dark-elf princess added distantly, "agreed that while they participated in the abductions, the decision to abandon the children as pirate-slaves was entirely yours."

Julanna made some sort of shocked noise. She seemed largely recovered, Thony was happy to see. Davril had gone quite pale and stepped away from her to reclaim his tiny daughter and stand in the circle of Istevan's arms.

Stillheart looked rather green as well, but she forced another sneer. "You would have made *peace* with those damned Light-elves," she said again. "Even after they killed my *brother*. And now you would take me to task for the sake of one of *their* brats? Or perhaps..." and now she recovered some and her tone became insinuating, "perhaps the rumors are true and you would *more* than *make peace* with *Lord Aspenheart?*"

Lady Opalsinger's expression didn't even twitch. "You will face the Queen – or you will take your chances with your own kind, Stillheart. I will not offer you the choice again."

Puck smiled then and... it was not a *friendly* smile. "*I* might add, however, that Her Majesty isn't particularly inclined to be *merciful*. It's been brought to Her attention that you had plans to overthrow *Her*, and in the doing you went far beyond the bounds She has set on what liberties one might take with *mortals.*"

Stillheart turned on him, snarling, "Lilysong's Lackey!"

Puck put a hand over his heart and gave her a very genteel – and mocking – bow. "At your service."

The God of Lies didn't take that so well. He stood up, leaving Kamauri's still-limp form to Daennor. "Show some respect for Prince Skiftglow, criminal."

Puck waved this aside. "Let her bluster, Aleri. 'Twill do her no good when she kneels before our dear Aunt's throne." He gave Stillheart a rather *nastier* smile than Thony would have imagined the cheerful fairy-prince could. But then... Thony hadn't really realized

Puck was a *demi-God...* "Our *other* Aunt took a fairly minor Evil Wizard who hurt our newest cousin under the ocean a few years ago. Didn't you tell me that he's *still* regretting his poor life choices, Aleri?"

"This might not be *quite* so personal," Aleri noted dryly. "After all, none of *these* children here are Her Majesty's *own*. And... She's been known to be more merciful than the Sea-Queen. Occasionally anyways." His own look at Stillheart was quite nearly as darkly sardonic as Puck's. "I'm not sure *I'd* want to take the chance... but *you're* a *brave soul,* aren't you Stillheart?"

"She told Quellarie Unicorn-Born that she was practically a Goddess herself," Amanita volunteered.

Her brother and the warrior women all looked incredibly unnerved that she'd drawn the immortal beings' attention. On the rooftop, Thony and Jost exchanged a look behind Dae's head. Just as well that the mercenette was up here with *them* – it was all too likely that she'd have done the same thing.

Puck exchanged a glance with Aleri. "Well, then you've nothing to worry about, have you, Stillheart? Perhaps it *would* be wiser to come before Queen Lilysong. Your own people look like they aren't in a terribly forgiving mood."

It appeared that they were *baiting* Raven'sWing's former collaborator...

...and it worked.

"Damn all your eyes," Stillheart snarled. She looked up at Lady Opalsinger on her high horse. "I'll take our people's justice. But when it's done, the Queen doesn't get me."

Lady Opalsinger's smile curved slightly. "As you have said it, so shall it be done. You will have until midnight before the Master of the Wild Hunt will take your trail for a full quarter of the moon. You may have whatever aids you wish – though none will be compelled to assist you."

The Dark-elf-woman who had thought to unseat a Goddess had started to open her mouth.

Instead, she frowned. "The *Master* of the Hunt? *You* won't lead it, Opalsinger?"

And now, Lady Opalsinger's smile became truly devastating – both because of her beauty and because of the vengeance in her expression. "I have recovered my sister, Stillheart, though she suffered much. Lord Aspenheart has claimed the honor, since his daughter will still not speak to him because of the trauma that shaped her."

She gestured, and the rider with the massive array of antlers ducked his head to come under the arch of the gate and into the courtyard. His face was still shrouded by the deerskin cape from Thony's perspective. The young prince found that he didn't mind – he'd seen Lord Aspenheart in Queen Lilysong's Court when the Light-elf-prince had merely been mildly annoyed. He wasn't at all sure he wanted to see what Aspenheart looked like *now*.

"But don't worry, Stillheart," Lady Opalsinger said casually. "*I'll* be right behind him."

It was clear that should *not* be reassuring.

Stillheart ran her tongue over lips gone thin and pale.

"I want your steed, Opalsinger," she demanded suddenly. "Your steed, and your promise that he'll obey me."

Lady Opalsinger dismounted without hesitation. "My other sister, Lady Embersoul, will ride at Lord Aspenheart's side."

Another huntress, this one on a bay mare whose coat could have rivaled the sunset, nodded and edged forwards, golden eyes gleaming with eagerness.

Stillheart stepped forwards to take the reins from Opalsinger. The horse...

Oh. My. God.

The *horse* bared pointed teeth at her. But he suffered the disgraced Dark-elf-woman to mount.

"He'll fly like the wind, Stillheart," Opalsinger said, not yet stepping away. "And take you where you wish. But should you mistreat him... well... you rode a *hrulga* once yourself, I believe."

Stillheart swore violently, but her hands were gentle on the reins, Thony noticed.

She trotted the magnificent creature out past Lord Aspenheart and the rest of the elfin contingent, affecting a great nonchalance...

...but the moment she was past the gate and out sight, she fled.

Like the wind, as Lady Opalsinger had said.

There was a moment of utter silence.

"Well." Lady Opalsinger gestured, and her hunting party began to dismount. "It isn't even sunset yet, so she has some time. And there's a great deal to be set right here, it seems. Shall we begin?"

And it finally occurred to Thony that they'd *won*.

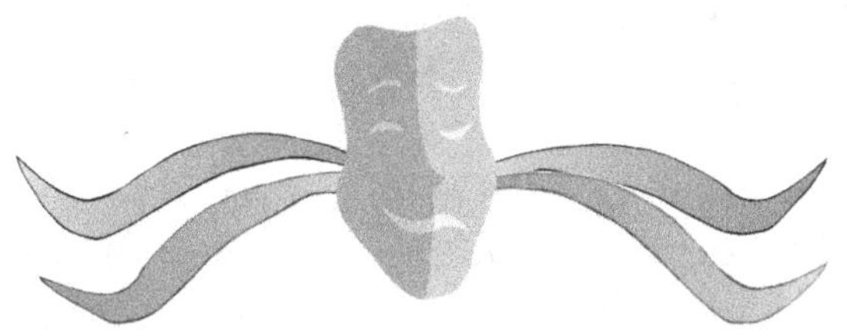

EPILOGUE

(Where we tie up every last little loose end – KNOT!)

CLEANING UP WAS EXACTLY THE right description, Thony reflected.

In addition to some seven thousand people who needed to be unenchanted by the unicorns, there were several hundred more Raven-troopers who needed to be sorted into the willing and the enspelled. The enspelled needed their *compulsion* spells broken, and something needed to be done with the rest.

Since those spells seemed *not* to be dissipating with Raven'sWing's passing, there were some *thousands* of other troops spread out around the south-central plains. And one might only guess at what proportion of *them* had followed the Raven banner by choice instead of by force. Nor what such men and women might do now that they had no leader *and* no money.

Raven'sWing's nascent empire would most likely shatter quickly back into its component parts… though after what painful contortions it couldn't yet be guessed.

And then there was the town of Flowerdust, which had been rather shabbily treated by both Raven'sWing and the youthful defenders these last few days. The Floridustians seemed ready to bounce back rather easily at least – the former mayor had turned up to reclaim his mansion almost before Stillheart had been out of sight.

"I suppose it was too much to hope that the *compulsion* spells would actually fade with Raven'sWing dead," Thony commented to his friends.

There wasn't a lot for them to do just yet.

The Dark-elves were collecting the Raven-troops and sorting them and breaking spells. Lady Opalsinger had made it clear that they were spreading goodwill to make up for the evil impressions that Shalladra Stillheart had given everyone of their kind.

The unicorns were moving through the masses of enchanted people, breaking *those* spells one at a time. It helped that the green-eyed zombie-people were all attracted to the horned equines, and that they all were sort of standing and swaying in place since the last set of instructions and prodding they'd been given had apparently long since run out.

But it still took a minute or two for each person.

And then, the freed human tended to collapse to their knees. And look around themselves in confusion.

The mayor had people following the unicorns and extracting the freed people, though where they would put them all was... kind of undecided.

"At least they don't seem to remember anything after they were enchanted," Amanita commented, and her brother nodded.

Prince Daffyd had been introduced around, but he seemed willing to stay quiet and in the background. Though it had come out in conversation that going hunting for Amanita had been *his* idea. There was a story there, but one for later.

Julanna and Kamauri were both alive and recovering.

It turned out that in addition to being the God of Lies, Aleri was also the God of Healing. And Politics. And Rogues more generally.

It was a weird set of 'responsibilities' in Thony's opinion, but he supposed it wasn't up to him.

Julanna was a little put out that she hadn't gotten to do anything particularly useful in the grand finale. She was also all mixed up about Valderon Raven'sWing. Apparently, she'd had stronger feelings for him than even she had realized.

Istevan had the baby in his hands – she seemed to be chewing on his fingers – and was trailing Davril around as the young banker worked with the mayor of Flowerdust to sort out logistics for what to do with all these unenchanted people and former Raven-troops. They were discussing an economic recovery plan for Flowerdust in the interstices of the rest of the work. Jost was staying at Davril's shoulder, taking mental notes and absorbing everything as fast as he could.

The other street-kids had gone off to the Mercenaries' Guildhouse with Evrien. There were a number of mercenaries – such as Tethro Fishglitter, who had formerly been the Keeper of the Flowerdust Guildhouse – who had been released from Raven'sWing's *compulsion* spells. They were dazed and ill – *they* remembered everything they had done. It was hard for them to believe that they'd really had no choice...

Aleri was wandering around everywhere he was needed, sensing pain and anguish as any normal non-divine Healer would, but able to fix more than any mere mortal.

Dae was sticking to Kamauri and Daennor. The young woman was still incredibly weak from blood-loss, but all of her injuries had been Healed without so much as a scar. She was complaining about that mildly, since how was anyone supposed to believe her without scars for evidence – Daennor stopped her complaints with a kiss. He was keeping both the girl and the woman he loved close.

Thony had fallen in with Amanita and her brother more or less by default.

Although he did have to admit it felt like a very *secure* place to be, given that the troupe of small, fierce women surrounded all three of them. They were sitting on the side of the marble stairs into the mansion now, watching the various groups and commotions and trying to stay out of the way of people running in and out. The women warriors were too busy watching everyone else suspiciously, so it was almost a bit of privacy, even though they were out in the open.

"Did you know Puck's real name?" Thony asked.

Amanita shook her head.

"Or that he was a *demi-God?*" Thony asked.

She gave him a quizzical look. "I mean, he told us that. He told us Queen Snowmistral is a Goddess. And that he's Her Son."

Thony glared at her. "You both said he's a *fairy-prince*. Prince of the Snow-Fairies, or something. And he talked about the God of Mischief from that other world – Eyola – like, I don't know..."

Amanita rolled her eyes. "It's not like the *one* thing precludes the *other,* Thony."

"So, what's he the demi-God *of?*" Thony demanded.

Puck himself strolled up right then, still in his fancy outfit. The women warriors looked very disgruntled, but let him pass into the inner circle they were protecting. "I should have thought that would be obvious, Thony. I'm the God of Mischief and Pranks. It's why Aleri and I get along so well. Our roles sort of dove-tail."

The God of Healing looked up from where he was doing... *something* with a group of people on the far side of the courtyard, and looked over at them as if he'd heard his name. Puck waved him back to what he was doing.

"Well, he's a lot more useful in the cleaning up stages," the fairy-prince-*cum*-demi-God said cheerfully. "At this point, I get to just sit back and watch."

"Hmmn." Thony looked at him sort of sideways. He didn't *seem* terribly different than before.

"*I* haven't changed, Thony," Puck pointed out with a grin. "All that's different is your perspective. Speaking of which, where's your unicorn-maiden outfit? I thought the plan was that you were going to be wearing that while I was gone. And *staying out of trouble?*"

Amanita rolled her eyes as Thony mumbled something about having left it in his pack. "Like you even thought that was in the realms of possibility."

Her brother seemed to have an extremely ironic expression.

Puck's grin grew even broader. "Actually, no, I didn't. And I figured that if I sort of told you to stay *out* of trouble, you'd be that much more likely to get *into* it. Though I must say you exceeded all my expectations. So, you can really chock up the way things went today to how awesome you guys were at *not* doing what I told you."

"Hunh?" Even Amanita seemed baffled by that.

But Thony was frowning as certain things sort of clicked together in his head.

"That lady who turned back and forth into a unicorn," he began.

"*Quellarie,*" Amanita corrected him.

"Fine, *Quellarie.* She said Power is always a matter of belief. And that your followers – I guess that would be me and Amanita and Dae – had built you a sturdy *belief-base.*" Thony looked at Puck thoughtfully. "You were stronger because of us?"

Puck gave him an approving smile as Istevan wandered over with the baby in his arms. The warrior women – the royal escort of the Prince of Pathremir – seemed to simultaneously trust and distrust the tall man. Thony had noticed they didn't seem to like tall people, but apparently the happy baby girl that he was jouncing in his arms made up for that to some degree.

Daennor followed him with an arm around Kamauri. Dae was under her other shoulder. The warrior-women seemed much more willing to let the three of *them* into the circle.

"Not just the three of you, of course," Puck answered. "You got all the street-kids involved in your pranks. You got them to *believe* that what they were doing could make a difference. That *pranks* could – or at least *might* – win a war."

He flexed an arm. "I don't think I've *ever* felt so strong. It was that belief which let me break through the barrier that Stillheart and Raven'sWing had placed around this grove of the Fairy-Wood. I barely made it out with the two of you kids the first time – and coming *back* was utterly impossible until you built me up a following that I could work with."

"Well, then you should give the credit to Prince Thony here," Daennor said, looking up from settling Kamauri on the steps. "Kamauri and Davril and I were all set to get the kids to safety, and then he gave this impassioned speech about why they *had* to stay. And why pranks had to be the main thrust of the effort."

Thony flushed as Amanita and Dae nodded.

"I... was freaking out about Shalladra Stillheart being a Dark-elf," Amanita admitted. "And the giant army of zombies bearing down on us. I was just about ready to head for home."

Her brother snorted. "Nice to know you have a modicum of common sense under all that thick hair somewhere, sis. Did you pick it up somewhere in your travels?"

"Your Highness," one of the women warriors said reprovingly, and Prince Daffyd dropped his eyes immediately, though his grin stuck.

Amanita jabbed him in the ribs, but didn't disagree.

"I..." Dae looked at Daennor and Kamauri. "I had just figured out that I had a family. If Thony hadn't spoken up... and *they* wanted to go..."

The poufy haired man grinned at her, then at Kamauri. "Just think of all the time we wasted chasing her all over the northern plains, love."

"I don't want to be stuck back at Sonoro's," Dae warned. "I *am* still a mercenary."

"*We* are mercenaries," Kamauri said, though her voice was still weak. "We'll do whatever we do... together." She looked a little wistfully out of the gate to where the unicorns were still at work, but she seemed content to have Daennor holding her.

"Though... maybe we can take jobs that are... more steady and less risky," the young woman added with a wince. "I think I've had enough to do with evil magick for a lifetime. Or maybe *two* lifetimes."

Despite that request, Dae snuggled happily under her friend's arm. Daennor looked like his world was coming together.

Puck clapped a hand on Thony's shoulder, making him step forwards a little since he hadn't been braced. "So, it's all on you, Thony."

The young prince rolled his eyes. "Hardly."

Julanna came into the circle with the rest of them and reached up to take the baby from Istevan. Apparently, a *woman* coming in close to the Prince and Princess of Pathremir wasn't a problem for their guards. Or maybe it was that Julanna had been named a Bard.

Daphne went into her arms easily enough, but she cried out "Papa!" and reached out eagerly for Davril when he and Jost approached. He'd looked like he was trying to decide between being suave or stubborn to get past the ring of women warriors, but when his eyes went straight to Daphne, they let him – and even Jost – by without a challenge.

Julanna's eyes were sad as she yielded her over, but she didn't say anything.

Davril's whole face lit up as he took Daphne in his arms. But he wasn't so completely enamored that he didn't lean in to kiss his cousin on the cheek, nor to walk over to Istevan and nudge the tall man until he got a long arm draped possessively around his shoulders.

Istevan chuckled as Davril leaned against him peacefully. He offered Daphne his finger to chew on again, which she did with great gusto and a small wince from the tall mercenary. "Well, your efforts paid off more than anything that those of us who were *professionals* did. All our efforts to stir up an insurrection in the ranks – and when Shalladra offered the boys money, it didn't do a damn bit of good. Pranks and esoteric banking practices carried the day."

"Repossession is hardly esoteric," Davril commented absently as Daphne reacquainted herself with his hair and ears and nose. Jost nodded emphatically.

"What we did *un*intentionally made a difference, though," Daennor said in a teasing tone directed at Kamauri, who blushed.

"Yeah, what *happened* in there to set everything off?" Dae asked. "I mean, Jost caught us up on the banking stuff, but then what?"

Istevan winced. "Well... Shalladra had decided that I'm... not as young as she likes her men. Why she set her eye on *Daennor*, I don't know..."

Thony remembered what he'd seen of Lord Aspenheart in the Fairy Queen's Court and guessed it might be that Daennor – with his pale, poufy hair and deeply tanned skin – looked like a... *tamer* version of a Light-elf. One that Stillheart could dominate without much effort. Istevan, come to think of it, had nearly the coloring of a Dark-elf except for his golden tan that looked like it would mostly fade in Winter.

Pets, the evil Dark-elf-woman had called them...

"Because he's an unmitigated *flirt,* is why," Kamauri said with some asperity. "He *flirts* with every woman he sees."

"Not any*more,*" the poufy-haired man assured her, and Kamauri looked somewhat mollified as she muttered, "We'll see."

"She's not wrong, though," Daennor admitted. "It's... a bad habit I'd gotten into, I suppose. After the morning review, it was pretty obvious why Captain Stillheart was sending for me–"

"She said the most... the most *rude* things to him at the review," Kamauri said fiercely. "Right there in *public.*"

Daennor was looking a bit red. "Well, not so much *rude* as... *inappropriate.* She didn't know I belonged to you, sweetheart. We'd tried not to let anyone see that, remember?"

Kamauri sniffed at that.

"Shalladra wasn't too happy when the troopers brought up Kamauri along with Daennor," Istevan went on. "The two of them started arguing, and then–"

"I was about to be put in gaol for insubordination," Kamauri sighed.

"She's such a *rules-follower* usually," Daennor said fondly... though his smile was shading over into a rather self-satisfied smirk. "I had never guessed she would fight for *me* like that. For *Dae*, certainly... but not me."

"Silly," Kamauri reached a tired arm up to bop him on the nose. "For either of you. Always and ever."

Dae looked... incredibly content.

"*Any*ways," Istevan went on. "Julanna and Davril were in the next room with Va– Valderon Raven'sWing, going over options for finances. Shalladra had been keeping me away from Davril as much as possible – and Julanna away from Val.

"She kind of looked at me like *I* was supposed to do something about Kamauri..."

Daennor winced. "Somehow she'd figured out we were all former students of Sonoro's."

Davril rolled *his* eyes at that. "'Somehow.' Do you even hear yourselves? You had to fill out some paperwork when you were drafted and the two of you used your *real names*. She and Valderon were *Evil,* not *stupid.*"

"That still doesn't explain why she would think *I* could do anything," Istevan argued as Daennor muttered *not-quite-quietly* enough to be under his breath about how neither of their names was particularly uncommon and trying to remember to answer to a new name would have had its own risks.

"Dark-elves are very hierarchy-driven," Puck inserted. "You all saw how quickly Stillheart backed down when Opalsinger showed up. Even though she was planning to overthrow and *kill* Opalsinger on her way to the Fairy Queen's throne. Likely she saw you as senior to the others."

"Hmmn." Istevan looked thoughtful. "Well, while Shalladra was looking at me to do *something,* Kamauri whipped out her sword–"

"I hate swords," the young woman muttered. "Always feel so clumsy with one of them."

"–and she knocked over this odd silver rose in a glass case that Val had brought along with him when he came in," Istevan went on. "The case shattered, Shalladra lunged for it..." and *he* smirked a little now. "So, I, ah, '*accidentally*' stepped on the rose..."

Davril snickered. "Duse will be *so* disappointed in you, Stev."

Julanna wrapped her arms around herself and looked down. "I think that was the moment Val cried out. He... suddenly there were lines in his face, though at that instant I thought it was just how he was shouting. And... there hadn't been any white in his hair when... when I met him. Two years ago." Her beautiful voice trembled. "It was *only two years* ago. I didn't know that he was... *what* he was. He was so sweet to *me...*"

One of the warrior women – their chief, Thony rather thought – looked over her shoulder with a look of pity. "It's not just evil sorcerers, lass. There's hardly a woman hasn't had her heartbroken if she's unwise enough to settle it on a man who doesn't know his place."

Her dark glance touched on all the males besides Daennor, who looked rather wry at his exemption, but *stayed* on her prince. Prince Daffyd's hands twitched as if he'd *like* to clench his fists but didn't quite dare. He stepped behind his little sister as if to take *her* protection, and the woman smiled slightly and went back to glowering out at the chaos in the courtyard.

"Valderon was sweet *on* you," Davril told her, ignoring the interjection. His tone was very dry, but his expression gentle. "And vice-versa. People in love don't think sense, Julanna. Jess saw what he was – or some of it anyways. *She* knew he wasn't good for you. It's why she sent to me for help."

"Good for you or... *good,*" Istevan added reluctantly. "I could see it as well, though you're right. He was utterly charming when he wanted to be."

He cast a glance at the other side of the mansion's entrance where nothing was left but a heap of fabric that no one seemed to want to disturb. Thony had gathered that the sorcerer's body had collapsed bit by bit until there was nothing left but dust.

It was... unnerving, even after the explanation about how Raven'sWing was over three hundred years old had come to light. It was also somewhat unreassuring. If you didn't have a body to bury, could you really be sure he was dead and *gone?*

And... Thony wrapped his arms around *himself,* unconsciously echoing Julanna. It had been just over two weeks ago that he'd ridden pillion into this courtyard on Valderon Raven'sWing's horse. He'd had his arms wrapped around the man's warm waist and had been treated kindly. The sorcerer had patted him on the head like Papa would and said – *twice* – that he wished he had a son like Thony.

Jost was giving him a worried look.

"Valderon rushed into the next room and saw the flower," Davril continued the story after the awkward silence had stretched on too long. "He fell to his knees and started trying to put it to rights. And..." he hesitated, looking at Julanna, "there was a sort of... *pulling in* feeling. Like he was trying to draw all of his Power together to... to save his own life. I think that's when he lost control over Stillheart. That *love* spell..."

"Is that what it was?" Daennor asked. "I hadn't seen them together in private before, but it was clear *something* had changed." He glanced at the silently weeping Julanna. "But if he dropped his spells – why didn't all these other ones–" the poufy-haired mercenary gestured out at towards the enchanted troops and the enspelled troops and... the Bard. "Why didn't all these others fall apart as well?"

All eyes went to Puck, who could, presumably, explain this better than anyone else.

The newly-revealed God of Mischief tucked his thumbs in his belt and sighed. "We'll have to get the final story on that from Lady Opalsinger, but I suspect she'll tell us that *most* of those men and women were *not* under *compulsions*. And the ones that were... it's a subtle trick, but Life generates magick. You can tie a person's own small spark into a self-renewing loop to maintain a spell – it takes a lot longer, but it means you don't need to use your own to maintain the spell – rather like lighting a fire with a candle."

"*That's* overstating it." Aleri had somehow appeared in the protected space – wafting by the women warriors without their notice, to judge by the disgruntled looks. "Fires can spread, and these spells don't. Healers use this trick more than most anyone else," he explained. "There's no way most Healers could manage even the *smallest* Healings without the help of the person's own Life-force."

"It was a *metaphor*, Aleri," Puck rolled his eyes.

The God of Healing... and, apparently, Lies and Rogues and Politics... snorted. "Right. Anyways. The large-scale enchantment on the Darjeeling people is entirely different. Raven'sWing tricked the inhabitants of Castle Mind into giving him that spell – they thought he was a theoretical researcher like they are. And he determined how to Power it using a unicorn-skill that he weaseled out of Quellarie Unicorn-Born similarly. Stillheart had apparently clued him in to the fact that unicorns obtain all *their* magick from the spaces between worlds. She didn't know how to do it herself – and it actually *was* a sort of amazing feat that he was able to tie that Power in at such long distances from even a small scrap of the Fairy Wood."

He frowned as Thony wondered if anyone else here than the demi-Gods had heard of this 'Castle Mind.' "Quellarie is working on sorting *that* out, I believe. And she has a couple representatives of the Castle with her to do it. But the spell was essentially Powered by unicorn-magick, so I'm sure she'll figure it out. Eventually."

"So *that's* why Raven'sWing smelled like a sweaty unicorn!" Thony burst out before he thought better of it, and everyone stared at him.

"Um, *what?*" Amanita asked.

Thony flushed. "It was only when I was extending my senses like Twinklestar taught me. You know, sharpening my sight and hearing and such. There was a sort of weird smell of... stale unicorn-sweat whenever I was focusing in Raven'sWing's direction."

"You did *what?*" Amanita's expression was shocked. "But *you* can't do stuff like that!"

"He did it, though," Dae agreed. She looked at Jost, who nodded. "He even managed to make it work for Jost and me when we were watching... so we could see..." She gave Kamauri a stricken look and her words trailed off.

"When we were watchin' th'fight," Jost finished for her. "Didn' notice no weird smells, though I was a mite bit busy payin' attention t'other things."

"It went away when he died," Thony muttered, feeling flustered.

He didn't want to look at Amanita, who appeared both dumbfounded and *betrayed*. He wasn't even sure what she was upset *about*. Hadn't she said *she* had some sort of magick? And that lots of royals did?

Daennor looked between Amanita and Thony for a moment, then looked back at the demi-Gods. "That explains the troops. What about...?" He waved a little in Julanna's direction.

Aleri's expression went very soft. "That wasn't a *spell,* Daennor."

Julanna crumpled a bit as she got a mix of sympathetic, horrified, and disgusted looks. Istevan stepped away from Davril and the baby to pull her into an embrace that hid her face from everyone else.

"She's still very young," he told everyone else severely. "Not that age prevents one from making mistakes. *Lack* of it simply means you haven't had your own chances to screw up so badly. *Yet.*"

The younger people all flushed and that chief warrior woman looked at him approvingly... if still seeming rather disgruntled. The rest of the troupe of Pathremiri guards were doing a rather better job of keeping their stoic expressions on and pretending they weren't listening.

Julanna lifted her head to look around a little. "I... I did so *well* in Selavan. I thought... Val *loved* me. I *know* he did. I thought... I thought..." She started crying again. "He... maybe if we'd brought Daphne in sooner. He was so... so *happy* to see her. And then he started crying because he wouldn't get to watch her grow up and then..." She was crying almost too hard to speak. "I didn't do *anything* useful. All I did was make it all *worse...*"

Istevan gathered her in again, running a hand down her hair and murmuring gentle, reassuring sounds. Davril looked guilty and stepped closer to put an arm around her, though he had to step back again when Daphne wanted to 'play' with her mother's long, unbound red-gold hair.

"Actually, you did a great deal, Julanna," Aleri said. "Your presence weakened the bonds between Raven'sWing and Stillheart – which *he* was maintaining at that point for *his* advantage. As she said at the end there, *she* no longer needed *him*, but he'd managed to tie their lives together using the spell bound into that flower.

"And it was your injury – and Kamauri's – that allowed Puck to summon me here." he added. "More yours, though. I'm... more or less Bound to the Merutian Sea for a variety of reasons. And this is pretty far inland. As Stillheart also noted. But our dear Aunt, the Sea-Queen, has a soft spot for Her pirates – *and* their princess. And because I could come for you, I could help a great many others."

This didn't seem to mollify Julanna a great deal. She hid her face in Istevan's chest again as everyone stared at her again, this time for being a pirate princess.

"I think we've just about taken this conversation as far as we can," Aleri said. "Kamauri and Julanna need to rest and finish recuperating."

He looked expectantly at Puck, but it was Davril who answered.

"The mayor has offered all of us a place to stay in the mansion, if we want it. He's setting up tents and billets outside the town for the various troops. And, last we were talking..." he looked out past their circle of protective warriors, "he was trying to figure out where to put the troops who weren't enspelled. There aren't enough pickle cellars in the whole town to hold them all. And we don't want any of the ones who were herding the Darjeeling people to get away."

Aleri's expression grew stern. *"I'll* take care of *them."*

He seemed... suddenly taller and more ominous than the rather congenial Healer he'd presented himself as so far. Thony wouldn't want to cross *any* Healer, but especially not *this* one, *now.*

The demi-God took a stride away then looked back. "You know that the job isn't done, right? Raven'sWing had the rest of Darjil's population left behind – babes and toddlers and the old and sick. They were enchanted as well, so they don't have functioning life-processes – they aren't eating or sleeping or eliminating – but they need their spells broken. The unicorns will go there and do that, but even when the rest of these people go home, a good half of them aren't going to be terribly functional. They'll need... a great deal of help."

Davril lifted his chin. "I'll see that it's done. Money is good for – how did Stillheart put it? For getting humans to do things."

Aleri gave him a serious smile and a nod and headed off. To deal with the most criminal of the Raven-troops, presumably.

"I guess we're staying on a while, love," Davril said to Istevan.

The tall mercenary nodded. "It's too soon to go home to Selavan yet anyways. Darjil after this, then?"

"And probably Vel-Garsh," Davril added thoughtfully. "That's where the closest large bank in the area is, so that's where I need to roust up resources. And I have this apprentice to train." He grinned at Jost, who looked startled.

The tall mercenary looked at his husband ruefully. "Hmmn. And it's coming on towards Summer. In the South-Central plains. And you want to take us right up to the borders of the Muana Desert.

What was it you were saying a bit ago, about people who are in love not thinking clearly?" Istevan heaved a sigh as he looked at Davril.

"I swore not to go any farther south than this after I campaigned on Summer in Ladoor. I had to replace all my fighting leathers," Istevan added mournfully. "They were irretrievably sweat-rotted by the end of the campaign, though I got them washed out whenever there was enough water. Goddess, but I hate hot weather."

Puck seemed to find the tall mercenary's statement absolutely hilarious for some reason.

Istevan glared at him for a moment, then focused on Daennor and Kamauri and Dae. "There's all those unemployed Raven troops wandering around the south-central plains. Would the three of you care to come along and help me take care of everyone?"

Daennor looked dubious, then relieved, as Kamauri nodded. "Just... just give me a few days..."

"Of course," Istevan nodded. "We're not going anywhere soon, are we, Dav?"

"Not for at least a week," Davril agreed.

Dae frowned suddenly. "Amanita hired me to be *her* bodyguard."

Amanita gave her a dark look as the chief warrior woman gave the mercenette – and then her princess – a very dubious look.

"Hey," Dae said offendedly as she noted the look. "I did a *great* job. I managed to get her to stay out of Flowerdust almost the entire time."

Amanita gave the mercenette a narrow-eyed gaze. "I *hired* you to protect *both* Thony and me. And *he* was in here the *whole* time. *Most* of that time in super-danger in the mansion to hear you guys tell it."

"Where I could keep an eye on him," Dae retorted, with a toss of her head. Her high ponytail bounced dramatically. "And I... I sub-contracted Jost and the other street-kids to help with that."

Thony raised an eyebrow at Jost, who gave him a half-apologetic shrug and a smirk. No, Jost hadn't minded deceiving the young prince about why he was sticking so close.

"You stuck me taking care of the *baby!*" Amanita yelled.

Well, it could be worse. At least Dae wasn't mentioning–

"I was *working* on Thony's plan to get *you* to safety," Dae continued on vehemently. "I took you in to meet Evrien so she could honestly say she'd seen you and send word, and I even had the grown-ups and the unicorns helping out!"

Oh. She *was* going to mention it.

Thony took a large, judicious step away from the seething Pathremiri not-quite-Crown Princess.

The look of absolute glee on her brother's face wasn't helping.

"Well done, young sister," the chief warrior woman said hastily, preempting an imminent Amanita-explosion. "And we got the word your Guild sent us so that we could arrive here in time. But she's ours now to guard. Come talk to me later and we'll discuss your compensation. Unless she already gave you a number?"

Dae shook her head, but looked a little disappointed. "I wanted to be the one to return her to her grandmother. I figured that bringing in the Lost Princess of Pathremir would make my reputation."

Daennor snickered and reached out to floof her ponytail. "I think you already have enough of a *reputation,* munchkin."

"We'll see that you're given adequate credit," the warrior woman told Dae. "It's clear you're, ah, *needed* in the south."

"I am, aren't I?" Dae preened. Kamauri and Daennor smiled at each other behind her back.

"We will start for home in three days, Your Highnesses," the warrior woman informed Amanita and Daffyd. "We will take rooms in this house as the Selavani banker suggested until then."

"Yes, Zaja," Amanita actually *backed down,* to Thony's surprise.

But where did that leave Thony...? It was clear there weren't any princesses with rich and powerful fathers in this region – or Raven'sWing would never have been able to overrun it so easily. But he didn't know anyone else here, and his friends were going their separate ways...

A friendly hand clapped his back.

"Thony and I will be traveling with *you,*" Puck informed the Pathremiri contingent with a grin. "My Mother wants to meet him."

MAP that the Amanita 'borrowed' from Captain Stillheart

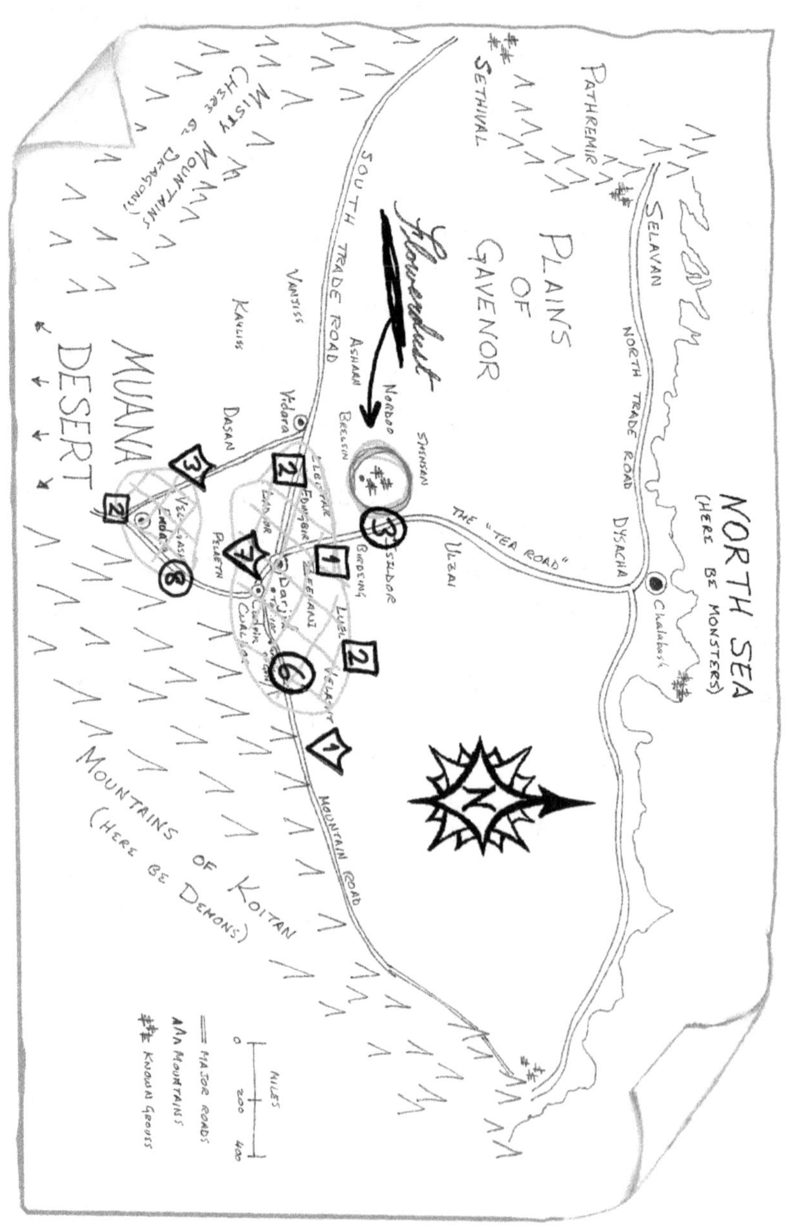

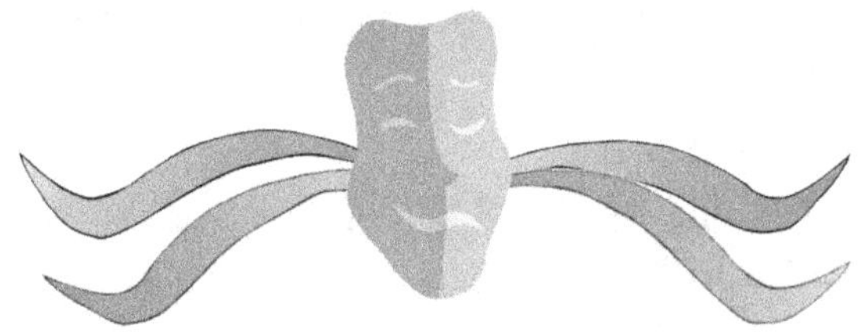

Index of Characters

<u>**Important People in Flowerdust when this Book Begins:**</u>

- Amanita (a.k.a. 'Nita, a.k.a. the Lost Princess of Pathremir). Thony's friend and co-prankster.
- Clarick. The nine-year-old son of the innkeeper of the Inn of the Starred Hoof in Flowerdust.
- Dae Goldeneyes. Youngest mercenary ever. A graduate of Sonoro's School of Soldiering.
- Daennor Cat'sFoot. Mercenary. Partner of Kamauri Spiralspear. A graduate of Sonoro's School of Soldiering.
- Daphne. Julanna Silversea's baby daughter.
- Davril (a.k.a., Dav). An associate of Julanna Silversea.
- Erroth. A Raven-soldier.
- Evrien Quickfoot. A very old mercenary. Temporary Guildhouse-Keeper in Flowerdust. A graduate of Arazia's Academy at Arms.
- Fayorn. A captain in Valderon Raven'sWing's army.
- Istevan Highblade (called Slyblade, a.k.a Stev). A mercenary serving as a lieutenant in the Raven-troops in Flowerdust. Also a spy helping Julanna Silversea. A graduate of Sonoro's School of Soldiering.
- Jost. Leader of a gang of street-kids in Flowerdust.
- Julanna Silversea. A Bard spying on Valderon Raven'sWing's forces in Flowerdust. She has a nursing baby.
- Kamauri Spiralspear. Mercenary and unicorn-maiden. Bound to Rainsparkle, partner with Daennor Cat'sFoot. Friend of Dae Goldeneyes. A graduate of Sonoro's School of Soldiering.
- Magritte. Clarick's sister, the fifteen-year-old daughter of the innkeeper at the Inn of the Starred Hoof.

- Rainsparkle. Unicorn. Bound to Kamauri Spiralspear.
- Rema. A street-kid.
- SAndy. Dae's horse.
- Shalladra Stillheart (called 'Icicleblood'). Valderon Raven'sWing's Captain-Mayoress in Flowerdust.
- Silverfoot. Thony's rather-too-energetic horse.
- Skylir. A street-kid in Jost's gang.
- Sterevor, Sergeant. A Raven-soldier. Raven'sWing's aide-de-camp.
- Thony (Prince Anthony Devinthal the Affable and the Affirmative). Crown Prince of Aldyrwald. Younger brother of Princess Joanna and Princess Priscilla. Unicorn-maiden Bound to Twinklestar.
- Twinklestar. Unicorn, Bound to Thony, friend of Amanita.
- Valderon Raven'sWing. An Evil Wizard.

Some Fairly Cool People Back on Thony's homeworld:

- Annabel (Queen Annabel of Aldyrwald). Wife of King Bill; mother of Joanna, Priscilla, and Thony.
- Bill (King Bill / King William Devinthal of Aldyrwald). Husband of Queen Annabel. Father of Joanna, Priscilla, and Thony.
- Eswith (Master Eswith). Protocol master of the Aldyrwald royal family. (Okay, he's not cool, but he gets mentioned in this book.)
- Jeremy. Centaur, husband of Priscilla.
- Joanna (Princess Joanna Devinthal the Wise and Wonderful). Eldest-born princess of Aldyrwald. Daughter of King Bill and Queen Annabel; sister of Priscilla and Thony. Wife of Prince Sir Roger. Goddess of the Earth.
- Priscilla (Princess Priscilla Devinthal the Bright-Eyed and Bushy-Tailed, aka Prissy). Second-born princess of Aldyrwald. Daughter of King Bill and Queen Annabel; sister of Joanna and Thony. Wife of Jeremy. Goddess of Animals (including humans) and of Love/Fertility.
- Roger (Prince of Schwannsberg and Knight). Second-born son of King Richie and Queen Janet;. Husband of Joanna. God of Air.
- Tad/Thaddeus. Stablemaster to Aldyrwald Castle, Amanita's boss.
- Wes. Amanita and Thony's friend, a stableboy.

People Who are Elsewhere when we get started, but are Still Important Anyways:

- Altaba. A Heroine or Goddess from the Mountains of Koitan.
- Aspenheart, Lord. Prince of the Light-elves, an attendant of the Fairy Queen.
- Aleri. Demi-God of Healing, Lies, Rogues… and Politics. Son of the Goddess Sifwisa of the Trade-Winds.
- Daffyd, Prince. Amanita's brother.
- Duse. A friend of Davril and Istevan's who is fond of flowers.
- Falmyra, fal-Princess. Princess of Pathremir (not in the line of succession), Duchess of Elaarwen in Ilseador. Amanita's aunt.
- Girona Starshine. A student wizard from Happy-Go-Lucky on Eyola, cousin to Midele.
- Goddess of Light and Darkness. Goddess of Selavan and Pathremir.
- Jessina Keetering (a.k.a. Jess). One of Davril's sisters.
- Kyri Keetering. One of Davril's sisters.
- Lilysong. The Fairy Queen… also the Great Goddess Who Guards the Ways Between the Worlds (a.k.a., the Waywalker).
- Lochea, Disciple of the Goddess of Light and Darkness, co-Disciple of the Lord of Light with King Mithral.
- Lord of Light. God of Selavan.
- Midele Featherspray. A novice priestess of the Golden Sphinx on Eyola, Girona's cousin.
- Mithral. King of Selavan.
- Naeel, Prince-Consort. Amanita's dad. Husband of Princess-Heir Ytheril, son of Eldest-Princess Reyalla.
- Namarina, Queen. Queen of Pathremir, Amanita's maternal grandmother.
- Opalsinger, Lady. Princess of the Dark-elves, attendant of the Fairy Queen.
- Puck. The 'King of Pranksters', a fairy attendant of Queen Lilysong.
- Quellarie. Someone who advised Amanita on how to travel the Fairy Wood.
- Reyalla, Eldest-Princess. Amanita's paternal grandmother.

- Ryan. Davril's uncle, Julanna's father. A 'captain' in the Western Ocean.
- Taridanae Foxheart (a.k.a. the Fox). Headmistress of Sonoro's School of Soldiering. Granddaughter of Sonoro.
- Tethro Fishglitter. Former Mercenary Guildhouse-Keeper in Flowerdust. A conscript into the Raven-troops.
- Ytheril, Princess. Princess-Heir of Pathremir, daughter of Queen Namarina, Amanita's mother, wife of Prince Naeel.
- Zaja. A warrior woman from Pathremir.

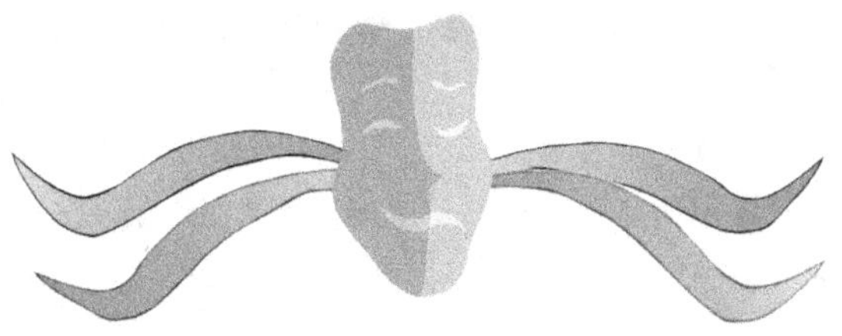

Index of Places

<u>**On Thony's homeworld:**</u>

- Aldyrwald. The country where Thony is Crown Prince. Three linked valleys, centrally located in the mountain region.

<u>**Other worlds:**</u>

- Eyola. The world that Midele and Girona are from.
- Fairy Wood. Ruled by Queen Lilysong. A forest that bridges the gap between many worlds. Only the fairies and elves know how to navigate it by nature, though others can learn.
- Happy-Go-Lucky. Girona's homeland on Eyola.

<u>**Amanita's homeworld:**</u>

- Brelsin. A country in the plains that regularly gets overrun by invaders. On Amanita's homeworld. East of Pathremir, Sethival, Selavan, Plains of Gavenor, Dawil, the Merutian Sea.
- Canador. A country on the North Coast where Dae Goldeneyes had serves as bodyguard to the young crown prince, Harper.
- Central Plains. The wide, grassy area that contains Brelsin and a number of other city-states that are perpetually at odds.
- Darjil. A town about ten days' ride from Flowerdust.
- Dawil. A prosperous country very far to the west of Flowerdust.
- Dynsfyor. Largest city on the North Coast. Home of Davril and Istevan.
- Flowerdust. A small nowhere-sort of town in Brelsin.
- Inn of the Starred Hoof. An inn in Flowerdust where only the desperate and down-on-their-luck ever stay.
- Ladoor. A city on the southern Central Plains. South of Flowerdust.

- Merutian Sea (aka 'The Western Ocean). An ocean very far to the west of Flowerdust.
- Misty Mountains. The mountain-range where Pathremir is located.
- Mountains of Koitan. Where Arazia's Academy at Arms is located.
- Muana Desert. A vast desert located to the south of the Central Plains.
- Pathremir. A country in the Misty Mountains. Amanita's homeland
- Plains of Gavenor. An area west of Brelsin.
- Selavan. A country ruled by King Mithral. West of Brelsin, adjacent to Pathremir and the Plains of Gavenor. Includes a famous school for Bards and an enclave for unicorn-maidens.
- Sonoro's School of Soldiering. Famous school for mercenaries. Graduates include the current headmistress, Taridanae Foxheart, Istevan Highblade, Kamauri Spiralspear, Daennor Cat'sFoot, and Dae Goldeneyes.
- University of the White Crystal Dome. An institution of higher learning located between Pathremir and Dawil in the Misty Mountains.
- Vel-Garsh. A large city located near the Muana Desert.

THONY
and the Much-Anticipated Adventure

MANGALA MCNAMARA

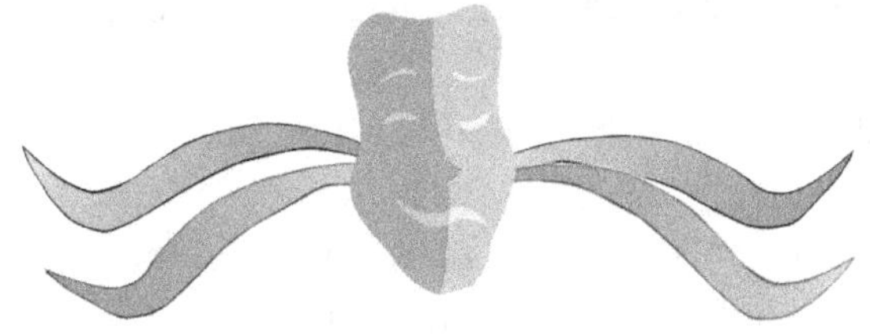

Chapter ONE

A Princely Punch

CROWN PRINCE ANTHONY DEVINTHAL THE AFFABLE (and the Affirmative) of the valley-kingdom of Aldyrwald – an inconsequential kingdom on a substandard continent on an unimportant world –slouched along a corridor of his father's castle, kicking a small rock that someone *(probably him)* had tracked into the castle earlier.

It wasn't *fair.*

His parents were ridiculously overprotective – all because Thony was Heir to the Throne. Queen Annabel had vapors when Thony went out of sight of the castle, even into the *very safe and well-maintained* woods beyond the village. King Bill started to *harumph* and look pale when Thony casually suggested a visit to the next valley-kingdom over, the one ruled by King Bill's best friend who also happened to be the father-in-law of Thony's older sister, Joanna – even *without* Thony hinting that a detour to check out the local giant along the way might be interesting.

Being a crown prince was *seriously boring.*

And anytime he tried to do something to *make* things a little less boring he ended up in trouble.

Today being a case in point.

It was his mother's fault really. She knew better than to come into his rooms.

For goodness' sake, the *servants* knew better than to come into his rooms.

Thony hadn't even been *in* there when Mama had opened the door, taken one look, screamed, and fainted.

Someone had been sensible enough to summon Joanna.

Someone *else* had tracked down Thony and seen him into the throneroom to face his father for a little chat about what King Bill called his 'misdemeanor'. *("You're the one who's meaner!" Thony had yelled in what was, perhaps, not the best display of behavior for a young man who was a few months away from fifteen. No matter that his parents seemed intent on treating him like he was five.)*

So now he was stuck with a fortnight of double-length protocol lessons with Master Eswith – the excruciatingly boring teacher who had reportedly convinced the eternally patient and polite Joanna to threaten to run away from home. *(That was the rumor anyways, passed on from Thony's middle sister, Priscilla. Joanna had been out from under Master Eswith's gentle care years before either of them had begun, though, so how Prissy knew this bit of intelligence was somewhat questionable.)*

An hour with Master Eswith was bad enough and what Thony had to suffer through on a regular basis. By two hours, the young prince was usually falling asleep and the 'gentle master' was beating him about the head and hands with a wooden ruler to *prove* that Thony had fallen asleep and Thony was plotting vengeance on Eswith and whichever parent had stuck him in double-length lessons. The one time King Bill had sentenced him to *three*-hour long lessons, Thony had plotted vengeance on the entire castle.

No one had ever considered doing that again, even though it had been almost five years and he'd grown a bit more of a sense of proportion. Apparently, the memory of caterpillars everywhere – in the bedsheets, in shoes, in the cabinets of clean dishes *(but not in the food. He wasn't an idiot after all)* – still lingered.

Thony kind of agreed that he'd deserved what he'd gotten for that one – helping clean up all the mess – but most of his pranks were much more amusing and innocuous. And he still got in trouble with his father over them. *(And <u>honestly</u>? How seriously could you take a man who let his subjects call him 'King Bill'? Thony had long ago decided that if anyone tried to call him 'King Thony' when <u>he</u> was crowned, he'd lop their heads off. Except his sisters. And their husbands; Roger and Jeremy were cool. And <u>maybe</u> his mother.)*

Princes were supposed to go on adventures and do interesting things. Instead, his *sisters* had gone off on The Quest a year earlier – and Left Him Behind. Instead, he'd been stuck *here* in *the most boring place in the Entire Universe.* And with no real hope that he would *ever* get to go *anywhere* or do *anything* interesting. *Ever.*

Of course, he didn't really blame his sisters *(or Prince Roger, the second-born prince from the neighboring kingdom)* for going on The Quest. They'd kind of had to, after the debacle that Prissy's sixteenth birthday party had become. But they'd left him behind.

They'd come back a few months later. Both of his sisters had gotten married while they were gone, though Mama and Papa had insisted that Joanna and Roger, at least, go through a second wedding ceremony *('for propriety's sake' – as if the very fact of Priscilla and Joanna secretly going off on The Quest hadn't taken everything so far beyond the pale of 'propriety' that there was no real way back. But the wedding had made Mama and Papa happier, not to mention King Richie and Queen Janet. Though Roger's older – and as yet unmarried – brother, Raymond, had kept giving both of the newlyweds odd looks as if he <u>wanted</u> to be happy for them, but couldn't quite stop wondering if they were planning to usurp the throne he was to inherit someday.)*

But Joanna had married *Roger*, whom they'd known forever. Mama and Papa were more or less refusing to acknowledge Priscilla's husband at all.

His sisters *(and Roger)* had also come back with the news that their magick-poor world was about to undergo a 'Ragnarök'. All the Gods they had been worshiping forever were about to *die* and be replaced by new ones. And the new ones just *happened* to be: Joanna and Roger and Priscilla – and the handful of friends they had brought back from The Quest.

Oh, and after all that, magick would be much more available to use. For everyone, not just the wisewomen and hermits and witches and sorcerers.

Mama and Papa's skepticism had been palpable. *(No one else than them and Thony had been told about the creation of new Gods at the time, although the word of the 'Ragnarök' had been duly passed along – no doubt with the tale growing less believable with every iteration.)* Princesses falling asleep for a hundred years and princes turning into swans and evil witches and ogres and such were par for the course in their opinion, but *Gods?*

And Joanna and Roger and Priscilla weren't even lucky-numbered children. Joanna was at least an eldest child, but she'd had the bad taste to then have a pair of younger siblings – nine years later, though apparently it hadn't been for lack of effort on King Bill and Queen Annabel's parts at attempting to properly produce three children *(of one gender)* or seven or twelve. *(Or even <u>thirteen</u>, though that number usually created more problems than it solved. King Bill was the oldest of seven brothers, and Queen Annabel was the youngest of seven sisters with three older brothers as well.)*

But Roger and Priscilla were both second-borns.

And then there was Prissy's tail.

Supposedly she'd been born the absolute epitome of perfect princesshood – golden-haired, bright blue eyes *(they were really more green, but for marketing purposes were blue)*, fair skin, the works. But somewhere in the handful of minutes between her birth and being Presented to the Populace, Priscilla had acquired a bushy, black tail that was nearly as long as she was.

When the tail had fallen out of her baby blankets during her Presentation to the Populace – and it was obviously attached to the baby – their father, King Bill, had fainted. *(Which wasn't a <u>manly</u> thing to do, but what can you do when the guy tells people to call him 'King Bill'?)*

*Un*fortunately, he'd been holding the baby.

Fortunately – despite all the adults frozen in horror around her – nine-year-old Princess Joanna was the only person who had the presence of mind to dash forwards and rescue her baby sister from their falling father. And then to stand up before all the people *(who had been seriously confused, I mean, <u>nothing</u> interesting ever happened here)* and declaim that it was a fine tail. That, in fact it was quite likely the finest tail a princess had ever had. And then she told everyone to call Prissy 'Princess Priscilla the Bright-Eyed and

Bushy-Tailed' *(which might be where all these ridiculous appellations attached to the royal children had gotten started, though at least Joanna had gotten 'the Wise and Wonderful'. Not that Thony begrudged his sisters theirs, but 'the Affable and the Affirmative'? Yeesh!)* and the poor, confused crowds had cheered enthusiastically.

That was all fine with the Local Populace and even their own minor nobility were willing to go along with things, but Word had gotten out *(Mama said Word always did)* and the royalty in all the neighboring kingdoms had decided the Devinthals had Bad Blood and decided to avoid them. Except for Roger's parents, of course, since King Richie and King Bill had been friends since they were boys.

But since the local nobility of a given valley tended to follow the lead of their king, it meant that all of King Bill's pages and squires were the scions of local families, and all of Queen Annabel's ladies-in-waiting were as well. This was potentially something of a problem, since the girls and boys were sent up to the castle to find a spouse as much as to learn some useful skills, but King Richie had traded them a couple *(which was how they'd gotten to know Roger so well in the first place, though it seemed likely he hadn't been granted permission from King Richie to ask for Joanna's hand – so perhaps even best-friendship only went so far in the matter of Bad Blood)* and if there were somewhat fewer of each group than the king and queen would like, because some of their own more remotely located nobility had sent *their* scions off to other kingdoms, it didn't bother *Thony* at all.

He was busy mulling over all this old history and the Utter Unfairness of having been Left Behind while his sisters had Adventures in the Fairy Wood and how his small attempts to liven up this deadly boring place were met with such an extreme underappreciation... So he wasn't really paying attention to where that rock was going and he nearly tripped over the girl scrubbing the floor.

Well.

Actually, his rock skittered into her bucket and knocked it over, even though he hadn't kicked it all *that* hard.

And *then* this midget-sized girl popped up practically under his chin and belted him a solid one in the gut.

And *then,* while he was stumbling away in surprise, he slipped in the soapy water and fell down, landing on top of the angry girl.

Who called him clumsy and overweight *(which he wasn't, thank you very much, either one. He'd been lanky until a couple years ago and now was sort of... stocky. Priscilla said he was just getting ready for a growth spurt, and she should know if anyone did, since she was now the Goddess of Animals – which apparently included humans, to Mama and Papa's even greater dismay).*

She also called him a thoughtless oaf... and that one struck a bit closer to home, given that he knew that a prince should always be considerate of his People and he really *should* have been more aware of where that rock was going. But he hadn't, because he hadn't been paying attention. Which was sort of the whole problem in a nutshell.

And anyways the whole thing was just too embarrassing. Getting beaten up by a teeny little girl who looked like she was maybe ten – and him almost fifteen? That dinky thing had a right hook that out-sized her for sure! And if he should have to try to explain this to someone...

No. Nope. *Not* happening.

Thony had sloshed halfway down the corridor and almost around the corner when he realized there was something in his *pants*. Something that was *cold* and *wriggling* – and in his *under*pants, or it would have fallen out down his pantleg since Thony didn't hold with hose or tight pants.

It turned out to be a frog and it was alive and relatively unsquished when he got it out... which was a relief, though what he'd had to do to *get* it out in good order had been somewhat embarrassing.

That was when he heard the laughter.

He turned around and saw the scrubbing girl, hands on her hips, and laughing her head off at his antics.

Thony's first reaction was to scowl resentfully at her, but after a scant moment his expression changed to a sheepish grin. He'd stuffed enough frogs down other people's clothes *(though never their <u>underpants</u> – and how had she managed to do that without him noticing?)* that he had a fair idea of what he must have looked like. And it *was* pretty funny.

"He's getting away! Help me catch him!" The girl splashed sudsy water as she darted after the frog that was merrily hopping away from them.

Thony followed her without a question. Frogs – as pretty much everyone from Mama to Joanna to Priscilla had informed him on more than one occasion – *didn't* belong in the castle. The stone floors were too hard and dry for a creature that spent much of its life submerged in water, and the servants did too good a job at cleaning even the remotest dusty corners so there weren't enough insects for it to eat. *(Though Mama's concerns were rather different than his or his sisters'.)*

And chasing a frog through the castle together was generally silly enough to make anyone either fast friends or mortal enemies.

Honestly, Thony didn't care which. Either one would lighten the incredible boringness of life in Aldyrwald.

Fortunately, they caught up with the frog just inches before it would have leapt into his mother's solarium to wreak havoc on ladies-in-waiting and embroidery hoops alike.

Not so fortunately, Mama came over to see the commotion at the door, spotted the frog, and fainted. Again.

Joanna was sent for and Thony and the girl were made to wait for her while the ladies-in-waiting waved smelling salts under Queen Annabel's nose and placed cold cloths on her head and gossiped in quiet, giggly voices.

"Twice in one *day*, Thony?" Even Joanna's ever-patient tone sounded exasperated. "What are you trying to do? Get Papa to keep you from ever seeing the light of day again? At this rate even Master Eswith will run out of protocol lessons."

"Um, no...?" She'd phrased it as a question, but Thony had the feeling it was rhetorical.

"And now you're involving the *servants* in your pranks again?" And *that* was disappointment, and if there was anyone whom Thony actually *cared* about not disappointing, it was Joanna.

"It wasn't a prank! The frog just sort of... escaped. And I knocked over her bucket. And then she helped catch it." Which was all true, if slightly out of order. And definitely gave the impression that the frog had been *his* to start, rather than that *he* had been the victim of the *girl's* prank.

There didn't seem to be any good way out of this one. Thony looked at his feet. The girl had the frog, so he couldn't even pretend he was looking at it.

Priscilla bustled up right then – presumably summoned by Joanna in that God-Way they had now, or else called by the frog in her role as Goddess of Animals. She plucked the frog out of the girl's hands and headed back out, cooing at it, and only noticing Thony by way of a quick ruffling of his red curls. She had that look she got when someone interrupted what Thony had nicknamed 'Jeremy-time' – though apparently part of being a Goddess was the ability to appear perfectly turned out in a proper, princessly pink and frilly daygown when one might be seen by one's mother and her ladies.

So much for his best friend since forever.

Jeremy was cool, of course – and how cool was it to have a *centaur* for a brother-in-law? – but Priscilla never had time for Thony anymore.

"The bucket got tipped over? I'd imagine that's how the frog escaped – and why the pair of you are dripping suds," Joanna said thoughtfully after Priscilla had disappeared.

Her eyes looked like she had rather more of an idea of what had happened than that... like she could just look into Thony's own *soul* and pull the truth right out of him. And maybe she really *could*, now that she was the Goddess of the Earth and all. Though she'd been giving him *that* kind of look pretty much ever since he'd first discovered frogs when he was two or three years old, so it might just be a Joanna-Thing and not a Goddess-Thing.

"I should probably get that water taken care of and finish cleaning the floor before anyone slips in it and gets hurt," the girl suggested. Thony decided he needed to remember that little crease between the brows that did such an excellent job of suggesting Concern and Responsibility. Not that it would likely do *him* much good, given that everyone in the castle tended to assume that if there was something crazy going on he was probably the cause of it.

To be fair, they were usually right.

And it was his honor and his privilege to liven things up a little.

Even if it did extend those interminable lessons with Master Eswith.

Joanna looked at him with a fair amount of empathy. "I'll tell you what, Thony, you go help this girl clean up all that soapy water and we'll just call it even. I'll make things right with Mama."

That was... not entirely unexpected. Joanna's approach to discipline was all about 'natural consequences', which translated into 'fixing what you'd messed up'. And since cleaning up the messes he'd helped create was *far and away* more interesting than protocol lessons, Thony far preferred it when *she* got to sort him out.

However, he did kind of have to admit that King Bill's approach was probably a more effective deterrent. Not only did it leave the energetic young prince less time to think up new ways to create havoc, but adding to the overall boringness of Aldyrwald – especially in his own personal life – went against every principle he tried to live by.

Though if he managed to stay *awake* while listening to Master Eswith droning on about what fork to use at dinner for which esoteric side-dish that would probably never show up on Thony's plate, he often could daydream up some of his best ideas. Unfortunately, Master Eswith dealt with daydreaming about the same as he did actual sleeping, and bruises from that ruler could really hurt.

"Thanks, Joanna, you're the best!" He stretched up and gave her a kiss on the cheek, then trotted after the girl. She'd taken Joanna's comment as a permission to leave and had almost disappeared around a corner already. He had to move fast to catch up.

Find out what happens nex in

Thony and the Much-Anticipated Adventure

Available in eBook, paperback and hardcover at all fine online bookstores!

Author's Note

Some of you may be wondering why I use so many *italics* and ***bold italic*** emphases. If you've stuck with me this long, you'll know that this is a part of my style.

As a teenager I ran across a wonderful book in the Colonie Town Library – completely by accident – that made an incredible impression on me: *The Last Word on the Gentle Art of Verbal Self-Defense* by Suzette Haden Elgin. Professor Elgin (who taught linguistics at San Diego State University, founded the Science Fiction Poetry Association, and published *dozens* of books) had a great many useful things to say about how to have more productive verbal interactions with other humans.

Dr. Elgin's incisive and very human approach to understanding humans made enough of an impact on me that her book is part of the homeschool curriculum that all six of my kids have had to go through. We're pretty flexible here and switch out what works for one kid, but not another as need be… but *The Gentle Art* stays constant.

(We've also added in *Thank You for Arguing* by Jay Heinrichs more recently, which elaborates in some ways and takes us into the realms of formal debate as well. Since all the kids love to argue and would prefer to be listened to than ignored, they really love these books.)

As a writer, however, the thing that stuck with me the most was that Dr. Elgin – who was herself a science fiction writer – pointed out that our written English language is deeply impoverished when it comes to trying to explain emphasis. And that where the emphasis is in a given sentence, both the primary and the secondary emphasis, can completely change the meaning of that sentence. (She also noted that upset people use a great deal of unusual emphases…)

Simply consider the sentence "Thony, you're quite a good prankster."

Think about who might actually say that sentence.

Amanita? Master Esquith? Can you tell if it's sarcastic, sincere, admiring, irritated?

Now try it with the following possible emphases:

"*You're* quite a good prankster."

"You're *quite* a *good* prankster."

"You're quite a good *prankster.*"

Very different implications, aren't they? And written without any emphasis, the sentence could be *any* of those things… and it's not always going to be crystal clear from context. Amanita might be admiring or sarcastic, for example. The emphases make it easier for the reader to pick up on the subtext.

Dr. Elgin used a combination of all-caps and italics in her book to demonstrate emphases. Her book was written in the early 1980s and her font-options were limited and constrained by technology as well as her publisher. Nowadays, good manners preclude the use of all-caps except in very extreme circumstances (such as when Amanita is yelling Fire! right under Sergeant Sterevor's nose, or when King Theolore's Court was so stunned to see Karana show up in rags on Midsummer's Day).

On the other hand, we now have access to a near infinitude of fonts and the options to alter how they look. (This is somewhat more restricted in eBooks, since those are supposed to be modifiable by the reader… and figuring out how to make *that* work well has been an… *interesting challenge.*)

You may also have noticed that the *Prankster Prince* series involves a great deal more extra emphases. Some young teens – in my personal experience – tend to be a bit on the dramatic side, and Thony and Amanita are definitely some of those, particularly Thony. Dae tends to be a lot more laidback and you see far fewer italics when she's speaking.

I strongly suggest you look up Dr. Elgin's work. (The last version of her Verbal Self-Defense series was published in 2009 according to Wikipedia.) It may change your life as much as it has mine!

And in more normal Author's Note news – you can look for *Book Five of The Prankster Prince* in October. *Diary of a* ~~RUNAWAY~~

~~PRINCE~~ *Bold Questing Hero* will take Thony to Pathremir – where he's going to have to challenge all of his assumptions and learn a few key things in order to get back out again!

If you enjoyed meeting Davril, Istevan, and Julanna – their stories will start to show up in late 2025 as the *Three With a New Song's Measure Cycle*.

And, of course, we haven't seen the last of Dae Goldeneyes, Kamauri Spiralspear, Daennor Catsfoot... as well as Puck (or rather Prince Skiftglow, since he's setting aside his title of Prankster-in-Chief to Queen Lilysong). Not to mention our fun new demi-God Aleri!

Hope you're having as much fun with all of this as I am!
Mangala

About the Author

Mangala McNamara lives in Flyover Country (the far northern end of the US South) with her husband, The Professor, and four of her six children. The remaining children are in college – you can blame the oldest for the excessive amounts of math showing up in Mangala's fantasy novels, the second one for better attention to staging of scenes, the third for all the economics, and the fourth for great attention to history – and all of them for a focus on political science! Mangala is a former professional bellydance instructor, and used to enjoy knitting, crotchet and embroidering Temari balls but now is much more boring as she rarely does anything but write... although she also fences (the sport) and plays D&D with her kids. She owes her love of books and reading to her mother, who was a professional folklorist and could recite – from memory – stories from every nation in the United Nations.

Her **Knightess of the Realm** and **Chronicles of Ilseador** series occur in Amanita's homeworld.

Also by Mangala McNamara

Fantasy in the World of the Living Gods:

The Prankster Prince

Thony and the Much-Anticipated Adventure: Book One of The Prankster Prince

Thony Goes Astray! (in the Deep, Dark, and Dangerous Fairy Wood): Book Two of The Prankster Prince

So You Want to Be a Hero? Book Three of the Prankster Prince

How Thony Stopped a War (and FIxed a Friendship): Book Four of th Prankster Prince

Knightess of the Realm

A Not-So-Sacrificial Maiden

Out of the Woods… Hopefully (a Prequel Novella)

The Fall of Taridawil (A Dtory Collection)

The Heir's Journey mini-series (3 books)

    A Not-So-Simple Mission: Book One

    An Entirely-Unexpected Revelation: Book Two

    An All-Too-Surprising Homecoming: Book 3

The Chronicles of Ilseador

The Rebel Duchess: Book One

The King's Champion: Book Two

The Pirate-King: Book Three

More Fantasy coming soon…

The Pale Sorceress: Book Four of the Chronicles of Ilseador (August 2024)

An All-Too-Obvious Choice: Book 1 of the Secret of Dragon Mountain (A Knightess of the Realm Novel) (September 2024)

Diary of a ~~RUNAWAY PRINCE~~ *Bold Questing Hero Book Five of the Prankster Prince (October 2024)*